The Dream's on Me

A Love Story

The Dream's
on Me

A Love Story

by DOTSON RADER

G. P. Putnam's Sons
New York

SBN: 399-11724-5

Library of Congress Cataloging in Publication Data

Rader, Dotson.
  The dream's on me.

  I. Title.
PZ4.R124Dr [PS3568.A27] 813'.5'4 75-34312

For Betty Anne Clarke

The only evil angel is love.
—SHAKESPEARE

The Dream's on Me

A Love Story

1

McFARLAND WOKE in the late afternoon, his eyes blinded by the white light shining in the windows of his rented guesthouse near the harbor of St. Thomas, shining intensely on the whitewashed walls and off-white furniture of the bungalow, shining on the white sheets where he lay naked and sweating. He was hung over from drinking in Katie's Bar the night before, the night his mother died, the night he flew to the island from New York. He looked around the room, squinting. The light hurt his eyes and increased his headache. He closed his eyes and tried to sleep. He hated white rooms.

White reminded him of ice and snow. As a kid he had been afraid of the cold, of freezing to death in rural Pennsylvania if he ran out of gas and was trapped in a blizzard. And it reminded him of hospitals and disinfectant and bandages and scar tissue and other paste-white things that mean you've run out of gas. And it reminded him of his mother before she ran out of gas.

McFarland's mother was crazy. However, she went crazy near the end, beginning to lose her marbles about the time he was born and then losing them more and more until at the end she was down to about four out of a dozen, and then they all rolled down the drain.

He did not like to remember his mother's madness because it was of the agonized sort, and to recall it made him unhappy, and it made him feel guilty, and he knew he had no reason to feel guilty. He didn't drive her crazy. His father did. And he knew his father also sent her away, awash with alcohol, her baptized Baptist body down to ninety pounds of

11

liver-damaged, jaundiced flesh. Pop sent her to a Lutheran banana farm, where they stuck miniaturized electrodes through the holes they drilled in her head and burned out her brain. When they were done, she was crazier than ever; only she did not know it, so she wasn't afraid anymore and so she did not have to drink anymore and take off her clothes and try to make her son's schoolboy friends who came home with him after football practice and try to make anybody else who happened along. Except her husband. Mom hated him, so McFarland knew she wasn't completely crazy.

No, he did not like to remember his mother's madness, and he consciously tried to avoid thinking of it, trying instead to remember when she was normal, sane, levelheaded, uncracked . . . but that was such a dishearteningly brief period in his acquaintance with her that it did not count for much. There was practically nothing he could remember which his mind could seize and say, See, Mom wasn't *always* bonkers. But maybe she was.

Part of the terror in that thought was the suspicion that madness was hereditary, that demented cells had passed from her blood into his and that they drifted there inside him like time bombs waiting for age or crisis to ignite them, exploding in his head. He was scared of going cuckoo suddenly, like his mom. And even if insanity were not hereditary, it might be contagious, caught like the flu with a kiss, bred incubating in the close proximity between mother and son. Whole families were retarded or Mongoloid idiots or dropped from schizophrenia, caught colds of dementia en masse; entire villages had gone mad during wars, and countries had gone mad before wars and thus waged them. And worse than the fear of madness was the attraction of it: to be mad was to be a child, free of responsibility for one's acts; it was to be dependent, the source of worry, and yet possessing great negative power, the power of unpredictable, incomprehensible and therefore awesome acts. He feared it and did not understand it. He grew up paranoid about paranoids. Under his normal guise lay trembling, like a tongue in a closed mouth, fears of madness. When he confronted crazed action in others, he froze inside, grew remote, unable to run or strike out.

How he dealt with the reality of madness was to treat it as if it were normal, ordinary, acting as if nothing remarkable were occurring. When his mother went through a genuine second childhood at thirty-five years of age, pedaling around the neighborhood on a toy scooter, hanging out at the corner candy store, mad for paper dolls, chocolate YooHoo, bubble gum, *Children's Digest,* hopscotch, jumping rope, doll tea parties on the front lawn, where she sat visible to the neighbors, talking hysterically to Raggedy Ann plopped on a folding chair at the other end of her card table, or when she set up her lemonade stand on the sidewalk and sold five-cent paper cups of the stuff to his friends on the way home from school, speaking baby talk to them, well, McFarland treated it as the most normal thing in the world. He acted as if everybody's old lady spent a summer wearing braids and big ribbons and carrying a teddy bear named Poo Poo with whom she held animated conversations as she rode down the sidewalk on her skateboard. And yet it was humiliating and embarrassing to him. He said nothing. He grew up a spectator to lunacy, watching his mother's brain go soft and finally run out of her ears. And growing up that way, he learned to know his paralysis in the face of what he could not understand, his helplessness before what he could not deal with. Faced with the possibility of dramatic loss, he became depersonalized. In moments of anxiety, life went skitzy, and he stood inside it as if he were outside it, watching himself and the others walk slow motion through mania.

When he was six years old, his mother got a blank look on her face for the first time. She stood in the living room and looked at the Chippendale antiques and the Colonial Americana her husband had inherited from his family and at the brocade sofa and chairs they had purchased when they were first married. His mother went *Tsk! Tsk!* and shook her head.

"*Germs,* Henry!" she said, grabbing McFarland's hand. She

13

pulled him out of the house and into her Ford coupe and drove to the hardware store, where she said, "Henry and me will have five gallons of pure white paint, and brushes, and paint rollers. And make it snappy!"

She charged it to her husband's account.

They went back home, Mom humming all the way, her mind a beehive of ideas. As she drove, she steered the car with her left hand, and with her right she caressed her son's thin legs. Every once in a while she stopped humming and looked down into her son's enormous eyes, and said, "You're so pretty, Henry. Pretty as an angel. Someday the women'll eat you up!" Or, "Henry, you have the very eyes of Jesus, don't you know?" Smiled at him, and he smiled back, feeling very safe.

The eyes of Jesus.

McFarland's mother once saw Aimee Semple McPherson at Angelus Temple in Los Angeles, preaching in a long white robe with long white angel cuffs; behind her stood a choir all in white in an all-white church . . . though your sins be as scarlet, they shall be whiter than snow. And there and then his mother decided to give up dancing and cardplaying and cigarettes and liquor and marry his father and go straight. She never remembered what Aimee Semple McPherson said that night, or precisely when that night was. But many times, over a gin and tonic and a cigarette, she told her son about that brilliant white robe, white enough to blind a soul, and that white church and that choir bathed in white, all of it pressed forever on her mind like footprints in cement. And finally when, unraveled and frayed, she came into confusion, when she could not tell night from day, son from lover, she still rattled on about them robes.

First they painted the living-room walls, his mother continuing to hum her Baptist hymns. McFarland started to hum, too. It was great fun. Then they attacked the ceiling, mother and small son slopping paint rollers into paint tubs and slapping the pure white against the ceiling. And finally, after a moment's reflection, Mom and he set about painting the Chippendale antiques and the Colonial Americana his

14

father had inherited from his family and the brocade sofa and chairs his parents had purchased when they were married.

Where was his father? He was in Lancaster for the week, trying cases at the county courthouse and spending his nights at the Grand Union Hotel in the flaccid arms of Elsa MacIntosh, who ran the Harbor Light Christian Bookstore in Lancaster. Elsa MacIntosh has since gone to her reward, there being no moaning of the bar when they erased her from the board. And so too has McFarland's father—cancer erased him—and now his mother, who ran out of gas.

But years ago, the day after the room went white, when McFarland was little, that day, when his father came home smelling of Elsa's Evening in Paris perfume, his wife met him at the door and trilled, "Close your eyes, honey."

Pop closed his eyes. She took him by the hand and led him into the living room, where their son stood in giggling anticipation of his father's delight.

"Surprise! Surprise!" she shouted happily.

His father opened his eyes and looked around the living room his wife had transformed into a pure white painter's dropcloth, whiter than snow.

At first his face blanched about the color of the newly painted armchair, and then he got very red. He dropped his briefcase. His arms went limp at his side. McFarland kept expecting his father to say, "Good work, kids. It looks *terrific!*" He was six years old, and he thought of his mother as being only slightly older.

Instead, his father stumbled back a foot or two and stared, baffled, into the smiling eyes of his wife.

"Why, Eve?"

"Henry and I worked so *hard,* honey . . ." she began excitedly, about to explain all the good they had accomplished in his absence.

"Henry?"

McFarland raised his hand.

"Your name is *Paul,*" his father said. "Eve, our son's name is Paul."

His wife giggled and ignored him and turned and twirled

15

around the middle of the room, raising her hands as Aimee Semple McPherson must have done on that big white stage in Angelus Temple long ago. "It's just like Christmas!" she sang happily. "Just like Christmas." Starry, starry night.

"Why?" her husband barked, returning to his normally commanding, abrasive self. "Why, Eve?" his wife's lunacy for the first time sinking into his law- and Elsa-befogged mind, sinking in and angering him because it scared him.

"Germs!" she screamed. "Germs!"

He took two steps forward and struck her in the face. He hit her again. She fell down, and he hit her some more. "Why? Why?" he kept repeating as he hit her and kicked her. McFarland stood next to the brocade sofa, its silk covering still sticky from the drying paint. He stared in horror at his parents, his mouth open wide, silent, unable to cry out. It was a dream to him, as if he were asleep, captive in nightmare, watching himself watching his father beat his mother. It took his father long to stop, and by then his son had learned to fear him, as he would until he died. And as he hurt her, she did not make a sound. Like her son, not a peep came out of her, nothing as he beat her up. She was quiet as snow. She said nothing. Years later McFarland wished his mother would have made noise, cried out, sobbed, wept as his father beat her up. But he did not know why he wished it, any more than he knew why, watching his father hurt her, hating him for doing it, why he envied his father's strength and found his cruelty transfixing and exciting. What he remembered was that he had watched, petrified with fright, and was helpless and had done nothing.

His father turned and walked out the door.

For several years, every time his mother would disconnect, those occasions when she was running on one piston, his father, feeling powerless, would beat her up, trying to knock some sense into her. And then he had her put away. And then they said she was cured and she came back home; only she wasn't cured at all, and so he beat her up some more . . . and it went on and on like that until McFarland's freshman year in high school, when she pulled her last mad-

16

ness on a city bus and someone told his father about electricity being used in brain surgery and how it was much cleaner and much more efficient than old-fashioned knives. They were right. It is.

The room stayed white for about four months, until they packed up and moved to another house, leaving behind the Chippendale antiques and the Colonial Americana and the brocade sofa and chairs. McFarland's mother always loved that room, probably because her husband refused to step foot in it. She read her son Bible stories there during the many nights her husband did not come home and she was scared to be alone, but with everything painted white and all the lights on, it was clear to her that no one could hide in that room and suddenly do harm to her. So she felt safe there. But McFarland never liked it, not after seeing her beaten there the very first time.

The last time he saw his mother alive she was sitting in a white wicker chair on the huge lawn at the Lutheran nuthouse outside York, Pennsylvania, sitting all alone in a white hospital frock with pink plastic flowers pinned to her bodice. She was fat now, since she was not drinking anymore, and she was very gray, like old bread.

When his mother saw him, she said, "Merry Christmas!" She didn't know him from Adam.

He was confused. "It isn't Christmas, Mom. It's August."

"Merry Christmas!" she repeated gaily, smiling up at him from her white chair planted by itself on that vast expanse of manicured Christian lawn. On her head were strips of bandage pasted to her skull. They were also white.

"Do you know why she says that?" the psychosurgeon asked him, beaming.

"Because she's loony?"

"We don't use those words. . . ." He pursed his lips. "They carry false value judgments. All healing is a relative art, young man."

He was right. They don't use those words. They called her "stabilized."

"Do you know why your mother says Merry Christmas?"

17

he inquired again. McFarland did not feel like answering because the doctor reminded him of those smartasses at parties who ask you dumb questions so they can come up with one-line jokes that make you look like a dummy. Anyway, his mother wasn't paying any attention to the doctor, so he didn't see why he had to.

"Do you?"

No, he did not know why she said Merry Christmas. And he wanted to turn away and not look at her anymore and not have to hear her silly, childish voice and her mad, benign, tranquil, sadly contented tones. He could not find his mother in his mother. Pennsylvania Edison had zapped her, short-circuited her, erased her from the board.

"She says Merry Christmas because she wants a *present*." The psychosurgeon smiled again, glancing pridefully down at the mother, his patient and creature.

"Why don't you give her this?" The brain surgeon took a green lime lollipop from his pocket, the kind dentists use to bribe recalcitrant kids, and handed the sucker to McFarland.

He bent down and gave it to his mother. She stuck it in her mouth.

"Not like *that!*" the doctor shouted at him. "What's *wrong* with you, young man?" McFarland knew he was in trouble. You always are when doctors ask that question. "You have to *remove* the *wrapper* first."

The doctor went to her and leaned forward. "Give me the sucker, Eve." Eve. That was his mother's name. He never called her that. He called her Mom. And she never called him Paul, not when Henry would do just as well. "*Give it to me, I said!*" She clamped her jaws over the lollipop, and the doctor clamped his fingers over the stick, and she held on for dear life, and the doctor wiggled it around, and then he yelled, "Look over there! Quick!" And dumb Eve looked and he yanked the lollipop from her mouth. Then, with obvious distaste, grimacing all the way, with the very tips of his fingers he gingerly pulled the saliva-sopped cellophane wrap-

18

per off the candy sucker and gave it back to her. She was still looking the other way.

"Merry Christmas!" she trilled, grinning up at the doctor. Starry, starry night.

2

MCFARLAND SPENT his nights at Katie's on St. Thomas.

Katie's Bar, its walls formed of shuttered french doors, sat in raffish disrepair on the side of a mountain. From its wooden deck one could see the harbor below and the naval ships, like cruise vessels, decorated with colored lights. At Katie's Bar, sitting in old wicker and rattan chairs, sitting in the open french doors trying to catch the weak, sweaty breeze, were men and women of various sexual and political persuasions, some of whom had been beached on the islands after World War II and who now, twenty-five years later, like aging, unsalable relics passed by history, each night occupied their accustomed places beneath the ceiling fans in Katie's saloon.

Why Katie's? Because it was, like them, a tacky monument to hope abandoned, to the decay of effort. Once a first-class joint, it was now, like its patrons, teetering on bankruptcy, making do on the cheapest of booze. Out of gas, and yet it had a romance to its rattan walls, a sense of former style and comfort, of life lived. It was a welcoming place.

So it was there one night, as McFarland worked his way through a debilitating hangover, that he noticed a young woman enter the semidarkness of the place and sit opposite him at a small table at the far end of the room. It was difficult to see, and yet he was certain that she wore a pale-blue, almost diaphanous dress and a straw hat with an enormous brim, also blue.

On her wrist were a dozen gold bracelets that jangled when she moved.

Because of the hat and the sunglasses she wore, it was impossible to see her face, but she appeared to be in her early twenties, and she was deeply tanned. She was well dressed, and she seemed to have money, so it was strange that she came alone to a dump like Katie's when there were better places in the mountains or in the town below.

On four nights McFarland watched her enter the bar. She came in at precisely eleven o'clock and each night did exactly the same thing. She took the same table, wrote a note and wrapped it over a five-dollar bill, and then called a waiter and sent the money and the note to the piano player, who would wave it at her in thanks and play "This Time the Dream's on Me." She would have one martini, straight up, and leave, glancing around the room as she did.

The entire affair was puzzling and absurdly romantic to him, as if the woman were living in a fantasy, having gone quietly bonkers in the heat. Then after several nights she no longer appeared, and McFarland realized that he, being alone on the island, having left his wife and son in New York, had come to look forward to her eleven o'clock visits. He was fascinated by her.

He asked the piano player about her.

"She first came in about a week ago, with a young guy about your age, dressed in one of those faggy white linen suits. The guy was blind drunk. They got into an argument, and he slugged her. The son of a bitch belted her across the floor. I guess that explains the sunglasses."

"And the song?"

"I haven't a goddamn idea what that's about. The guy punched her and then walked out on her. She paid the bill and left. The next night she was back by herself asking for that old Harold Arlen number."

"But why?"

"Who the hell knows? Her visa ran out, you know?"

"Her visa?"

The piano player rolled his eyes. "When they picked her off the floor, they asked her if she was all right. She said, 'Treacherous floors. . . .' They helped her to her feet, and I asked her who the son of a bitch was who hit her. She looked at me funny, crazy, you know? And she said, now get this, 'He's both the net and the wire.' Then she laughed. See what I mean about her visa running out? She's not all there.''

The net and the wire.

Sometime that night McFarland returned to his guesthouse near the long pier at the harbor. The place was large, and he disliked the white emptiness of it. He had rented it expecting his wife to holiday on the island with him; since she hated motels, the guesthouse was the only suitable alternative. At the last minute she had refused to come.

He made himself a drink in the living room and sat on the sofa and debated with himself whether to go out or not and attempt to find the woman he had seen at Katie's. He fell asleep on the sofa, the booze and heat having decided the debate over whether to go out again or not. He woke in the darkness to hear a group of French sailors yelling obscenities in bad English in the street. He thought of the woman and slept again.

The following day he saw her for the last time. He had driven to the other side of the island, to a resort called Pablo's, a very expensive hotel with a series of cabanas built along the beach in front of its private cove. He enjoyed sitting on the beach, listening to the steel band and having a drink.

She was also there, sitting some distance away at a white cast-iron table by a grove of date palms. She wore a white one-piece bathing suit, a wide-brimmed hat, and large sunglasses, and her gold bracelets.

McFarland studied her, intrigued by her pose. There was a fine contrivance to the manner in which she sat, to the way she held her cigarette and sipped her drink. He called a barboy and ordered another drink and decided to approach her.

He walked up the beach, past the outdoor bar, toward her table. Some distance away she noticed his approach, for she raised her fingers to her lips, as if she were about to throw a kiss. But her hand remained on her mouth, her fingers trembling. There was something to the gesture that was inhibiting and cautionary, and he knew she wanted to be alone. It was a gesture that his mother often made when her face went blank, drained white, some inarticulate fear passing over her broken mind. Then his mother would halt suddenly, her eyes wide, and her hand would go to her lips, her fingers trembling.

McFarland smiled at her and nodded and then returned to the beach.

3

WHEN McFarland came home from St. Thomas Island, he found his apartment empty. His wife, Adele, had flown to the Coast, taking their son, Jaime, with her. There she joined her lover at McFarland's beach house at Malibu as they waited out the divorce. He was not surprised. The marriage was a dud, its visa expired. He had known that for months, as he had known of her affair for months, long before she had told him of it.

Adele left the apartment in disarray, the beds unmade, breakfast dishes piled on the kitchen table, dirty towels scattered about the bathroom, strands of her black hair like veins on the white porcelain basin. He walked about the apartment and smiled at its disorder.

On the mirror in the bedroom Adele had scrawled with lipstick "Gone to Malibu. Will call. Water the plants." And then it hit him. She was gone for good, the marriage collapsed like a tent in a windstorm, and there was no help for it.

He watered the plants. Adele was crazy for plants, holding cooing, insufferable conversations with them as she sprayed their leaves and tended the roots. She believed that plants were sentient beings, that they could feel and understand although they could not speak. Eight years before, days after they met, she moved into the one-room studio in the Village where he lived for a time; she came to him dragging with her two boxes full of houseplants, each with its own Christian name and special requirements. The studio apartment went to hell, dust balls formed like tumbleweeds on the Panhandle, the stove went from white to grease brown and finally caught fire, roaches nested in the sugar bowl, drains clogged with hair, the toilet went·unwashed until it smelled like an army honey wagon, but each day she sprayed the plants and poked and tended the soil. Months passed, the freezer froze shut, and finally McFarland gave up. Thereafter he did the cleaning. Adele cooked and talked to the philodendron.

So she walked out on him, and he watered the plants, lugging a silver Georg Jensen watering can around the five-room apartment on Central Park West, a cooperative they had bought when McFarland sold his second movie script six years ago, two years after they married, moving the houseplants from the Village to the place above the park. A small silver plaque with the MGM logo was on the foyer wall. MGM had produced the movie.

McFarland carried the can into his son's bedroom. It was dusk, and the room was dimly blue in the evening light. As he entered it, he stopped suddenly, overcome by a curious, unsettling premonition regarding his small son, an undefined sense of endangerment. He glanced around the room, half expecting to find his son lying wounded and unconscious in the semidarkness. He looked at the bed with the boy's Doctor Denton pajamas twisted among the sheets; the walls covered with yellow paper across which painted cowboys and Indians chased and fought and danced and flirted endlessly; stuffed bears and dolls and plastic fish and pull toys heaped about the room. Adele and the boy had been gone for two weeks, and still the room smelled sweetly of him and of sleep. He missed his son.

McFarland did not believe in premonitions, although his mother had sworn by them. Nevertheless, he had a premonition that his son would not live out a normal life. Jaime, with his small size and frightening vulnerability to adult chaos, Jaime at five years of age already appeared to evidence unmistakable signs of emotional imbalance—and the boy still had to grow up among those like his father and all the others, most of whom he did not know, all the others who had already grown up and could not handle it and never would learn how.

26

Jaime was a mixed-up little boy who spent more time talking to picture books than he did to his parents, who was afraid that the string that held up the moon would break and it would fall on him, and whose great delight in life was pretending he was a goldfish in a bathtub . . . and yet whose hands were too small and muscles too weak to command the strength to open his bedroom door, to say nothing of being any match for his mother's rages or his father's drunken flight from them and him. To say nothing of his suddenly crying over nothing, breaking down into sobs, crawling under the bed or pulling a blanket or towel over his head and crying for hours from some sorrow or fear beyond his capacity to speak. And it drove his parents to desperation, scared them in the face of their inability to end an unhappiness they witnessed and could not understand or relieve. So they blamed each other for it. He was a mixed-up kid, his son, and McFarland believed that he would get more mixed up, crazier, until he came to hate both his parents with good cause, a hatred as seemingly inevitable as it was regrettable. They were mixed up, too.

McFarland had his initial premonition about his son a year before St. Thomas, a year before his mother died. It occurred when he and Adele spent the summer at Malibu, where he was writing a television script, having sublet their apartment in Manhattan for the season. One afternoon Adele threw the two of them out of the beach house. She was having some of her California girlfriends over for a women's consciousness-raising session in the kitchen, where they would discuss sexist oppression over martinis. That allowed McFarland to take Jaime down to the beach, where they played alone.

He watched Jaime as he sat in the sun, digging madly away in the sand with his red plastic shovel. He was four, and he was laboring to enlarge a hole in the beach for his father to fill with water so he could sit in it and pretend he was a goldfish. Jaime was terrified of the ocean, and as a result, the boy required bathing pools, and so they had to build them together in the sand.

McFarland watched his son work, the tip of the boy's tongue peeking out between his pressed lips, his concentration singular and intense, his shovel tossing sand with abandon over his Snoopy T-shirt, and McFarland said, thinking of their exile from the house, he said, "James McFarland, we're going down, and the pressure is making your mother and me a little crazy. And the world is nuts, too. Dig deep, Jaime, and maybe you'll find gold or oil or sludge or whatever it is one finds to make the digging pay."

That is what he said, but what he really meant to say and did not say because his son was four and would not understand it, not that *he* understood it, was that he thought the world was out of rope and out of steam and out of luck and its history was catching up with it. He wanted to say that something out there was dying because we were stepping on its throat killing it and we didn't seem to know we were. Some people did, but it was a foot grown too heavy to lift. The children of the earth whose throat we were crushing into the ground were growing up, and they were beginning to come after us. Only he did not think he would be around to protect Jaime when they reached his potholed beach, and he would have to face them off alone, with his small hands that could not turn a doorknob and tiny body that was happily convinced it was a goldfish in a tub. And there was no help for any of it.

The drama of the sentiment was lost on Jaime, who continued tossing sand over himself.

Adele stood in the kitchen, holding a vodka and tonic in her hand, swaying slightly. She was dressed in a sheer nylon robe, and in the light McFarland could see the outline of her breasts and the black area of her sex under the material. She leaned against the kitchen counter, which was filled with ashtrays and liquor glasses and a dozen half-eaten plates of tuna salad and cottage cheese.

"Nice party?" he asked, smiling at his wife.

"Wasn't no fucking *party*. It was serious stuff. . . ." She made a dismissing gesture with her hand and then looked at

Jaime's sunburn. "Jesus. I can't leave the kid with you for five minutes without disaster overtaking him. . . . You're goddamn incombbadant . . ." she slurred.

"Incom*petent.*"

She reached down to pick up Jaime, her breasts swinging forward heavily, clumsily against her nylon robe, stumbling forward as she tried to raise him up. McFarland steadied her.

"I'll take him."

"The hell you will," she said, straightening up and then taking her drink. "There aren't any cigarettes in the house," she whined, forgetting about Jaime. "And if I don't smoke, I *eat.* You know I have to *smoke* or I'll get fat . . . fat-*ter.*" She groaned.

"There's some in the box on the mantel."

"I gotta lose some goddamn weight . . ." she mumbled, shuffling dejectedly out of the room.

McFarland carried his son into the bathroom and undressed him and wiped his pinkly sunburned arms and legs with warm, soapy water, the boy standing in the washbasin as his father cleaned him off. He stood a moment looking at the boy, who was spraying shaving cream on the bathroom mirror above the basin and then vigorously swirling it around with his hands, making abstract designs as he did, giggling as he did.

"Snow . . . snow. . . ." He looked at his father, smiling delightedly. "Cold snow," he said.

"It's shaving cream, Jaime."

The boy stopped his rubbing against the glass and looked at his father, the boy's eyes very large and lightly blue.

The eyes of Jesus.

"Shaving cream," his father said again, and then made motions with his hands as if he were shaving.

The boy seemed perplexed, staring at his father's shaving pantomime, and then he decided that his father was wrong and he had been right. "*Snow!*" he exclaimed, laughing, and continued playing his fingers on the glass as if it were frosted with a winter's day.

He looked at his son's small body, his sex with its foreskin pink and loose at the end, his round ass, white as milk glass, and he wanted to take Jaime in his arms and cry over the beauty of his son. Instead, he carried him into the kitchen and fed him Franco-American spaghetti and chocolate milk as Jaime watched cartoons on the television, and then he put him to bed.

Put him to bed—that is, McFarland, who could not find his son's pajamas and did not want to ask Adele—who was sitting outside on the terrace drinking—McFarland laid his naked son in his own bed and then lay beside him, holding him high against his muscular chest, and hummed songs to him, caressing his son's head until he slept. And as he slept, he rubbed his hands softly over his son's body, down his tender back and legs, over his small chest and stomach, feeling his breathing and his heartbeat, and over his son's sex and feet, touching all of him, awed by the softness and delicacy of the boy, fascinated as he rolled his strong hands over his son. And then he kissed his lips and smelled his body, concentrating on the texture and odor of Jaime's body, all of it, in order to remember it. And only then, when Jaime was asleep, did he take white Noczema creme and rub it lightly, coolly on the mild burn.

"Is he asleep?"

Adele was lying on long overstuffed cotton pillows that she had pulled onto the wooden deck of the terrace. It was a warm night, late dusk; the breeze was up. In the distance along the beach surfers walked toward home, carrying their waxed boards under their arms like schoolbooks.

"Yeah."

"Get me another drink, please." Adele gestured toward her glass, which sat on the grayish redwood planking, and as she did, her nylon robe opened a bit, revealing the inside edges of her suntanned breasts bordered by the white cloth.

"You've had enough to drink."

"I . . . suppose, I uh, have. . . ." She grunted and closed her eyes.

He looked down at her as she lay in the dying light, her

hair ruffled by the breeze. The first time he had ever seen her she lay on the south lawn at Columbia in the afternoon sunlight, her head resting on a cashmere sweater on top of a pile of books. "You haven't really changed," he said quietly. It wasn't true. And he knew it.

He pulled off his swim trunks and stood for a few minutes watching her lying at his feet, feeling his penis, tugging it hard as he looked at her. He was very tan, the tan running dark to his waist, his chest and stomach hairless except for a briarly trail of dark blond hair that ran from his crotch to his navel. McFarland was an attractive man, indeed a man of intense physical appeal; his body was tight and healthy, tall and as finely honed as a long-distance swimmer's. His hair was bleached by the sun, and it curled at his neck above his shoulders, it toppled over his ears in waves, and it swept, blown and snarled, over his forehead like Jaime's tousled hair. He had a strong, manly face, a high forehead and a rather long, broad, somewhat insistent nose and a firm jaw. The only softness to his face was found in his eyes and mouth, and it was there alone that his features resembled those of his mother. His eyes were large and pale blue, too pale, too large. They seemed lazily to express openness and a kind of wonder, and they were what gave to his face its youthfulness and tentativeness of expression. His mouth was soft, his bottom lip larger than the top, twice the size, like two overstuffed cushions piled together in lazy disproportion. His mouth was feminine and sensual and fatigued and inviting and sultry in expression and a touch untrustworthy. His face was a becoming contradiction.

He lay down beside Adele.

"I'm worried about Jaime," he said, not touching her.

"Uh-huh. . . ."

"He lives in a dreamworld all the time. He put shaving cream on the mirror and said it was snow."

"He's a poet." She was disinterested.

"He really believed it was snow. He's in a dreamland all the time. . . ."

"So are we. Only it's called a zoo. . . ." She opened her

31

eyes. They were onyx black. Her eyebrows were unusually thick, and they kept her deeply set eyes in a permanent shadow, like dark, wet jewels enshrined in white grottoes. He loved her eyes.

She glanced at him tiredly and then closed her eyes again. "Uhhh, if you wanna talk . . . uh, then talk about our marriage. Christ, it's a. . . ."

"It's a *what?*" He rolled on his side and looked at her. He moved his hand between her breasts, feeling the bone, and then squeezed her breasts, pressing each of her nipples between his finger and thumb, and then he pulled her nylon robe off her shoulders.

"Stop it," she said sleepily. He continued feeling her breasts.

"Our marriage is a what?" he asked again, shoving his hand down her stomach.

"I have to be, uh, more independent, honey. I really, really do. . . ."

"Sure." He undid the belt of her robe.

"You never listen to me. I feel like an object. Housewife shit. Independence. . . . I have to get out by myself more and . . . I don't know . . . I . . . what are you doing?" She opened her eyes a second and then closed them, rolling her head to the side. "*That's* what I mean . . . hell, I feel drunk."

He pulled open her robe. He leaned on his elbow and stared at his wife's body, her clumsy breasts lying heavily above her thick waist, and beneath it her coarse, abundant pubic hair black and vacant in the evening light.

"Jaime'll be all right. I'm the one falling to pieces . . ." she said quietly, as if in sleep, as she spread her legs, rubbing her knee against his upper thigh.

"I'm worried about him, though. He cries too much."

"You think he's really *crazy?*" Her eyes were closed as she moved her leg on top of his and moved her bottom to a more comfortable position. She bent her leg and shoved it up so that her knee pushed against his sex. "You're hard already," she said without emotion, and bent her shoulder toward him as she reached down and took his penis and began sliding her hand up and down the shaft. "The first time I felt you was in the dark, remember?" she mumbled to herself. "And I couldn't get my fist around it and it scared me being that big. It don't scare me anymore. . . ."

"I know . . ." he said, and he began thrusting himself into her hand, the friction exciting him.

She moved her hand lower and squeezed his balls. "You've got sand in your hair," she said. "You're as bad as Jaime. He's always full of sand. . . ."

"No, I haven't." He laughed, the comparison pleasing him.

"Hell, I can feel it, honey. You should've showered. That would've been, uh, nice, you know. . . ." She trailed off.

"I'm clean," he said, and kissed her. She twisted her head away.

"Jaime, if he's nuts, it's because of you . . ." she mumbled, "I'm going nuts, too. Because of you. . . ."

"No, precious. . . ."

"Honey, you're the only man I ever had. God, ain't that *sad?* Now I'm older and fatter and, oh, Christ!"

"I love you. . . ."

"The only one. . . ." She pulled her hand away from his cock and spit into her hand and then brought the spit to his cock and lubricated the head of his penis with her palm, pulling back his foreskin as she did, and he, lying on his side, pressed his sex against her hip. He groaned, and then swung his leg on top of hers, and finally mounted her, gripping her shoulders, her arm and hands still pressed under his stomach, pumping his cock as he moved it toward her sex.

"I'm not crazy," he said, laughing.

"Your mother was. . . ."

"*Don't* . . . please." He was afraid Adele would break off and begin attacking his mother. He did not want her to because he wanted sex and an argument would ruin it.

"Well, what the hell . . ." she said, pulling her hand from under his stomach and putting her arms around him. "Wet

33

as hell, honey, uh, I get so fucking wet." She groaned, "I'm crazy, that's where Jaime gets it."

He reached under and grabbed his cock and arched his pelvis and ass and then directed his penis inside her as she wrapped her arms around him, her fingers kneading the skin of his back. Slowly he penetrated more and more, moving in response to her sighs and breathing.

"Why are you crazy, love?" he asked facetiously, his breathing short, his face pressed hot against her cheek.

"I married you. I got to be plumb crazy." She was serious, and he laughed. He thrust his arm under her back and gripped her head from behind, cradling her.

"You smell of Noczema," she said. "I like the smell."

"Is Adele there?" McFarland asked late that night after he had unpacked and watered the plants and had his premonition about his boy and called the maid service to send someone over in the morning to clean the apartment and undressed and decided to put off calling Adele until the next day. He then had two double martinis, became lonely for his wife and son—it had been two weeks of separation since St. Thomas—and changed his mind and called the Coast.

"Who is this?" her lover demanded suspiciously, a bit gruffly, in what McFarland considered a decidedly proprietary tone.

"It's her husband."

"Mr. Charlie. I'll be damned."

McFarland had no idea why he insisted on calling him Mr. Charlie, but it irritated the hell out of him. That was probably why he did it.

"Where is she?" he repeated. It was ten o'clock on the Coast.

Silence.

"Cat got your fucking tongue?" McFarland regretted the expression at once. It sounded like his old lady out to lunch.

"Adele's taken the kid to Westwood—"

"At this hour?"

34

"—to buy him some clothes. They've been gone since the afternoon." McFarland had charge accounts at several stores in Westwood, so he surmised that Adele had gone to buy herself some clothes while the accounts were still good. "She called an hour ago and said she was taking the kid to the movies. You want to leave a message, Charlie?" Snide tone of voice.

Burning. "Tell her that I called. That I returned from St. Thomas all right."

"Sure." Pause. Bored. "Anything else?"

"Tell her . . ." He was about to say, Tell her that I miss her. But he thought better of it. He could not admit that to him. He did not know why unless it was because he refused to give him the satisfaction of knowing what he had cost him. "Tell her to kiss Jaime for me."

Laconic. "That kid needs discipline. He's spoiled."

"Listen, you son of a bitch, you so much as touch my son, you *breathe* on him, and I'll kill you, if I have to *hire* someone, fucker, to do it." He was incensed, his anger fueled by his sense of impotence. How would he ever know what they did to his boy, and how could he prevent it in any case? His lease had run out.

"Wait a damn minute."

"You touch him, you motherfucker." He was yelling into the phone, his arm shaking with rage.

"You got me *wrong*, mister. I *love* your kid. Why, he's like my own. . . ."

It cut deep, *like my own, like my own.* . . . McFarland went silent, fearing his voice would break in anger and loss if he spoke. *Like my own.* . . .

"Okay, Charlie, calm down."

Silence.

"Oh, listen . . ." her lover said, brightening, the crisis passed.

"I've got to go." McFarland regretted the call. He felt like a fool in having vented his feelings, allowing himself to be easily provoked.

35

"Listen, did you water the plants, Mr. Charlie? Ha-ha-ha."
Bang.

Then he knew; her lover was at the apartment when she wrote on the mirror her message to him, and they probably laughed as she left instructions for him as if he were household staff given orders before the mistress went on holiday. They probably laughed.

McFarland had never met her lover, although he had briefly seen him once the day before he left for St. Thomas, the day before his mother died.

Adele and he had gone to Saks, where she shopped for resort clothes. As they left the store, she pointed out her lover to him. She saw her boyfriend across the street, on the other side of Fifth Avenue, walking uptown dressed in tight Levi's with a red bandanna tied around his head. He looked about twenty-seven years of age, and McFarland thought that he was dressed too casually for his age and training (he was a former schoolteacher), and it struck him as affected, dressing down to complement the age of those you once taught, for whom you now hoped to write pop music. He was carrying a bowling bag, and McFarland thought that odd on Fifth Avenue.

"He bowls?"

"Don't be idiotic." Adele rolled her eyes heavenward in disgust. "It's his *stash*." She felt proud of her lover. She saw his unconventional ways as daring and provocative. They made her feel young.

"He's handsome, don't you think?" she asked, her eyes focused on her lover bounding up the avenue.

McFarland glanced at the man disappearing in the distance, and then he looked at his wife. Her expression was full of longing and defiant pride. She not only didn't give a damn that he saw her enthralled at the appearance of her lover, she wanted him to see; it excited her. He laughed, finding her infatuation both silly and inexplicable.

"What do you think?" she inquired again, not looking at McFarland.

36

"I think he's losing his hair."

She glanced at him, wide-eyed, her expression slightly stupefied. It had never occurred to her that he was losing his hair. "What difference does it make? I'm too fond of him to care."

"You mean you love him?"

"Have it your way."

In the beginning she had tried to conceal it, lying by omission; then she began referring to the affair fleetingly, in passing, lightly as if it were a matter of no special importance, a nonsexual friendship that had little significance for her. She was testing the waters of his feelings and at the same time trying slowly to acquaint him with the situation, to make him adjust to it and finally to accept it. She did not want to leave her husband, yet she could not face living without her lover. She wanted both. More, she hoped in time that they would come to like each other, respect and even admire each other, and she, like some primordial link between land and sea creatures, would bridge two lives and unite them in herself. She sensed his jealousy and disquiet. Therefore, she moved slowly.

In the beginning, seven months before, when he first suspected the adultery, she said, "We're simply *friends*, honey. He works part time at the [health] club. He was a schoolteacher, but it was impossibly confining. He wasted his time and talent teaching those damn kids. He writes music. Di*vinely*."

"Is he handsome?" He was sullenly interested.

"I never noticed." She touched McFarland's chest, smiling tolerantly.

Months later she said, "He's been terribly hurt by life. He's shy and insecure and very gifted. He reminds me of you when we first met. You were bursting with talent, too, and you had nothing to show for it but ambition. You were a promise and a smile. . . . Let me give him a chance. Help *me* to help *him*." Civilized, rational, patient, understanding. She wanted her husband allied with her to promote her lover's career. She did not comprehend why that notion offended him to the quick. "Get him an assignment writing music for the movies. You can do it." Soothingly, speaking to McFarland in bed after sex, her head resting on his shoulder, her warm breath tingling his ear as he lay open-eyed, hating her unseen lover and imagining what he did to her in bed and what she whispered in his ear, what pleadings and flatteries and breathless jokes and vulgarities.

"Have you sucked his cock?"

"What?" She raised her head and laughed. "Oh, honey, you are impossible. . . ."

"Bitch."

"All I asked was for you to help him get some recognition. It'll reflect well on you, I must say. You take everything so goddamn serious."

"A job?"

"I'll love you for it."

"I could do it. . . ."

"You're wonderful, Paul. I love you."

"But I won't." He was offended that she would ask. It was enough that he slept with his wife; now McFarland was supposed to act as his agent and promoter and public relations man? He was humiliated by the idea.

What was he to do? He loved his wife, and he believed that she loved him. He tolerated her affair, at first responded indulgently to it, feeling essentially unthreatened although he did not like it. He knew it would take a long time after it was over before he could forgive her for the infidelity. Yet he loved her, and he did not know how to deal with her infatuation with someone else. He ignored it. Or tried to when she let him. He believed it would exhaust itself, that what they had known between them in eight years, their son, all of it would hold her to him irrevocably. He would not compete for what he thought he had won eight years before. And so he lost.

Adele was frightened of aging. She was thirty-eight years old, and she felt ten years older. Worse, she felt useless and extraneous, dependent and confined, and she held her husband responsible. She was fat, and her inability to hold the line against armies of calories, to saying nothing of pushing it back, sandbagged her with hopelessness and physical self-dislike. She dieted compulsively and put on weight. She adopted starch diets and water diets. She fasted. She devoured Weight Watchers' frozen pies and diet-depressant pills and No-Cal sodas and instant Skinny-Thin breakfasts at dinner and toast without butter, coffee without sugar, cottage cheese and plain yogurt and celery sticks, denying her appetite, wrestling with an unending hunger, and she put on weight.

Adele often stood naked and looked unhappily at herself, at her breasts, which had become unattractively large, cowish, sagging and netted with blue veins running out from her nipples like traffic diagrams, at her stomach, which had widened and now flowed without indentation into her ample hips, her bottom expanding accordingly. Her weight and age and the drear predictability of her married future mortified and frightened her, and her mind was a nightmare vision of days to come: that like her Italian mother and aunts, she would continue to inflate until she was gathered to them at Leone's in matron sack and hair bun and "sensible shoes," large as a cow buffalo chewing cud, gathered to gossip of food and grandchildren, exchanging recipes for pasta. She held other hopes, God knows, and they all rested on escape.

Her weight had come with her pregnancy and then remained after her son's birth, like surplus goods after a war. It was distressingly clear to her that her son's prenatal feeding had enlarged her own appetite and broken down some obscure mechanism in her metabolism, leaving her looking forever snared in the early stages of childbearing. She felt a mess. And then Adele, eight years married, overweight, with dyed, jet-black hair, met a lover who cut the ice.

In New York McFarland missed her, and he missed his son as he waited out the divorce. He had always associated the beach house at Malibu with the best part of their marriage.

His son had been born at UCLA Hospitals in Westwood, and it was to Malibu they had gone when he sold his first script, and they were happy for a time, loving each other, giddy with the sudden release into freedom that his success at scriptwriting had provided.

Many nights after he returned from St. Thomas he was lonesome for her and for Jaime, and he wanted to try again to call them on the Coast. Jaime was five years old, and the New York apartment was bleak without him. His voice, high and tinny, given to easy giggles and cries. He worried about Jaime drowning in the tub playing goldfish while Adele and her lover were having sex somewhere out of mind. Or his waking in the night alone and terrified and no one there to hear, although he knew that was unlikely because Adele, when she wanted him to sleep, and Jaime slept badly now, slipped him half a Seconal.

But he did not call the Coast again because he knew, more likely than not, Adele's boyfriend would answer the phone and say, "Shit, it's you. Hey, Adele, Mr. Charlie's calling."

When he said it, McFarland knew he would get angry, and when Adele took the phone, he would start an argument about her Bonwit's bill or her goddamn plants or something else to avoid saying what he had called to say, which was that he missed her and he missed his boy. He would not tell her because he felt she had betrayed him in walking out, and thus he took it silently and hated himself for doing it.

Sometimes he fantasized about flying unannounced to the Coast to enter the house and find them. He tormented himself imagining her lover on top of his wife, fucking her. It was difficult for him to accept the fact that Adele had left him out of free choice; therefore, he consoled his pride by imagining that the ex-teacher-cum-masseur possessed some secret power, some strange hypnotic force, a kind of Charles Manson holding his wife in bondage through sexual magic, bizarre implements and a bowling bag stuffed with addictive drugs. He wanted to act ruthlessly and throw out her lover with a rain of curses and anathemas like heroes of old, to wipe the goddamn floor with him. He wanted to punch him out. To castrate him. To wipe him from the board. And yet he knew he would never take the milk-run flight to catch them unawares, and he would never punch him out, as he had never punched out his father, although he grew up daydreaming about punching him out. And he would not fly to them, not even to protect his son. He knew that he could not endure finding her in bed with another man. He could not go through life hounded by the memory of that.

McFarland's problem was that he wanted his wife back, but he could devise no way to get her back. So he temporized and avoided reprisals and kept paying bills. Even with her gone, he clung to the belief that in time she would come back to him. He was blinded by conceit and longing. He felt cheated and betrayed. Enraged, choking on it, he did not understand that she had left him not because her lover was better, but because he was different. That's what cut the ice.

The night before he left for St. Thomas was when he knew the end had come. The needle pointed to empty. Adele cooked dinner for Jaime and him. She ate nothing herself. She was dieting for the island beach. You could not lose twenty pounds in a night, but he thought that was her goal.

"I've lost four pounds this month," she said proudly.

He looked his wife over and smiled. "You look terrific. Much better." He patted her ass. She looked no different to him from before.

After dinner they watched television, McFarland holding Jaime on his lap, the five-year-old boy laboring over a dish of ice cream, now and again pushing a dripping spoonful of strawberry to his father's mouth, saying, "Here comes the old *witch*, Daddy!" Giggling as he shoved the spoon against McFarland's tightly sealed lips. And then he would open his mouth, which had become the witch's cave, and the boy would fly the cold pink witch into it, and McFarland would clamp his teeth over the spoon, as his son, giggling, tried to free it.

Jaime fell asleep in his father's lap, and McFarland carried

41

the boy into his bedroom. It was winter. The windows over-looking Central Park were frosted. The streetlight hit the glass, and the cold panes glistened as if smeared with stars. Jaime had drawn his finger over the frost, leaving oddly shaped trails on the glass, tracks paved by his finger's heat, silvery ribbons laid in the icy field.

He looked down at his son asleep in his Doctor Dentons. Jaime's small hands were curled tightly at his sides, the fists facing upward as if the child were expecting attack.

McFarland undressed and returned to the living room. He turned down the lights and put records on the stereo. He made drinks for Adele and himself. He liked occasionally having sex with her in the living room. It seemed spontane-ous that way, as when they were first dating and the urge to sex suddenly overcame them, wherever they were, and they gave over to it, indifferent to their surroundings. There was also the fact that one wall of the room was covered in mirror which allowed him to watch himself and Adele as they had sex, and that increased his excitement.

Adele came into the living room wearing a long black ny-lon nightgown. McFarland was sitting on the sofa. When he saw her, he gripped his penis and smiled at her. "I want you."

"What else is new?" She sat down next to him on the sofa, not touching him. She was irritated that he was naked. She did not feel like sex, and she did not like it being pushed at her. "Act your age," she said.

He leaned over and kissed her.

"I'm tired, Paul." She looked at him, her eyes vacant. "God, I can hardly wait until Jaime starts school. He wears me out."

He touched her nightgown. "Is it new?"

"Yes." She smiled, flattered that he had noticed. "Ben-del's."

He smiled and gently ran his fingers through her hair.

"Is anything wrong?"

"Why do you ask?" She spoke too fast, leading him to be-lieve that something *was* wrong, a bitchy edge to her voice

42

as if the question were improper and intrusive. Why doesn't he leave me alone?

"You seem nervous."

She shook her head no, puckering her lips sullenly. He watched her and thought how much her face had grown to resemble her Italian mother's, oval, and heavy, the eyebrows too thick, shading the eyes too deeply. He did not like the resemblance because he disliked her mother, and her mother hated him since he refused to involve himself with his in-laws' lives. He had not seen his in-laws in years, and he knew Our Lady of the Passion's Sorrows had been beseeched many times for a conclusion to Adele Theresa Loopo's renegade marriage to a non-Italian Unbeliever. Our Lady must have heard.

"I wish you'd stop lying about naked. It's not very goddam attractive. Why do you do it?"

"Let's ball," he said, kissing her.

She looked at him, lazily turning her head, and gave an exasperated sigh. "Stop it."

"Come on. . . ." He tugged playfully at her arm, grinning at her, her resistance and indifference habitual by now, and still she excited him. "Look. . . ." He touched himself; she refused to look down. "I want you."

"That's supposed to be sexy?" She laughed. "Because your thing's hard I'm supposed to get excited? I ain't a dog lathering at the mouth when a bell goes off. Grow up." She stood up. "It's too late."

He grabbed for her arm, and she shoved his hand away. Her rejection, as usual, hurt him. He had come to the point where he did not care whether she wanted it or not, whether she fell asleep in the middle of sex with him inside her; he did not care. He did not want physical rejection. He would rather she just spread her legs and permitted him in, without invitation, than be rejected. He felt that he had earned the right.

"Don't you ever get enough?" she asked tiredly.

She left the room.

43

He finished his drink, angered by her refusal. *She's getting it somewhere else, that's why.* "You're my wife, remember?" he shouted. She did not answer. He decided to try again.

He found Adele standing naked in the bathroom, one foot resting on the rim of the toilet bowl, cutting her toenails, her breasts swaying against her upper arms as she worked the scissors. Her nightgown lay discarded on the floor.

"Don't you ever knock?"

He reached down to pick up her nightgown.

"Leave it there. It has to be washed."

He moved and stood behind her and looked at the rough hair between her legs, her sex visible under her raised leg. His erection returned. He moved closer to her, and his penis touched her hip. He placed his left hand on her back and leaned forward, over her bent body, and kissed the middle of her back, his right hand moving between her legs and on to her sex, feeling the damp warmth. "Beautiful. . . ."

"Get out," she said. "It doesn't belong to you anymore."

He moved his index finger into her sex and then pressed it against her clitoris.

She elbowed him in the side of his stomach. "I said, get out, goddamn it! I don't want to be groped. It doesn't belong to you anymore."

He moved off her. "It's become a public utility?"

She continued her pedicure, not shifting her position, refusing to look at him. She wanted to be left alone. She did not like the touch of him now. "I'm not going to have sex with you ever again."

His stomach tightened. "Don't ever joke about that." He laughed it off.

"I'm not."

He did not know whether to believe her or not. How do you unilaterally stop having sex after eight years of it? He was angry, suspecting it was true. He wanted to hurt her.

"You should lose some fat, Adele. Or nobody'll want to ball with you. I'm the only one who *has* to." It hurt her, as he

44

knew it would. He regretted the remark at once. "Adele, I'm. . . ." He lowered his eyes. "I didn't mean it."

She straightened up, staring fiercely at him, her eyes wet. She jabbed the scissors toward him, shouting, "What the hell do you want? Leave me alone! You want a blow job? You want to fuck my cunt? Here, fuck it!" She shoved her hands between her thighs and thrust her pelvis forward, parting her lips with her fingers. "There it is, you bastard, *fuck it!*"

"Adele." He reached toward her. "I. . . ."

"Get the hell *out* of here!"

He returned to the living room, grabbed his drink and refilled the glass. He sat down in a chair across from the sofa and put his feet up on the aluminum glass-topped coffee table. He felt defeated and scared. He knew, at that moment, she hated him. He did not know what he had done or failed to do that made her hate him.

After she showered, she came into the living room. She wore a housecoat. Her hair was wrapped in a white bath towel. She glanced at him, her face rigid. She was still angry. "Jesus. . . ."

"What now?"

"Put on some pants, for God's sake. This isn't the YMCA."

"*You're* naked half the time. . . ." Petulant.

"Not anymore." She began nervously pacing the room. "*Well?*"

"Well what?"

"Put on some *pants.*"

"You used to like to see me strip. . . ."

"Mother of God. *That* was in the beginning. *That* was when we were broke and there was no money and no air conditioning and one lousy room in the lousy Village and it was *summer.* So put on some goddamn pants."

He ignored her. That was his standard procedure when she was angry: ignore and drink until it passes.

"I want to talk."

"Okay, talk. I've got no place to go." Immediately he felt

45

self-conscious being naked in front of his wife. He pulled a scatter pillow from behind his back and shoved it on his lap. He rested his drink on top of it.

"I want *out*."

"What?" He pretended not to have heard her.

"Please turn off the stereo."

He did not move. He was afraid to move or to speak because he sensed she was looking for an argument, that she had finally resolved to leave him and she wanted a fight to make the leaving easier. She wanted to walk out as the injured party, guilt-free, pinning the onus on him.

She flicked off the phonograph.

"I want a divorce." She pulled the towel off her head and shook out her hair; it was straight and long and black, looking silky, almost liquid in the light, like water at dusk, placid on a windless night.

He smiled at her, remembering the first time he saw her bathe, sitting in the tub in his studio in the Village with its rose-colored wallpaper stained and peeling, sweating like him in the summer heat, its windows overlooking the chimney pots and sooty roofs of Little Italy shimmering in the heat, in the heat as she laughed, splashing water at him, laughing, laughing, Sugarboy, I love you, Sugarboy, shoving herself deep into the water as he watched, her breasts rising in it as she sank, her hair wet and shiny; kissing her in the bath, kneeling beside the tub, his trousers soaked, his hands gripping her head, tangling in her wet hair, kissing her, biting her lips, his tongue filling her mouth, her breasts bobbing in the water. Now eight years later she had finally asked for a divorce, and he discovered with relief that he welcomed the request, the end of tension. Out in the open. It could be dealt with. So he smiled, as if a heaviness had been lifted and he were released. He felt stronger than she, he always had, and morally superior, knowing that the initiative for the break had come from her. He was clean of it.

"What the hell are you smiling at?"

"I was thinking. . . ." He continued to smile.

46

"About what?"

"Rose-colored rooms."

"You're nuts, like your mother." She twisted her hands together. "Wipe that grin off your face."

He continued to smile, could not help smiling. She hated him for it.

"Stop it!" She threw the towel at him, narrowly missing his drink. He put the towel around his shoulders, like a prayer shawl, and gripped the ends of it against his chest.

"Just look at you. So smug. Like you never fucked anybody but me. You hypocrite. *You* abandoned *me*."

He did not know what she was talking about, and he could not accept her anger as real. He felt like the one betrayed, the cheated against. Why was she angry? She was the adulterer, not he. His mind kept drifting back to the rose-colored room where they had spent their first year together, to the steaming summer, the breezeless nights she lay beside him, the hours of sex when they sweated fucking, leaving the bed wet, and did not care, no money, little prospects, making do, and did not care; and now she was playing a moral advantage she did not have, accusing him of guilt and disloyalty he did not feel.

McFarland was a curious anomaly: he deeply believed in what he could not defend. That is, he believed in fidelity. He knew that without it any marriage he was part of would collapse in time. His jealousy and insecurity and what he considered his sense of justice and honor would break it up. He did not know where this insistence on fidelity came from. His father had played around constantly, and after his mother had been locked away, his father was open about it, even flamboyant, and his son looked on, hating him. Maybe that was why McFarland clung to the *idea* of fidelity. He had hated and feared and envied his father and resented his father's adulteries, seeing them as gross disloyalty to his mother; and yet it was his father's very infidelity that provided his son the comforting assurance of moral superiority over his father. He knew no rational, moral argument to support his convictions. He was not religious, and all the ascendant moral conventions of his time denied what he believed. He tried to convince himself that whom Adele slept with did not matter, not as long as she loved him and did not leave him. *It gives her pleasure, and it costs me nothing.* Nevertheless, it mattered crucially, and he knew it, and he could not tell you why. Perhaps unhappily, there was to the emotional fabric of his nature, to the very knitting of his cells, to his deepest expectations something that required the disciplines of physical exclusivity for a relationship to survive. He was ashamed to admit he felt that way. He thought it was conservative and old-fashioned and lamentably insupportable. And so he raged against her quietly inside himself, baffled and angered and humiliated by her recent and persistent adultery.

"You may not have left me *physically*," she said, her voice loud and incensed, "but you sure as hell left me psychologically."

"Who told you that, your boyfriend?"

"No one told me." She slapped her hand against her forehead. "God! I want to get *out*."

"What's your boyfriend's name?" He smiled again, briefly hating her.

"Who?" She had not heard him.

"That unemployed teacher you ball?"

"Fuck you."

"Odd name."

"Fuck you double."

"You drink too much, Adele." She did. It was the major reason why she had trouble losing weight. Since meeting her lover, who did not drink, who considered liquor to be a narcotic manufactured by the capitalists as an opiate for the oppressed masses, she was not drinking as much as before. Her weight was down as a result.

"*I* drink too much!" She grabbed his drink and threw it against the living-room mirror, cracking it. "*He* doesn't drink at all. *He's* not into all that middle-class, prematurely middle-aged crap. He's . . . ah, the hell with it." She stopped shouting, and shook her head, and began to laugh. "Now I *really* need a drink."

He watched her walk to the bar and pour herself a vodka on the rocks.

"Are we out of Rose's Lime?" she asked, turning toward him.

"I think so. Sorry."

"Doesn't matter."

"I suppose not."

"I'm not going to St. Thomas tomorrow," she said, sitting opposite him on the sofa. She sipped her drink.

He shrugged. "It doesn't matter, Adele." He lied. It did.

"The only thing you need me for is instant sex and to baby-sit Jaime. . . ." She yawned. "I really am tired. And you never listen to me."

"I'm listening now." He did not know what she meant. Never listen to her? She talked all the time.

"Listen, Paul, please." She stood up and walked to him and touched his chin, lifting his face to her. "I mean, really listen. . . ."

"Do you love me, Adele?"

The question startled her. She stepped back and looked oddly at him, distrustfully, not sure whether he was asking honestly or was trying to trap her.

"Do you love me?" he repeated.

"Oh, Paul"—she cupped her drink in her hand, turning it slowly like someone taking the cap off a bottle—"it's so complicated. Why do these things happen? Poor darling, I never meant it to go this far. . . ."

"Do you love me?"

She stared at him, chewing her lip anxiously, and then breathed deeply, tiredly, and her face grew hard.

"I'm very unhappy, Paul. I want to take Jaime to Malibu. I'm not going to St. Thomas. But I want you to go. And when you return, I want a divorce." She said it flatly, and he thought, catching her matter-of-fact tone, that she must have rehearsed those lines for months, saying them into the mirror, testing their effect on her current lover: this is how I will tell Paul.

"You're not taking my son." Coldly.

"Just until the divorce."

Later they lay in bed together. Neither touching the other.

"Paul?"

"Yes?"

"Do you know why I've stayed so long with you?"

"Because you love me. And because of Jaime."

"Jaime? No." She spoke softly, knowing what she was about to say would hurt him and still saying it because it was necessary to her that he understand. "I'm tired of playing second fiddle to your career."

"Wrong. That's untrue."

"I feel like a piece of furniture you push from room to room and sit on when you feel the need. I'm like an employee. Kitchen help."

"You know that's not true."

"Don't tell me how I feel."

"We'll talk tomorrow."

"Tomorrow you go to St. Thomas."

"And you to Malibu."

"Yes."

"Don't. Please." He touched her hand. "I wish to God we had never left the Village, that we were still in that room."

"You know," she said, rolling on her side and looking at him, "it wouldn't make a goddamn bit of difference. Even sex with you bores me now. It has for a long time. I once thought you were the most beautiful man in the world. I couldn't take my eyes off you. I couldn't believe how lucky I was to have you. And then you changed. Or we changed. I don't know. Life changed. You're right. It was better when we had no money and nobody ever heard of you. It was better before Jaime."

"Don't say that."

"It's God's truth, honey. And now I look at you, at your body, and I don't want to touch you anymore."

50

"He's so much better?"

"In some ways."

"Name one."

"He's circumcised."

McFarland laughed. "You're so full of it, Adele. You've gone dizzy." McFarland wasn't circumcised. He never thought it mattered much.

"Quit laughing, honey. Believe me, it makes a difference." He said nothing. He now felt no anger, simply a small, numbing fear in the hollow of his stomach quieted by fatigue. He did not want to be alone. He had never wanted to be alone. That was why in the end he had married her. He loved his son and could not tolerate his absence. He could not imagine life without Jaime in it. He felt depersonalized, as if he were standing at some distance away, watching and overhearing his wife talking to someone else.

"Can I tell you something?" He squeezed her shoulder and then slid his hand down her arm, the side of his hand brushing against her breast, and took her hand and pulled it to his chest. "I love you."

"I know." Indifferent.

"But you're becoming a very silly woman."

"Honey." She drew her fingers from his hand, speaking matter-of-factly as if she were asking her son to look both ways before he crossed into traffic. In that kind of deadpan, cautionary, yet condescending tone, she said, "I don't think I ever loved you."

"No?"

She thought a moment. "No. Not once."

He woke early, the bedroom semidark, the dawn light a thin corona shining in at the edges of the drawn, beige window shades, strips of light falling narrowly across the bed, like white traffic lines painted on a highway, the lines serried and bright and severely distinct across Adele's body. Adele lay zonked in her Seconal sleep, snoring quietly, oblivious to his dressing. He watched her a moment as he stood pulling on his shirt, buttoning it; she stirred in bed and rolled from

51

her back onto her side, her breasts under her nightgown sliding as she moved, their weight pressing against the material, tugging open the top of it, her breasts partially, suddenly visible, one nipple uncovered, erect as in sex, one strip of window light now falling like a binding rope across her breasts. Asleep, she reached out her hand and fumbled on the bed where McFarland had slept an hour before. She's searching for me, he thought, asleep, and she senses I'm gone. Old habits. She found what she wanted and pulled his pillow to her, wrapping her arms around it.

In the kitchen, reading the *Times*, having coffee. The phone rang. The flat Pennsylvania accent. Bureaucratic tone. His mother dead. To whom was the bill to be sent?

Later. He did not feel shock but completion, numbness, conclusion. The other shoe. Dropped. She had died before her death, face it, years ago, when they toasted her brains, leaving her crumbs as hard and dry as crystal for a mind. Face it. Half a mind. Better off now. Face it. His grief gave out then, years ago, in small horrors and shocks, petty, sadly funny insanities witnessed and witnessed again, hysterics, husbandly beatings, lemonade stands and a white wicker chair seated alone on a perfect green blanket of a lawn. Literally too late, too late, absolutely too late for tears. Jesus wept only once, pal. Even Jesus.

He packed what needed to be packed, and called the airport and confirmed his St. Thomas flight, and called the florist to send some flowers and on the phone suddenly remembered and had white lilacs sent.

Lilac and pine. As a boy she stood him on the counter in the kitchen in the house in Hanover in the late fall when all the leaves were down or falling, and only the pines in the grove across the street, by a mock-Tudor house his six-year-old mind was convinced was inhabited by a witch, only the pines were still green. His mother stood him on the counter; he faced the window and the pines, the window open, the smell of burning leaves, masses of songbirds on their way south chattering and quarreling and bickering unseen in the pine grove as his mother said to open his mouth so the witch riding the silver spoon, his dinner, could fly in, her hand the wind holding the broomstick and its rider. And he asked her where the birds went in the winter. And his old lady, not so old then, younger than he was now when she ran out of gas, his old lady cackled, laughing, "They fly up high. And their feathers turn to snow and fall on us." For a short time, one season, young as he was, he saw the snow as feathers fallen from dying wings.

"Adele," he whispered, leaning over the bed. "My mother . . ." he began. She did not wake. To hell with it.

He kissed his son good-bye. Starry, starry night.

4

FIVE months after McFarland returned from St. Thomas Island, Tom Stein told him about Jesse. Tom was his best friend, a tennis fanatic, a backslidden Jew and a sexual compulsive. Jesse was a real whore, Tom Stein said, but she was special. She was different. A whore. Special. Different. Tom had said the same thing about scores of other women because he liked to believe that all women were whores. And that was that.

"Jesse spent a weekend fighting off David [their host, David Rothenberg, a television producer]. She's not very politic."

"Rothenberg's a pig."

"Not politic." Tom sat back. He looked at McFarland and shook his head. "He's one of the majors. Jesse needs work. She's done a few commercials. We handled one of them for her at the agency. It's self-destructive of her to make enemies when she needs friends. She should've put out a little. God knows, she's fucked half the Avenue, so why not ball with David, huh?" Tom's logic. Sex had no moral content for Tom, and he placed no emotional value on it, as McFarland did, and he could not understand how women could see it differently. It was all combat and barter to him. "You give a favor. You get a favor."

"What happened?"

"About three in the morning Jesse schlepped into my room. She pounded on the door. She was crying. It embarrassed me. You'd think she'd have better taste. She wanted protection. David apparently had been pawing her. You know how he gets with a few drinks in him."

55

McFarland knew. He wrote television scripts for Rothenberg.

"She came to you looking for protection, right? And you fucked her."

"*Jesse?*" Tom looked astonished. Then he glanced around the restaurant. They were eating at the Back Table, a café on Third Avenue where they often ate. The place was frequented by advertising people. Tom Stein was one of them.

"Did you fuck her?"

"No." Tom put his finger in his drink and swirled the ice around.

"I don't believe you."

"What's it to you? She was sobbing. Christ, I'd have to be a sadist to get it up. And she was trembling. . . ." He leaned forward, lowering his voice, his face almost touching McFarland's, who looked back at him and wondered, as he always did when he saw Tom Stein, how anyone that homely could make so many women. He was more attractive than Tom. Taller. But Tom pocketed all the marbles.

"It unnerved me," Tom said. "I think she was on *drugs.*" He nodded his head knowingly and sat back in his chair. Drugs! Good Lord. Both men had grown up on the cusp of the eras, that dead stasis between Nixon and the Flower Children, although their young manhood was from Nixon to Nixon, and they were older by a year than the optimum age to sink into drugs. They were also somewhat established, certainly McFarland was, and while company types tolerated liquor, drugs sent them into panic, reaching for the pink slip. Of everyone McFarland knew, David Rothenberg was the only one who used hard drugs, and he was big enough and careful enough to get away with it.

"I think you laid her."

"I wanted to. But I didn't. I must be the only guy on the block who never had her. I'm too goddamn decent." He was serious, in an aw-shucks way.

"Who else has had her?"

"Nobody I know." Tom hesitated, and McFarland suspected he was lying. "But she has that reputation."

They ordered another round of drinks.

"Have you had any lately? I mean since Adele, uh. . . ." Tom fumbled for the word, knowing McFarland was unhappy about the separation.

"No, not in a couple months."

"But why? I know you're depressed and everything, I mean about your wife, but God, you're really, I mean you can be such a stud now, being free and everything. . . ."

"Sex makes me lonely."

"What?"

"Casual sex, sex with strangers, girls you grab drunk and toss out before they sober up, where they never even know your last name. . . ."

"What's wrong with that?"

"It makes me lonely. You shouldn't use women like that."

"Bullshit. You go to the bars. . . ."

"Sometimes."

"And you go to get laid."

"I go *thinking* I will. I'm looking for it. But once I get there and stand around holding a drink, and all that vapid conversation and desperation, Christ, that fierce unhappiness, after a while I decide just to stay long enough to get drunk and go home. I go to the damn bars because I'm depressed, and once I'm there I get more depressed. If I pick somebody up and ball, when they leave it knocks me out. And I want them to leave because they are never what I want. I think they are what I want, but they're not. So what's the point of it? I don't need it, Tom."

Tom grinned. "You got it wrong. You do them a favor. They all have an itchy crotch. You're only scratching it. It isn't a big deal. They don't *want* to know you. That's the point. They don't give a damn about your last name. They want to ball and leave. They stay drunk so they have an excuse for what they do and so they don't have to read the name of the fuck ship passing them by in the night."

"It isn't my ticket. It's never been."

"Eight years you were married? You'd think it was fifty. What the hell is your ticket?"

57

"Someone with feeling. Someone who'll stick. That's my ticket."

And so a week later, the night he chanced upon Jesse, McFarland thought he found his ticket.

It was late at night, and McFarland was slightly bombed, and Tom Stein was slightly bombed, too, although he was still eager, only giving up the game when morning called it. Tom never ran out of gas.

The game was dressing down and making the singles and honcho and dinge and glitter bars, pretending you were not what you were because you were oddly ashamed of what you were, as if what you were between nine and five desexed you in competition with junior execs and salesmen and graduate students and PRs passing as Venezuelans for that night's brace of secretaries and clerks dolled up in Ohrbach's copies and platform shoes and, the really stylish ones, mock thirties' makeup. However, the makeup and the dress, and the forced, boozed hilarity could not hide the outer boroughs' accent in the voice or the future yenta lying in ambush in the years ahead. And nothing could disguise, not the diet Dex or liquor or the mimicked Hamptons' laugh, the sorrow in the future no one wanted and no one could avoid.

The bar, called Bottoms Up, was located in a warehouse building in the Village across from the West Side Highway. It boasted a Victorian pool table, and it had walls covered with Christmas decorations, and Easter bunnies with red lightbulb eyes, and plastic Halloween pumpkins, and a clientele fitted to the decor: aging longshoremen and a few uptown heads slumming and young men who fancied themselves as pool sharks and hung around wagering small bets loudly, never winning more than pocket change, procrastinating against the last possible moment before they had to follow their fathers onto the docks and assembly lines and Jersey workshops. The bar was badly ventilated, the air filled with the acrid smell of cigarette smoke and grass and beer breath and Old Spice and the slightly dizzying odor of amyl nitrate, the amyl coming too sweetly from an area near the jukebox and pinball machines where couples danced slowly together, a few breaking poppers and breathing deep.

Jesse was with Durk, a young man with his name tattooed in blue on his upper arm. Durk was twenty-one years old, six years younger than Jesse. He was playing pool. He wore a sleeveless T-shirt, tight denim shorts, shorts made from jeans with the legs torn off at the crotch. And tennis shoes. It was a big year for tennis shoes. He looked dumb and over-built. Long brown hair fell over his forehead as he leaned over the table to pocket a shot, his crotch rubbing against the table's lip.

Jesse was sitting on a stool several feet behind Durk. She was sitting out of the light, her shoulders slouched, clutching a drink in her hand. There was something about her, about the way she sat and held her drink, the alert passiveness to her pose, the elegance of her, that he recognized but he could not place. He was intrigued by her, and he was glad that he had agreed to Tom Stein's importunings that he needed to get out among people, that it was unhealthy to sit around the apartment at night drinking alone. So he watched Jesse, her face hidden out of the light, as she watched Durk play pool. Behind her, above the bar, was a nativity creche and above it a sign that said, -ERRY CHRIST-AS It was July. Starry, starry night.

McFarland noticed Jesse's face when she lit a cigarette; her auburn hair, like Durk's, fell over her forehead as she bent her head to take the match. And then she tossed her head back, shaking it so that her hair fell away from her face, and blew the cigarette smoke toward the ceiling. It was that gesture that reminded him of the woman he had seen on St. Thomas.

McFarland was high on vodka, and he found Jesse attractive, so he decided to approach her. As he began to move toward her, she turned and noticed him. She raised her fingers to her lips, as if she were about to throw a kiss. But

59

her hand remained on her mouth, her fingers trembling. McFarland knew at once who she was and where he had first seen her.

He smiled at her and stepped forward, about to speak.

"Watch him," she said abruptly, nodding toward Durk. "He plays very well."

McFarland watched him play, and strut as he played, his pelvis forward. Every time Durk pocketed a shot he gave Jesse a wink or a sharp, barking laugh. McFarland did not like handsome, overbuilt men much on first sight; he did not like Durk, the dislike based on a sense of competition and reinforced by the fact that Adele had walked out on him with a man younger than he.

"What'd you do?" he asked Durk, his tone insinuating that whatever Durk did was disreputable and valueless. McFarland was slurring his words, and he was conscious of doing it, and he was unable to stop from doing it although he wanted to stop because he was aware that Jesse was listening to him slur his words. He wanted to catch Jesse's attention, to impress her, and he was sounding like a drunk, and he knew that wouldn't cut the ice.

"Play pool. Whatcha think?" He laughed at the obviousness of the question and flexed his shoulders. He winked at Jesse, who smiled in return. McFarland, seeing them, felt the first gnawings of paranoia. In the wink was conspiracy. The air made him nauseated. He wanted to leave. But he also wanted to meet Jesse, to speak to Jesse, who sat watching Durk play. The reason Durk's laugh offended him was she. He did not like the fact that she was with a pool hustler. But then he did not like the fact that his wife was having her insides balled sore at that moment in his house in Malibu.

"You a hustler?" he asked. He was convinced his wife's lover was.

"Huh?" Durk narrowed his eyes, glancing up as he bent over the table.

"You don't look smart enough."

Durk straightened up, stopping the game. He shifted his

60

weight to his right side. He flexed. He leaned against the pool cue held like a centurian's spear.

Jesse got up and stood beside him, and she seemed very small standing next to him, her movement unsteady. She looked up at him and then over to McFarland. The overhanging light above the green felt-topped table reflected in her eyes, emphasizing their pale green. Under her eyes were circles, like charcoal smudges, skirts of shadow, that increased the wet green of her eyes and added to the handsomeness of her face. Jesse was not beautiful, her features were too uneven; striking is what she was, commandingly so. She looked younger than she was. McFarland studied her a moment, deciding whether or not to mention St. Thomas. He concluded that he shouldn't, sensing that she would resent it. In any case, he did not want to take the chance. He had seen and been intrigued by her once, once having attempted to meet her and failing, and now that he was inside the circle again he did not want to risk not knowing her. She fascinated him. He did not want to risk not knowing her, and yet he was convinced she was better than Durk and did not belong with him, as she had not belonged in Katie's Bar. And there she was, and he could not account for it.

"Hey," Durk said, jutting out his hand toward McFarland in a stabbing, Brandoesque gesture, like that of someone testing the stuffing of a convertible sofa, "ya know what you look like to me?" Pause. "An asshole. Yeah. That's what you look like to me." He chuckled. McFarland sensed a fight was about to begin, and he knew, looking at Durk and at the cue stick, judging their disparities in age and weight and sobriety, that he would lose it. He had not fought since he was a school kid, and had lost all those fights, too. When he came home after school, beaten up, his mother would look at him oddly, her eyes not quite focused, and the blank stare would begin and her hand would go to her lips, the fingers trembling. "Henry, is your father back? Henry, is he back?" Then: I got beat up by the boys at school, Mom. Then: "Your father's a bully. He should be expelled! Henry, they must

61

throw him out! Pronto!" No, he didn't like to fight. As a boy he was small for his age and was constantly being attacked by the larger boys in his class, and it wasn't until he was in his late teens that his growth spurted so that by the time he left high school he was taller than average. But by then he had spent most of his life as a runt with too long, curly blond hair that his mother insisted he wear, being the angel he was, when all the other boys looked like prisoners or platoon sergeants in their crew cuts.

Jesse reached over and touched Durk's upper arm, caressed him gently below the ridiculous name tattoo, not looking at him as she did, the touch indifferent and yet effective because it relaxed him.

She stared expressionlessly at McFarland.

"He's with me," she said quietly, meaning don't push him too far because I cannot be involved. And then she laughed. Her laugh was vastly tentative, a vocal shudder, weak and too breathy and high, unsure of itself, like a small boy's hand extended defensively, suspiciously toward a stranger. If a laugh can be said to be sad, hers was.

"An easy mark." Durk pointed his thumb derisively at McFarland. "An easy roll." He scratched his crotch.

"Forget it, baby," Jesse said.

Durk shrugged, losing interest. He turned back to the table, eyed the balls and did a little body business before he made another shot. "Hot shit!" he exclaimed, pocketing three balls.

"Did you see *that?*" he asked her.

"Terrific." She smiled.

"I'm *baaad* tonight!"

"Baby, do me a favor. . . ."

"Sure," he said, resting his cue on the table, "I bet you want music."

She nodded. Durk touched her cheek and then moved off, pushing himself through the crowded bar.

Jesse sipped her drink. She stood, one hand resting on the edge of the pool table as if she needed the support. She wore white cotton, flared slacks and a T-shirt with BORN FREE printed on it, and she wore no bra. On the right side of her slacks, hanging from a belt loop, were several keys dangling on a steel chain.

A few minutes after Durk parted from them, the jukebox came on again, and they heard above the noise of the room Peggy Lee singing "This Time the Dream's on Me."

"St. Thomas?" McFarland asked.

She said nothing, simply looked at him as if she had not heard. Before he could repeat himself, she asked, "What do you do? You might even hustle."

"Not that way." He laughed.

"You're handsome enough. . . ." She smiled, for the first time flashing a very broad grin, one that implied you are beyond reaching me. It came automatically to her when she was tense and anxious. It was the kind of smile celebrities are conditioned to make, a defensive expression that is so open and dazzling and yet so patently insincere that it neutralizes a stranger's advance at the same time that it flatters him. She used it to distance herself from the world. It was both correct and condescending, like a big restaurant tip.

"I write. . . ."

"Yes?" She reached out and touched his hand. Her fingers were cold.

He nodded in agreement. He was flattered by her touching him and yet depressed by it, and he did not know why unless it was because he had not stood up to Durk as he felt he should have done. He had provoked him and then backed away, protected by her.

"Why do writers drink so much?" she asked.

"Do they?"

"I only know one writer. He's always drinking . . . if he's not stoned. . . ." It was difficult to hear her. She mumbled as if she were speaking to herself. It was a manner common to her, mumbling and looking down as she spoke; when she was saying something hurtful to someone, she would glance down as she said it and, when finished, lift her head slowly, gazing up disinterestedly as they took it in.

"I have no idea. Why do they drink so much?" He did not

think the question was interesting, but his mind had gone blank, a dry field, and he could think of nothing to say. He wanted to keep the conversation going, to know her, and yet he couldn't organize his thoughts. He felt tongue-tied and stupid in front of her. He wanted her to like him. He did not know how to go about it.

"Because they have so much self-contempt."

"I'll drink to that." He raised his glass.

"Do you know Mike Rhodes?" she asked. "He's the writer I know."

"I went to college with him. Columbia. We both hated the place. I haven't seen him in years."

She nodded. She raised her glass to her mouth and sipped her drink, watching him as she did. On her wrist was a round pink scar, about a half inch in diameter. "Mike was good at it once. . . ." She meant good at writing. "He isn't good at it anymore." She spoke more to herself than to him.

At that point Tom Stein came over. "I see you've met." He seemed very pleased.

"She knows Mike Rhodes."

"No kidding."

"Yes, don't you?" McFarland smiled at Jesse and touched her hand.

She nodded.

"Mike Rhodes is crazy as hell," Tom said.

5

THEY left Tom Stein and Durk in the bar and walked down West Street to Hudson and then across to the Morton Street pier. It was a warm night, and the tide was up, and the odor of the harbor hung heavily in the air. It was dark, although they could see indistinct forms cruising along the pier, cigarettes glowing.

Moored next to the pier was an old ship that the city used as a marine high school. Long, thick ropes swung from it down to the pier. The pier creaked as the ship tugged with the tide against the ropes, the ropes groaning.

Jesse and McFarland balanced themselves on the ropes. They sat facing the Jersey shore, the hi-rise apartment buildings on the Palisades twinkling in the night.

Being out of the bar, he was more relaxed, and he was delighted she had agreed to walk with him. He asked her where she was from.

"I grew up in Minneapolis." She pronounced it Minn-ne-an-*na*-polis. He had never heard it pronounced that way before, so he suspected she was lying. "The river isn't as wide there. I used to play on the sandbars beneath the Lake Street bridge . . . there were high sandstone bluffs, the color of wheat. . . ."

"Like the Palisades?" He had never been to Minneapolis.

"Starker. Like claws. In the winter the Mississippi is solid ice. Every winter someone jumped from that bridge."

Jesse stood up and walked to the very end of the pier. She swayed. He came up behind her and held her a moment. He thought of his wife as he did, and it gave him a tinge of guilt because he knew he wanted to go to bed with Jesse, and then

65

he felt angry that he would feel guilty. He still felt a habitual sexual loyalty to Adele, and that was one of the reasons why he did not like to play around. He felt betrayed by his wife, robbed from and cheated. She damaged his sense of sexual adequacy. In avoiding fucking other women, even after she left him—and for his age and station he was remarkably faithful—he felt morally superior to her, as he had felt to his father. And that superiority fueled his contempt, and it was his contempt for his wife's adultery that held his loneliness for her at bay.

Jesse leaned back, her head lolling against his cheek. He tightened his hold. She was thin and fragile, and he felt he could snap her back between his hands as easily as breaking a pencil. The thought of hurting her excited him. He did not know how to account for it.

"I've only been home once," she said. "Mike and I spent the entire week holed away in a suite at the Northrop Inn, like two invalids. . . ."

"Mike Rhodes?"

"He was drunk or stoned or both all the time . . . he writes that way, and what he writes makes no sense. Listen"—she pulled away from him—"I paid for that goddamn suite. I had a lot of money then, residuals." She was suddenly angry as if he had accused her of something false. "It isn't true what they say. I even did the magazines. I don't care what those bastards say! So let the dogs bark . . . I made more money than *you* make!"

"Probably." He moved toward her and grabbed her hand. Her outburst made him uneasy. He did not know how to handle flashes of hysteria in women, particularly women he loved, and he had faced them all his life. His response was to speak quietly, to be reasonable. But reasonableness rarely worked, only seeming to incite their hysteria further, and he knew violence would most often work, but he could not bring himself to use it, not against a woman he cared for, not after seeing his mother beaten down that first time in the white-painted room.

"Calm down." Quiet. Reasonable.

She struck his hand away.

"Don't hit me!" she yelled. "Don't *touch* me. Leave me the hell alone!"

She swiveled around and backed away from him. He couldn't see her face, but he could hear her fast, labored, frightened breathing, and he knew she was alarmed. He did not know about what.

"Hey, it's all right." He moved toward her, speaking softly. He was suddenly aware that her panic sexually aroused him.

"Don't hit me. Please don't hit me."

"I would never hit you. Never. . . ."

"I'm not a whore . . . I'm not."

He put his arms around her and gripped her tightly. She was very rigid, and then she relaxed. He kissed her. "Hell, they won't hire me anymore. Thanks to Mike." She laughed. And then he did, only a beat too late. He had lost the thread of what she was saying.

They turned and began to walk off the pier toward the street. McFarland's foot hit an empty beer can, and he picked it up and threw it toward the river. It clanked in the darkness at the edge of the pier and then splashed into the water. "You dumb fuck!" someone yelled in the darkness. French sailors yelling obscenities in bad English in the streets of St. Thomas the night his mother died. He had thrown too short.

They went along the promenade at the entrance to the pier and then across Hudson Street past a group of trucks around which about thirty men were milling, and then they smelled the odor of grass.

She pointed to the trucks.

"That was Mike's kind of scene. He liked to stand outside and listen to them banging away. He liked the cries. He liked the noises they made. That's what he liked to write about. Everywhere he was, he saw and heard animals mating and snarling and tearing at each other."

"People are only animals to him?"

"Well, scientifically speaking, at any rate. What do you like writing about?"

"Me?" He thought a moment. "Whatever pays the rent." It

67

wasn't true in terms of intentions, but it had been true in terms of fact. He said it because James Baldwin had once said it and it seemed clever at the time.

"You're a hack, too." She sounded both cynical and disappointed.

He laughed. "Do you still see Rhodes?" He was jealous of him. Rhodes was crazy.

"Mike?" She considered a moment. "He's in Los Angeles now. I don't know what he's doing. I don't care."

They walked to Seventh Avenue. He put his arm around her waist. He wanted her to come uptown with him, and he wanted to have sex with her in the dark.

"Come to my place," he said.

"Some other time, baby." She pulled away from him.

"No, come home with me now. I want to be with you. I feel lonely." It was very important to him that she come because he did not want to be alone anymore, and he had not and would not adjust to the apartment without Adele and his son living in it. More, he was beginning, at thirty-five, to fear that he was missing out, and at times the fear of missing out was more important than keeping his contempt clean. And she was his ticket. So he made the request. "Come with me."

"Mike used to say that the only people not lonely were the blind. They were most blessed because they never saw an empty room or someone walking away."

"You're making fun of me."

"No."

"Then come."

"I forgot," she said, smiling. "I have his keys." Then she reached up and touched his cheek. "I have to get back to him, my angel." She said it sweetly, caressing him. He melted.

"*Please* come up."

She looked at him, cocking her head to the side, and then she flashed the movie star grin. "I hate men to beg." She jangled the keys at her side. He remembered the bracelets jangling on her wrists in St. Thomas.

"Whose keys are they?"

"Durk's."

And for no reason understandable to him, since he did not know her, his feelings were profoundly hurt. His reaction to the hurt was anger.

"How much money do you want?"

She stared at him, her eyes misted. She ran her hand through her hair, and took a deep breath. "Oh, baby," she said, and once again laid her fingers against his cheek, "you have too much pride."

He turned to hail a taxi.

Jesse stood on the sidewalk as he went into the street and stopped a taxi. In the minute that passed before he entered the taxi he regretted his remark and wanted to take it back, and yet he could not bring himself to apologize for it. He did not know what to say or how to begin saying it. He got into the taxi. He looked back at her. She raised her hand to her lips, he thought at first to throw a kiss, but her hand remained on her mouth, her fingers trembling.

6

SHE was on his mind all week, and he saw her everywhere and nowhere. And late one night, driving home in a taxi through the theater district, he saw her standing out of the rain under a marquee at Forty-sixth and Eighth Avenue. He yelled at the taxi driver to stop, pounding on the plastic partition between them. It took the driver two blocks to stop, and when he did, he swore violently at McFarland in Spanish. He threw money at the driver as he left the cab and ran down Eighth Avenue to the marquee only to find Jesse gone. And like a man whose mind was derailed, he stood in the rain shouting her name as a crowd gathered. She never answered.

It rained most of the week in New York. The island was a haze of gray, and the air atypically clean and summer-smelling, although the heat was great, and the trees in Central Park below his apartment window were a blur of green in the wet fog between the rains, and their color reminded him of her eyes.

McFarland stayed in most nights, working on the script he was contracted to write for David Rothenberg. It was a television movie about a Nazi doctor hiding out in the United States after the war. The picture had been optioned by Paramount, and Rothenberg was working on foreign sales before production. He did not know much about the war since he was not born until it was well under way in Europe, and what he knew about the death camps and the Jews came from reading in school long ago. It had no immediacy for him, and no reality. There was so much horror in the world, its sorrow so unremitting, that he could not take it in. It seemed to him that the human capacity for grief was never as large as its penchant for disaster, and so he let it go by. However, he was required to know something about the camps and medical experiments for the script, and through Paramount a screening was arranged for him to see footage taken of the Holocaust.

It was during the week after he met Jesse when it rained all the time.

He took a subway to Rockefeller Center and walked to the screening room on Third Avenue, past the spot where six months before Adele had pointed out her lover to him.

He sat in the screening room for four hours with a librarian from the Columbia University Library who had provided the film footage from their war archives. The librarian was a middle-aged man who kept averting his eyes from the more heinous visions on the screen and who, when wide-eyed, would light a cigarette prefatory to getting up and whispering to him that he was off to the men's room, sweetheart. When he returned, he would sit one seat closer until at the end of the screening they sat side by side, his herringbone pant leg rubbing against McFarland's. It made him uncomfortable. The herringbone made his leg itch.

Gross-Rosen. Buchenwald. Chelmo. Ravensbrück. Sobibor. Natzweiler. Belsen. Auschwitz. Treblinka. The Warsaw Uprising. Hours of it, millions slain, and McFarland watched it all knowing he should never forget but would always forget the ovens and the endless lines and the piles of stripped clothing and mounds of stolen hair, God, the answerless sorrow; he would forget, as others had and would, and what of it? Still, he sat in the screening room crying, embarrassing the restless librarian, and he was there to write what he knew was a lousy commercial script about a camp doctor escaped to America, to make money off it, and he felt no guilt about any of it, and his lack of required guilt made him guilty.

He did not know why he cried. He did not know why he did that. Nor why later he was never able to forget the small boy in that film with his hands raised in the air, his fingers trembling, his face bewildered by terror, being marched out of the Warsaw ghetto by men with big guns meant to wipe him out, while all about chaos and madness reigned . . . and he wasn't even born then. McFarland would be *younger* than that boy now. He wasn't even Jewish or circumcised. He was raised a *Baptist* by a mother with Wonder Bread for a mind, and he was taught that the Jews made hamburger out of Jesus. But since that moment McFarland always wondered where that boy was now, that small Jewish boy with almond eyes large with panic, who had straight black hair and a mouth opened wide, baffled by terror. He was wearing a small black cap and a winter coat made of black cloth with large white buttons down the front and short schoolboy pants and little shoes turned up at the front from schoolboy wear. Someone's son, someone's issue. He wondered if they had erased him, wiped him from the board. *He needed to know what had happened to him.* He would never know. He wept. So what? He wept more for Jaime than for the Warsaw boy, more for himself than for the boy, more for his mother, who had scrambled eggs for brains, than for him. More than for him.

"What happened to that boy?"

"What boy?" The librarian smiled, wiping his tongue over his lips, his eyes staring at McFarland's crotch and glancing up. McFarland did not like his wetting his lips or his hungry eyes or the way he said "boy."

"The one in Warsaw in the little coat, the one with his hands in the air?"

"Warsaw? The Uprising? Let me see, that would be May, 1943, under SS General Jürgen Stroop, who I believe is still alive. Curiously enough, the Jews fought back. The SS murdered some fifty-six thousand, and it took four months and three thousand troops, and they used flamethrowers and artillery and tanks and armored cars—"

"But the boy? What of him?"

"I wouldn't know. He may have escaped, but it's highly unlikely, a child, a Jew. No, no. In any case, it's too late to know. It's lost to us, historically speaking."

Lost to us.

7

HE LEFT the screening room and stood outside for a few minutes deciding what to do. It was raining, and the weather was hot, and the rush-hour traffic was jammed up Third Avenue past the movie houses in front of which crowds of young people grouped, waiting for the shows to begin.

He was disturbed by what he had seen moments before. He felt disconnected, vulnerable, his safety, his life itself contingent on powers and sudden intrusions, on evil without a known face. The small boy of Warsaw in his coat . . . and he felt as if he had encountered the other side of things, as if he had overturned a delicately beautiful gazebo out of doors and discovered under it nests of vermin. He knew no way to reconcile the young Americans lined in the rain before the movie theaters on Third Avenue with the young Poles lined at Belsen in the bloody snow. There was no way.

This he understood: around us all was madness peeking through, and he could hear its scratchings, like mice clawing behind a wall, breaking through. There was no help for it.

He was saddened and depressed by his own futility. He needed sane human company. He needed someone to talk to. He felt as wasted as he had felt when his mother blew her fuse the last unhappy time in Hanover, Pennsylvania. It was a Saturday in the winter, and he was home watching television. His mother was on a bus going to see the doctor. She had been released from the loony bin months before on condition that she check in with the shrink every Saturday. She had started attending a Pentacostal church and while it should have been obvious to anybody that she had unraveled somewhere in her attic the Holy Rollers saw her mania as the Infilling of the Holy Spirit, and in no time flat she had become something of a big wheel in the little church. Even at home she managed to function if one overlooked her newly acquired and fanatic piety. If one ignored her shouted prayers bursting forth from her at odd moments like steam shooting suddenly from an overheated radiator. His father and he did their level best to ignore the hollered benedictions, as at dinner when she began to shout grace and was still at it, head bowed over her cold plate, an hour after the two of them had finished dessert and wandered into the living room to watch *I Love Lucy.* Or if one ignored her "witnessing" every time the phone rang, something her husband didn't do since his clients were the usual victims of her religious hysteria via Bell.

"I don't care who you want, mister! I'm talking about *Jesus!* God Incarnate. And that ain't small potatoes, don't cha know! Why weren't you in church on Sunday? Cat got your tongue, huh? *Speak up!* Don't be a 'fraidy cat! *Or you'll burn in hell, cocksucker!*" Bang!

His father had a lock put on the phone.

One afternoon McFarland got a call from the Sunoco filling station. It was the bus driver.

"Your mother has hijacked my bus!"

He got dressed and walked ten blocks through the snow to the Sunoco station. Sitting across the street from it, parked at an odd angle and blocking one lane of traffic, was an old green city bus. He could hear his mother's voice singing "Throw out the lifeline, someone is sinking todaaay!" She was holding revival services on the bus. Starry, starry night.

"She's stolen my bus! She must be off her rocker!"

"What?"

"She must have beans for brains! Cuckoo! A loony bird!" The bus driver stood in the snow, stamping his wing-tipped oxfords up and down in the slush, twirling his index finger wildly at the side of his head. "Brazilian nuts upstairs, I tell you! A *toaster* for a *brain!* A religious screwball, a menace to the public safety!"

76

"I'll get her home," McFarland said, by now used to the townspeople's decidedly negative response to his mother's religious vocation. He didn't care anymore. He just didn't want her hurt.

"Get her home? You bet your sweet ass you'll get her home. *But not before she's paid the goddamn fare.* She didn't even pay her *fare.*"

McFarland gave him a quarter, and then he and the driver walked to the bus. His mother stood inside the front, by the driver's seat, dressed in her bridal gown and wearing over it his father's long white terry-cloth bathrobe that had long angel-cuff sleeves. The robe hung down to her bare feet.

He climbed into the bus. She stood with her feet together in a puddle of snow water and slush melting on the rubber floor, and her arms were outstretched at her sides, her hands gripping the aluminum ceiling straps to prevent anyone from getting off until the service was over. When she finished singing, she moved down the aisles toward the two old ladies who huddled together on the green leather seats, their faces pictures of stupefaction and unholy dread.

"Mom," he said quietly, tapping her on the shoulder, "Mom, the ride's over. It's the last bus stop."

She ignored him, as she often did, and went up to the two old ladies and boomed out, "Tell Sister Aimee your heartache, sisters, tell her your *pain!*" His mother had recently adopted the third person in speaking of herself. "Tell Sister your troubles. Arthritis? Jesus can *heee*al it! Cancer? Jesus can *paaa*ss it! Goiters? Jesus can *wipe them out!*" The two old ladies, the only passengers on the bus, stared up at her, tentative, appeasing grins breaking out helplessly as if they sensed their time had come.

As McFarland came up behind her, his mother slammed her hands down on the head of the first old lady, pushing the old lady's beflowered pillbox hat down over her ears. And she shouted, "Be *heee*aled! In the name of Jesus of Nazareth and before the Company of Angels! Be *healed!* From the top of your old head to the soles of your old feet!"

"Mom!" He went up behind her and pulled her hands off the old lady, who looked as if she were seconds from cardiac arrest. "Mom, it's me, *Paul*."

She dramatically swiveled around, her white sleeves slapping in the old lady's face as she swung around. She faced her son, her countenance flooded with heavenly joy.

"Henry!" she shouted. "Jesus *saves!*" And with that she clamped her hands over his skull and yelled, "Be healed! In the name of Jesus of Nazareth. . . ." And he began backing out of the bus as his mother stumbled along, facing him, her hands glued to his head, her fingers messing up his greasy, carefully combed duck's-ass hairstyle, her white terry-cloth robe and white bridal gown flapping, flapping against seats and posts as they clumped down the aisle, mother and son. "Before the Company of Angels, in the name of Jesus of Nazareth. . . ." Screeching as they stumbled out of the bus and stepped into the drifting snow and backed away through the snow past the gas pumps and piled tires and Coke machines and the two cars filling up, their drivers staring in fascinated horror, as they lockstepped through the snow and into the filling station, her hands clutching her son's head, "Henry! Be healed!"

He called his father, and that was that.

And so he decided to find Jesse. He did not know why he hesitated so long in calling Tom Stein to ask for her number, unless he harbored the hope that somehow his marriage would be patched up, that he would get a late-night call from the Coast and hear Adele conceding defeat and begging to return. No call had come. None was likely. It was on the rocks for sure.

Stein didn't have her number, nor did Information. But Tom did have her address on Greene Street in Soho.

McFarland stood in the rain for five minutes watching empty taxis rush by with their off duty signs lit, the drivers grinning fiendishly as they roared by the crowds of the rain-soaked begging for rides. Finally he took a subway down to Houston and walked through the rain to Greene, where he climbed five flights of steep wooden stairs in an old loft building to the top floor. He knocked on the door. There was no answer. He pushed against the steel fire door and found it unlocked and entered the loft, his stomach tight with anticipation.

Jesse stood in the center of the enormous room, holding a joint of grass in her hand. She looked passively at him, his face and clothes wet from the rain, all out of breath. She started to speak, and then she laughed, covering her mouth with her hand as she did. He laughed too.

"God in heaven," she said, "you're the last person in the world I wanted to see."

McFarland stood grinning at her, rainwater dripping down his face, his blond hair slicked wet and flat against his forehead, his eyes wide and full of delight. "Beautiful . . . beautiful . . . beautiful . . ." he mumbled, staring at her. She was dressed in shorts and a V-neck sweater, and her hair was piled on top of her head, held in place with bobby pins. Her skin was tanned, and to him she looked about five years old, a child. "Beautiful. . . ."

She shook her head in disbelief. "Snap out of it, baby, before you wear out the word."

"I . . ." he began.

"You what?"

"I'm very sorry about what I said to you when I left you in the Village the night we met. . . ."

"Oh, that." She shrugged. "It's been said before."

"I was jealous and angry, and I didn't mean it."

"Forget it. I never take drunks or politicians seriously."

She walked up to him. "You're soaking wet." She unbuttoned his raincoat as he stood grinning foolishly at her, feeling relieved and happy. "That's right, take it off." She felt his trousers. "They better come off, too." She knelt down in front of him and untied his shoes. He laid his hand on her head. She moved away. "Now take them off." He stepped out of his shoes.

"You must have walked miles in the rain. . . ."

"I swam the *Hudson* to reach you."

"Then why don't you smell like shit?"

She touched his wet hair and then let her hand slip down his face, feeling its wetness. "What beautiful eyes," she commented. "He was right about you. . . ."

"Who was?"

"Durk."

"Oh, him." Dejected.

"Yeah. Him. He said you were an easy mark."

"It was a cheap shot." He unbuckled his belt.

"Well, he's right. You are. It's in your eyes. You have big farmboy eyes. You look like you're seeing the Empire State Building for the first time, and you find it a real knockout."

He smiled, embarrassed by her teasing him, yet flattered by it. He was hooked, going ga-ga, swimming toward the boat. He felt an immediate intimacy with Jesse. Her directness disarmed him, although in point of fact her apparent openness was highly provisional and limited. She was as defensive as the rest; only she hid it better since her capital defense was the appearance of having none.

"My mother said I had the eyes of Jesus," he boasted, somewhat astonished at hearing himself make the remark.

"Did she now?" She looked into his eyes, standing on her tiptoes in order to be nearly eye level with him. She opened her eyes exaggeratedly wide and stared into his. Then with her index finger she pulled down each of his lower eyelids in turn, as if she were an examining eye doctor.

"Damn it all if she wasn't right! You sure do. And that's about the saddest thing anybody could say. How'd your old lady know?"

"Know what?"

"*Jesus.* I never met the gentleman myself, although I think we would've gotten along, Jesus and me. But I wouldn't know about His eyes."

"The very eyes of Jesus, that's what she always said," he repeated humorously, the observation now seeming crazy and funny to him. He remembered riding home from the paint store with his mother, her hand resting softly on his leg the first time her lights went out. Soft as snow.

80

"Now take your pants off, and I'll get you a towel, and a drink. Scotch, right?"

"Vodka. Straight."

"I always thought shit-kicking farmboys went to bourbon and whiskey. Live a little. Learn a little."

He took off his trousers. She took them from him and hung them on a chair in front of the floor fan at the far end of the loft. She returned with a towel and his drink. "Sit down, Paul. *Paul?* It *is* Paul?"

"Yes." He sat on an old, dog-bitten, soiled and badly torn sofa. "Nice," he said, his bare legs feeling itchy from the particles on the seat. "Does it rain *crumbs* in here? God, it feels like a beach."

"We do our best."

She stood in front of him and rubbed his hair with the towel and then gently, with the ends of it, patted his face dry. He noticed the scar on her wrist.

"That's good. Nice and dry. Don't want you to catch cold, baby."

She stepped back and looked at McFarland sitting on the broken-down sofa, his blond hair teased as if he had just been juiced with thousands of bolts of Con Edison, the light shining on his hair glowingly, his shirt hanging over his crotch, his bare legs, his calf-length socks. The combination of his seriousness and boyishness of expression, his dishevelment and bashful attempt at dignity, the ease with which he had complied with what she had asked, his apology, his obvious delight in her and his patent desire to be liked, his handsomeness and vulnerability—all of it won her affection. She started to giggle. She could not help herself. She felt lucky and relieved and found it all mildly cockeyed and silly, this tall, intense, pathetically decent and attractive man suddenly bursting in on her out of the rain; and there he sat toweled dry, grinning like an athlete anxiously waiting to be sent back into the game. She felt stronger than him, tougher, more cynical, wiser to the world, more lived, less trusting; she had been around the block more times, more desperately in worse ways. So she giggled, shaking her head at the kind improbability of it all.

"Why are you laughing?"

"Good God! Look at what the cat's dragged in! *Look*"—she pointed at him, wagging her finger, giggling—"look at what fell from the sky, across the Hudson, right into my life. Jesus *Christ!* It must be Christmas."

It was August. Starry, starry night.

He sat gazing at her, seemingly preoccupied, his mind off somewhere.

"You seem dazed. I know it isn't me."

"It's you and—"

"What?"

"I was remembering something I saw this afternoon. The boy—"

"What *boy?*" She was immediately suspicious. "Oh, God, don't tell me you're a faggot," she said nervously. "Not that, please."

"No. . . ."

She sat down beside him, and he recounted to her what he had seen at the screening and about his crying when he saw it. She did not altogether trust what he was saying because she could not fathom his reasons for bringing it up, and she said, "Tears are cheap."

"But the kid with his hands in the air that goddamn day. . . ."

"Why are you so sentimental about kids? There were seven kids in my family. My old man worked for the telephone company as a lineman climbing poles. He hated all of us. He hated his job, his boss, stormy weather, my mother. Boy, could he hate. He hated feeding us and wasting all that hard-earned money he made shimmying his ass up those icy telephone poles. He beat the hell out of us. When I think about it, I don't know many men who really like kids. . . ."

"You met one now."

"Sure. But you're a sucker for affection," she said. "I knew right away."

"Maybe I am."

She snorted. "There's no maybe about it, baby. No maybe, baby. Ha-ha."

She was right. He knew he was a pushover for kids, especially if they were injured children. He did not know why that was, but that was part of the architecture of his heart, and there was no denying it. As a boy he was given to sitting up all night watching charity telethons. His mother loved them, too. It confirmed her notions about faith healing; loony, yet she understood the potential. He was always pulling for the telethon and hoping the pledges would go over this year's goal and they'd win one for the little kids streaming in as the band played "The Impossible Dream." Kids tripping and falling and twitching and hurting spastically, laughably, horribly in their shiny stainless steel crutches and braces, slouched in brand new wheelchairs and baby-blue stretchers, sealed in iron lungs like beans in tin cans, their uncontrollable muscles and their large, tormented, unfocused eyes. It was better than *Queen for a Day*. For sheer sentimental gorging on guilt, what could beat their silly, lunatic grins as if it were a big deal to be on a theater stage making a spectacle out of your six-year-old hopelessness, commercializing the bald fact that your distressingly beautiful, malformed, ugly, contemptible, haunting, twisted child's body would be a dead duck in no time, moments from then, unless the viewers all pitched in with their nickels and dimes to give the little tots a chance at life? McFarland loved it and he hated it and he couldn't help himself. He kept thinking through the years, Where was Jesus when we needed Him? Why wasn't He in Warsaw with the others? After all, where was He now? Somebody had to take up the slack. It was McFarland. He canvassed from door to door for Birth Defects, Cancer, TB, MS, Diabetes, Retardation, City of Hope, MHA, and more, for March of Dimes and CARE and Sister Kenny and Boys' Town and the Community Chest and the Red Cross and the Heart Fund and the Lighthouse for the Blind. And still he had this compulsion to slip white charity envelopes under his neighbor's door. And he wondered why. He felt responsible and he knew he was not, and he also

83

knew that even if he were responsible, there wasn't a god-damn thing he could do about any of it. He was certain that long after he had dropped dead, they would still be hobbling across that television stage in steel frames, drooling spit from tiny pink mouths as they appealed for money. God broke a few cups when He made the dishes, his Mom used to say, and there's no mending them now.

"I want you to come to a party with me," he told Jesse.

"Is that why you came by, to take me to a party?"

"I have to show up at this damn thing, and I'd like you to be there."

"When is it?"

"Tonight."

"Who's giving it?" she asked disinterestedly.

"David Rothenberg. He's a—"

"I *know*. A bastard." She screwed up her face, and then she laughed. "Why, he hates my guts. You can't bring me there."

"Yes, I can."

"You better call and ask, baby. You don't want a scene."

"I'm writing a script for him. He won't make a scene." Only then did he remember Tom Stein's telling him of meeting Jesse in East Hampton at Rothenberg's.

"It's your life," she said. "Okay, give me time to change."

Holding the drink, he wandered around the loft in his stocking feet, without his trousers, following her as she pulled off her clothes, throwing them on the floor. She walked naked into the doorless bathroom and washed herself and put on false eyelashes and light makeup and combed her hair.

He stood in the doorway of the bathroom, watching her, her eyes very green, the shadows under them not as insistent as when he had first seen her. Her body was small. In fact, seeing her naked, he was surprised at how petite she actually was. It was endearing to him. She was five feet two inches tall, a full foot shorter than he. She had lovely breasts, not as large as his wife's, but nice enough, and a round, small, tea-cup ass. On her back and on her right shoulder were dark, bluish yellow bruises, as if she had taken a bad fall recently. He reached out and felt her bottom. She slid his hand away. "Later," she said, as she looked into the mirror, combing her hair, her head tilted to one side while she pulled the brush rapidly down and away. She caught his eye in the mirror, and she winked at him, wrinkling her nose. "You're a big looker, aren't you?"

He did not answer.

"Well, baby, so am I." She stopped brushing her hair and stared at him. "What are you thinking, Paul?"

"I was thinking how nice it is to watch a woman brush her hair. And I was thinking how lovely your nose is." Jesse had a small, turned-up nose. She was half-Dutch in descent, and it showed in her green eyes and small nose.

"I never liked my nose," she said. "I always wanted a nose like yours, straight and long, very patrician. I have a peasant's nose, and that's not the least of it." She grabbed a comb. "Here, comb your hair. You look like a bushman."

He combed his hair and handed back the comb.

"Good. Now get out of here a minute."

McFarland stepped away from the bathroom.

"What happened to the door?"

"What door? The bathroom? There never was any. They never got around to putting one on."

He heard the toilet flush.

The loft was filthy; the furniture, what there was of it, was old and soiled, Salvation Army stuff found in the street. The back area of the loft was divided by two plywood partitions into bedroom areas. There were two double beds, each enclosed in its own partitioned area. It reminded him of the Bowery old men's hotels with their floors broken by plywood walls that did not reach the ceiling, in each cubicle a bed, and stretching over the entire thing, like steel lace, chicken wire netting to keep the men from climbing the walls into their neighbor's area. There was no chicken netting here, but the place had a similarly jerry-built appearance. The loft, like others in the area, had until recently been occupied by small manufacturers. However, in the last few years more and more of the small plants, mainly textile and carpentry concerns, had moved away, and the landlords had illegally rented the vacated space for apartments. What one rented was totally empty space. Bathrooms, bedrooms, kitchens had to be added by the tenants, most of whom were poor, so that the Soho lofts, largely warrens for artists, had a nearly uniformly tacky, unfinished appearance.

In the far corner, under the ceiling space heater, lay a small foam rubber mat with a dirty sheet covering it. On it, asleep, was a mongrel dog.

"Don't you ever clean this place?"

"This dump? What's to clean?" She turned and looked at him, her eyes wide in mock innocence.

"Is that your dog?"

"It's a stray."

"What's its name?"

"Anything. Call it what you want. It's deaf."

He was troubled that Jesse would live there. The dirt and barrenness. It made him uncomfortable. He associated it in his mind with drugheads and dopers and weird sex, with his wife's lover, with losing, and with everything else he feared—the loss of money, friends, position, hope, self-respect—that meant defeat. He was middle class enough to believe that when conventions and manners went by the board—neatness, politeness, cleanliness—what it signaled was the loss of self-respect. And that was why her living in the loft troubled him. It hinted to him of bad times.

"You should live somewhere else."

"That's what Pat Nixon used to tell the slum kids. She'd go on tours through the ghetto, see, in her Peck and Peck suit and I. Miller shoes and her Mr. John hat, clutching her Delman pocketbook, and she'd say to the people, You should move your ass to a nice all-nigger suburb. Ha-ha-ha. Patty never caught on. It takes *cash* to live somewhere else. Anyway, it's only temporary. Ha-ha. Come to think of it, that's what terminal cancer patients say, it's only temporary. Me?

86

I'm waiting for da big ship to come in—" she said the last in a Southern drawl—"for de Emancipation. Den me and Miss Scarlett and Prissy'll shake our ass ou' da hee-ah!"

"You're too good to live here."

She laughed, pulling on a beige knit dress that buttoned all the way up the front. It clung to her, revealing the outlines of her body, its hem breaking at the knee. She wore no underwear. For the first time he lowered his eyes and looked at her sex; her pubic hair was sparser and lighter in color than his wife's, and it appeared far less coarse. Its color was dark honey. She noticed his look and ignored it. "Too good to live here, huh? I don't buy that line, baby. That's what I told you before."

She buttoned her dress.

"How do I look?" She smiled, doing a brief model's walk, hand on hip, swinging her shoulders, chin up.

"I could eat you up."

"Later. Now I'll have a drink." She fixed herself a vodka and tonic. They sat together on the torn sofa, and she put on Peggy Lee, and one of the songs played was "This Time the Dream's on Me."

"St. Thomas?" he asked.

She tensed, her jaw tightened. She narrowed her eyes, glancing suspiciously at him.

"I saw you there."

She lowered her eyes. "It was a long time ago."

"Who were you with? Who was the man in the white linen suit?"

"You don't know?"

"No."

She smiled and shrugged and did not answer. "Lousy weather," she finally said.

"The ducks love it."

"Yeah? Well, they're too dumb to come in out of the rain." And then, remembering he was pantless, she laughed. "Nothing personal, baby."

She stood and took his hand, pulling him to his feet. They

87

danced, McFarland moving somewhat awkwardly. He held her tightly to him, his arms around her, feeling the warmth of her body. They danced slowly together as she laid her head against his shoulder. He pressed his face against her hair. She smelled of lilac. He wanted to tell her that he loved her, but he was not sure how she would take it, and he was not certain that it was true. Before and after Adele he had loved no one. Adele had been the ball game, so it was difficult for him to think of loving someone else again. He was not sure how one went about it. And he did not trust his emotions or other people's enough to know when to chance it or when it was truly there. Because he was excessively given to sentiment, he distrusted it. He kept it bottled up inside. He sat on it. What he did know was that it was good to be close to a woman, *this* woman, and that he was greatly attracted to her, but as to how much of the attraction was sexual and how much was affective, that he did not know. When he first knew Adele, she had asked him what he wanted, and he had said, "To make a life with somebody." He wanted the same thing now as he danced with Jesse to "Crimson and Clover." To make a life. Crimson and clover, over and over. . . .

"I have no jewelry," she said. They were standing by the door about to leave for Rothenberg's party. McFarland was back in trousers and shoes. "I need a necklace or something. What do you have?"

"Nothing. . . . No, wait. I forgot." He lifted his right arm. On his wrist was a gold link bracelet that Adele had given to him when they were first married. He prized it.

"You want to wear this?" he asked, smiling at her, touched that she would want to borrow something of his.

She looked at the bracelet, thinking it handsome and very expensive. She knew by the slight reluctance in his voice that he did not want to part with it, that it had some sentimental value to him. She declined to borrow it.

"You *have* to have a goddamn necklace." She started unbuttoning his shirt. "I thought all men wore chains with dog tags on them."

"*Dog tags?* Where have you *been?*"

"I've been around the block, baby. Everybody wears a gold necklace. All the boys in Rome do."

She laughed as she undid his shirt, and he laughed, too, more out of self-consciousness than anything else. She pulled his shirt off his shoulders, pulled it roughly off, in one thrust. He stumbled back, and she stumbled with him, gripping his shirt in her small hands. He leaned against the wall, and she fell against him, and he felt her breasts under her dress against his chest, her breathing, as she pressed against him a moment. He was so used to his wife's heaviness that Jesse seemed air-light to him, excitingly small and delicate. "No, necklace, baby. But a pretty chest."

She kissed his chest, moving her tongue catlike over his nipples, and then she ran her fingers down the sides of his stomach, making him shiver, and then shoved her hand under his belt, leaning her body against him and kissing his neck.

She smelled of lilac. White lilacs grew on large bushes in front of his mother's house. Summer, and she would cut them and place them in urns throughout the house. Ever since then lilacs reminded him of the dead summer heat in that house and many other things he knew as a boy. They grew in massive white bursts on thickly leafed bushes, flowers like bunches of grapes covered in frost, like thousands of tiny trumpets made of snow, exquisite minuscule mouths of white ice. She was very proud of them, boasting that white lilacs were extremely rare and therefore expensive. They were the flowers of princes and holy people and other big shots. They had been Aimee Semple McPherson's favorite flowers because they had been Miss Mary Mother of God's favorite flowers, and now they were hers.

She smelled of lilac.

He had an erection, and for a moment he felt Jesse's cool hands encircling it. He feared he might come at once, wrongly, come then in that moment her hand encircled his erection. He thought of glass vases stuffed with lilacs and heavily perfumed lilac rooms of closed summer windows and argument. He grabbed her wrist and pulled her hand away.

"Please, let's do it now," he said. "Let's ball."

"Don't ever *beg*," she said sharply, high on booze and grass. She withdrew from him. "You have to learn the rules if you want to play the game."

He pulled on his shirt, confused by her advances followed so quickly by rejection. And the odor of lilac confused him, and the memory.

She knew he was disappointed and frustrated, his ego hurt. She decided that she did not care. To hell with it. For a moment she had been sexually aroused by him, and then he had requested her permission, politely, too goddamn politely, and her desire went. Not that it mattered to her one way or another. Most of them, yes, almost everyone she had ever slept with had not aroused her, and she had slept with many, most of whom she could not remember. She had merely closed her eyes and faked it while she thought of other things. While she thought of the few she had both loved and sexually wanted, two, three at most, who were there or had taken her there to the house at the river where the first had come at her drunkenly, erect, as she froze terrified against the screens staring at him, cowering, wanted what she feared. All the others, all of them, maybe this man, too, would only act as sexual surrogates for the two, three at most, she had wanted and loved and known and lost. And it didn't matter a good goddamn. Not anymore.

"I'll take the bracelet."

He undid it and put it on her wrist, the bracelet large and manly, the links thick as twigs, making her wrist appear small and breakable. It excited him. She held out her arm to display the bracelet for him. He saw the scar, like a tiny moon fallen on her wrist.

90

8

THEY arrived at Rothenberg's apartment about nine o'clock. The apartment was large and it was crowded with theatrical and movie types, some actors and agents, a writer or two and a small number of tall and very beautiful women making the usual small talk.

Rothenberg was standing at the far end of his living room. McFarland waved at him as they entered. The room was cluttered with pieces of uncomfortable thirties' furniture that had come back into vogue recently.

As they approached Rothenberg, he smiled at McFarland and then nodded coolly to Jesse.

"It's good I bought extra booze. There's always a goddamn few unexpected guests."

"I'll be goddamned." Jesse laughed. "David, you're so rightly famous for your charm."

"You got a drink?" he asked. McFarland held up his glass. "Good. Sit down, I want to talk to you. Long time, no see." He slapped him hard on the back. Rothenberg spoke very quickly as if he were consistently behind schedule and trying to say something urgent, like someone speaking rapidly as they boarded a moving train. It was cocaine that sped him.

Jesse and McFarland sat down next to each other on a low boxy sofa. Rothenberg sat opposite them, on the other side of a small table.

"When did you get rid of the slipcovers?" Jesse asked. The question irritated him, as she knew it would. And it surprised McFarland to learn by it that she had been in Rothenberg's apartment before, and then he remembered that he had identical slipcovers at his house in East Hampton, all made from shiny clear vinyl.

"Those *are* new."

"New?" They were the same ones McFarland had seen there months before. Rothenberg could not stand having his clothes wrinkled or his furniture soiled. He covered everything he possibly could against the disaster of a spilled drink.

Rothenberg leaned forward, brushing unseen dandruff from his shoulder. He opened a small silver box on the cocktail table. McFarland rather liked the table. It was made of blue glass set in an odd white geometric frame, with an abstracted woman etched into the blue glass, all in a subdued Art Deco manner.

Rothenberg dipped a tiny silver spoon into the box and drew forth a touch of cocaine.

"Want some?" He offered the spoon to McFarland. He declined.

"What about you, Jesse?"

"Not tonight." She knew he was baiting her. She hated him.

"But every night, huh?"

"No."

He gave a dirty chuckle. "Since when? Only thing I thought you wouldn't do is poke it."

Jesse stood up.

"Where are you going?" McFarland was suddenly anxious that she was about to walk out on him. He did not understand anything concerning what had happened between her and Rothenberg, although according to Tom Stein, nothing had occurred, and that was possibly the basis of the hostility between them. But he did not want to know. He felt jealous, and he thought it absurd.

"I'm going to get some food."

"I'll come with you."

"I can find my own way. You stay here and talk with David. No one else will." She leaned down and touched his

92

cheek. "You're the best man in the room, my angel." He grinned like a kid at a home run.

"What'd she say?"

"I said, he's the only *man* in the room."

They watched her walk through the room, greeting people. He was surprised that she knew as many as she did, and it occurred to him that he knew almost nothing about her, and it did not matter much at all.

"How'd you get hooked up with that? I thought you had more brains." Rothenberg leaned over the table again and dipped his spoon once more into the coke.

"It happened."

"She's trouble."

"I don't care."

"Then you're a fool. Let me tell you. . . ."

"I don't want to know."

He shrugged. "Don't ever say I never warned you, Paul." He lifted the spoon held in his right hand and rolled his head back, placed one finger against his right nostril, brought the spoon up to his left and snorted the crystal snow.

"Keeps me going. Keeps me going," Rothenberg said rapidly, repeating the same procedure with his other nostril. He closed the box.

"Priscilla's talking divorce again, the bitch." Rothenberg groaned and slumped back into the low boxy chair. Priscilla was his wife, and McFarland had known her for several years, during which she had continually attempted to begin an affair with him and he had never responded. They had become friends, and he liked her. David and Priscilla had their main house in Benedict Canyon in Beverly Hills. "Look at those assholes." He gestured toward his guests in the crowded living room. "Parasites and sharks. The mayor's coming later. Every goddamn time that creepy hack sees me it costs the company several more grand in kickbacks. Between paying off the asshole unions and the scumbag politicians you're ten fucking percent over budget on a picture. And the jack-

93

ass, His Honor, wonders why we try to stay out of New York. Stupid pud."

"Forget the mayor. . . ."

"I wish the Honorable would forget me."

"And forget about Priscilla's threats. She's always talking divorce. It doesn't mean a thing, David. She won't leave you."

"No?"

McFarland looked toward the windows. Beyond them he° could see the East River and the barges moving up it toward Harlem. McFarland remembered standing with Jesse on the Morton Street pier the night they met, the sky packed with stars.

"I suppose not. Where'd she go, for Christ's sake? You know, the bitch thinks I don't love her. Maybe I don't, who the hell cares? But I *like* her. The only complaint I ever made, and I never complained about her boozing it up and about the money she spends and her birdbrain romances, all I ever bitched about was her lousy makeup. I mean, I'm a successful man, and my wife should look it. God, if only she'd let up on the makeup. She shovels it on with a trowel. You'd think she had skin cancer or fifth-degree burns the way she piles it on."

Rothenberg began to run his fingers through his hair, and then he abruptly stopped. His hair was a blond toupee. He had a tendency to forget.

McFarland wondered when it would finally exhaust itself between David and Priscilla, after twenty years and how many comings and goings and threats of divorce until the last was believed. Priscilla was constantly walking out on him, flying from the Coast to Hong Kong or Tunis or Nice, anywhere his credit cards would take her where she invariably met a man who invariably stayed with her until the credit suspensions and the overdrafts arrived from New York and the cards were worthless and she wired Rothenberg for a ticket home, enclosing apologies and veiled threats. He buckled under because he honestly liked his wife and he

94

liked very few people, and they had grown used to each other's ways, and more important, he felt she knew too much about him to trust her on the loose. His drugs and his prostitutes, as pathetic as those habits were, and yet in his position as a producer he believed he could not afford a public scandal, and he was probably right. Who wants a brigade of street walkers named as correspondents in a divorce action? No matter how he comforted himself that a wife could not testify against her husband, or so he believed, and regardless of how sophisticated he thought he was about his use of drugs, he was unhinged by the idea of Priscilla drunk and at Le Bistro shouting *J'accuse!* across the velvet ropes. Better pay up and shut up. The more he paid, the less she respected him. She knew he was a bully and a coward, and she hoped he would change; she wanted him to call her bluff. He never did. And McFarland was convinced that she would finally call it quits when she knew he never would.

"How's Adele?"

"We're getting a divorce."

"And your kid, how's he?"

"I said, we're getting a divorce."

"Tough break." He couldn't have cared less.

"Adele's out in Malibu now with her lover. . . ."

Rothenberg raised his eyebrows. "Anybody I know?"

"I doubt it. Jaime's with them. He's fine, to answer your question."

Rothenberg reached across the table and patted his hand, playing at sympathy. He didn't give a damn. As long as what one did did not interfere with him or one's ability to produce work for him on deadline, he didn't give a good goddamn.

"Probably for the best. It'll give you more time to devote to the script. . . . I want you to take over another project for me."

"I've got the Nazi thing to complete."

"Balls. That'll only take you a couple more months. But I want a strong script, you know? Stress the angle about antidiscrimination, that's the message, but not too hard."

95

"What is the new project?"

"Oh, that. This is a movie about an *up* suicide, understand? A couple of beatnik kids in New Orleans who make a suicide pact because they fall in love and the girl gets knocked up and they can't get an abortion because they're broke and under age and the two of them check out watching a drive-in movie."

"It sounds like crap."

"So what? It's based on an actual case in Idaho and it's pd so we don't have to negotiate rights. Maybe it is crap, but the networks will eat it cold. I'm thinking about casting the kid from *The Waltons,* Johnboy whatever the hell his name is, and some unknown girl. He'll bring us a top Nielsen. . . ."

"I'm tired of writing crap."

"You'll have to give it a happy ending, Paul. Maybe they recover, what do you think?" He was leaning forward, his elbows on his knees, trying to sell McFarland.

"I don't know, David." What he meant was, how much will you pay?

"Got to know soon, kid. I leave for the Coast next week and won't be back here for a month. We had a writer working on it on the Coast. An asshole. An ar*tiste.* He let us down. I pulled him off it about six months ago. Couldn't even find the son of a bitch. He was flying around the place, spending my advance money at hotels. . . ."

"Who was the writer?"

"A schmuck named Rhodes." Rothenberg raised his middle finger and whirled it in the air.

"Mike Rhodes?" It startled him.

"That's the cookie. He cost fifteen grand in advances. I don't know what happened to him. He wrote a bestseller once. We had hopes for the guy. . . ." Rhodes had published one book, a thinly disguised autobiographical novel. It had made his reputation. That was seven years ago. He had not published a word since. "Oh, I never read the book. But he seemed to be up on the script. Your friend, Jesse, she knew him. She was on the Coast with him, poisoning the waters.

And then they took off together. . . ."

"I know." He lied. He had not known she had been on the Coast with Rhodes.

"Yeah? Well, she didn't help him any. Son of a bitch. I fired the cocksucker. So I want you to take the goddamn property over."

"I'll think about it." He stood up. "I'll let you know."

"Sure," Rothenberg said, dismissing him with a wave of his hand. "Hell, I don't believe this business. I don't believe this town."

"Is it getting you down, David?"

"We got the NAACP on our ass and the Human Rights Commission, and they want twenty percent of the technicians and actors to be minority and half to be women. How you going to have jungle bunnies playing Jews in the camps? I ask you, how is that possible? Shit, with the jiggies and the spics and faggots and goddamn women libbers you might as well close the goddamn store. I never liked those damn militants, and I never will. A crowd of schwartzers that don't want to work. . . ."

"You don't talk like a Jew, David. You talk like a racist."

"Screw you. What's it mean? It's English language, kid. It's *words*." He started to backtrack, to mitigate, to drag out his liberal credentials. "If they put the schwartzers in camps I'd be the first to die to get the bastards out. I'm a liberal, don't forget. I raised two hundred grand for old broken-down Hubert Humphrey. I *care*. Listen, I'll tell you something. . . ." He stood and put his arm around McFarland's shoulder. "A couple of years ago I brought my mother, may she rest in peace, to meet George Burns, the comedian. He was doing an act here. When I was a kid the only fight I got in was at P.S. 11. Some fat goy called me a jewboy. He was bigger than me. I beat the shit out of him. Years later I take my mother to meet George Burns. He says a few words, and then she leans over and whispers in my ear, 'Sonny, I didn't know George Burns was a jewboy!' Ha-ha-ha." He slapped McFarland's back. "Go get another drink, kid. It's free."

97

He found Jesse sitting in the library, talking with a short, very fat, red-faced Englishman. He was wearing thick bifocals. Jesse introduced them. She extended her hand to the Englishman and said, "Now I think Paul and I must leave." She glanced over at McFarland and winked.

"You're the writer on the Nazi script?" the Englishman barked, coming up to him. He stood with his left hand thrust into his suitcoat pocket and his right extended before him, gripping a cigar in his fingers.

"Yes, I am."

"You a Zionist?" he demanded.

"Yes, I think so." McFarland had never been asked that question before. But he believed in homelands, thus he assumed he was indeed a Zionist.

He jabbed his finger hard against McFarland's chest, cigar ash flaking off onto his shirt and tie. "Don't fuck with the Jews, boy. Don't fuck with us. . . ."

"I . . . I won't. I mean. . . ." He did not understand what he was getting at: don't fuck with the Jews?

"They gassed the weak and the feebleminded and the bloody unfit. Only the best survived. Is that clear?" Banged against his chest. "Only the best survived, boy. Only the strong. So don't bloody fuck with the Jews."

He nodded and took Jesse's hand. They turned and left. As they approached the door he yelled out behind them, his voice booming and hoarse, "Don't fuck with the Jews!"

The boy of Warsaw. He didn't understand.

9

THEY were both a little drunk when they arrived at Jesse's loft. As they entered the dark apartment, Jesse went *Shhhh*. They fumbled their way to one of the double beds. They kissed in the dark. She smelled of lilac. He unbuttoned her dress and let it fall to the floor. He kissed her again, holding her to him. She pushed herself away and reached out and began unbuttoning his shirt, in her haste fumbling at it. He tried to help her, and she whispered, "Let me do it alone." And then she unzipped his trousers and pulled them down. He had an erection. "Tell me to suck it. *Order* me," she said in an urgent, thick whisper. And he said, "Suck it, bitch! Now!" And she pulled down his shorts and went down on her knees, and in the dark he could feel her hands playing with his butt and her mouth roll over his erection, her arms hugging his hips, her breasts rubbing against his thighs as she rocked back and forth against him. She made small noises, and it felt good, and he came in her mouth. "Swallow it," he said, and she did.

When he awoke the next morning, she was lying beside him on the double bed, the sheet off her body and tangled around her feet. She slept with one hand resting on his chest, the other hand lying on his groin. He studied her a moment, caressing her hair as she slept, looking at her small body, at her face which was damp and flushed in sleep, and he whispered, "I love you, Jesse." And maybe he did.

He slipped quietly out of bed, without waking her, and dressed. He went into the bathroom, and when he returned, he looked down at her as she lay on her side, her knees now drawn up against her stomach, her hands thrust between her legs as she lay curled fetus-like on her side. Her hair fell over her eyes. He leaned down and smoothed her hair away. She murmured, and he kissed her.

He wrote her a note: "Let's make it work. I need you."

Before he left the loft, he looked into the bedroom area on the other side of their partition. Lying in the other bed were two men. One was Durk; the other was older than he and Hispanic. They lay asleep in each other's arms. He stared at them a moment, his feelings confused. He thought, Durk and the other man are her roommates. . . . He felt relieved, safe, superior, even happy; she lived with queers. The competition he had imagined and feared wasn't even in the game.

The following day Jesse met him at his apartment on Central Park West. It was five o'clock on a Sunday. She was dressed in a summer frock and sandals. She wore a white ribbon in her hair. She was damp with sweat from the heat. She was out of breath.

"I got off the wrong subway stop, like a fool. And I ran ten blocks. I'm wet as rain."

"You shouldn't have run. . . ." He smiled, pleased.

"I didn't want to be late. Not the first goddam time in your apartment." She looked around the living room. "Not bad. Enjoy it, you won't have it long."

"No?"

"After the divorce your wife will pick your bones."

He made her a gin and tonic. She sat on the sofa and pointed to the mirrored wall. "What happened?"

"An argument. Someone threw a glass. I keep meaning to get it fixed. I never seem to get around to it."

A few minutes later Adele called from the Coast. He could not believe her bad and too appropriate timing. As soon as he answered, she said, "Honey, Jaime wants to talk to you." He knew by that ploy that she was after more money.

"Hi, Daddy." His voice was high and very distant, as if he were speaking underwater. McFarland pictured his son floating under the sea, and he shuddered.

100

"Talk louder, Jaime. Daddy can't hear you. . . ."

"Hi, Daddy."

"How's my boy?"

"Daddy . . ?"

"What, Jaime?"

"Daddy, when you coming home?"

In the background he could hear Adele saying, "Give the phone to Mommy." And another voice, her lover's, saying, "Just take it from him. We gotta go, goddamn it." McFarland now hated them, and there was nothing he could do about it.

"Daddy, can I—"

("Jaime, give Mommy the damn phone!")

"Daddy. . . ." Frightened.

"What is it?"

"Paul?" Sweetly.

"Put Jaime back on."

"I haven't much time. . . ."

"Put him on, goddamn it."

"We're about to leave for Carmel. For a rock concert. . . ." Her voice was brittle. She disliked talking to him.

McFarland gave up. "How much do you want this time?"

"I need two thousand. Right away."

"For what?"

"It's for *Jaime.*" Adele was indignant that he would inquire after the purposes for the money.

"It's always for Jaime. He must spend a hell of a lot on Kool-Aid. . . ."

"You calling me a liar?"

"Wait a minute." He put his hand over the phone. "It's my wife," he told Jesse, smiling sheepishly at her. He put his finger to his lips. He rolled his eyes. She smiled and nodded.

"Are you alone?" Adele demanded.

"Pardon?"

"Are you alone? You must be deaf. Are you alone? A-L-O-N-E."

He didn't answer. He didn't know what to say.

101

"Speak, you coward. I know someone's there. You cheap bastard. Someone's there, aren't they?"

"So what?" He didn't care anymore.

"You two-timing son of a bitch! Just *wait* until I tell my lawyer. You can't do this to me!" Bang.

He turned to Jesse. "Hearing from her always makes my day." He shook his head.

"Do you still love her?" She held her icy glass to her forehead, rubbing it on her skin. She was still hot and perspiring.

"I don't know anymore. Sometimes I do. And sometimes I detest her."

"I know what it's like."

"She ran off with a twenty-seven-year-old former teacher, some punk who gave her back rubs at the health club. It makes no sense. . . . I really tried with her. And I woke up one day, and she wasn't there anymore. You know, Jesse, sometimes at night . . . oh, to hell with it."

"Sometimes what? Tell me."

"I'll wake up in the dark and stretch out my arm in bed, feeling for her. I can't get used to the emptiness."

"No?"

"And I miss my son. I'm sorry."

After they finished their drinks, they left the apartment and walked to McDonald's on Broadway, where McFarland used to take Jaime for milk shakes and Ronald McDonald cookies. The kid loved cookies with his milk shake, and, like Jesse, he loved junk food. It was a warm day, and Seventy-second Street was crowded with people, mainly blacks and Puerto Ricans heading to and from Central Park. McFarland bought a bag of Big Macs and two Cokes. They went into the park at Seventy-second Street and walked under the grape arbor and down the path to the upper lake. They held hands as they strolled. The sun reflected off the towers of Fifth Avenue, and the towers reflected in the waters of the lake, golden pickets soaring to the west like bayonets shining quivering in the heat. They sat on a bench under an iron gazebo and ate their bag lunch, hearing the sound of steel drums and the staccato of Spanish music in the distance.

He told her about Jaime.

"See over there?" He pointed to a sandbox surrounded by an iron fence erected to keep dogs out. "I used to take him there in the summers. He wouldn't play with the other children. I don't know why. I remember sitting on that bench, watching him play on the other side of the bars. And a little boy with one of those plastic rat-ta-tat-tat guns came up to him. Jaime must have been about three then. The boy fired the gun at him, and it made this god-awful noise. Jaime was frightened, too frightened to make any noise. Instead, he sort of crawled and tottered to the iron fence, and gripped the bars, and stared at me through them, scared over nothing really. I don't know. I felt helpless to protect him from so little."

"Does he look like you?"

"No, he's more like his mother, although he's blond and they say he has my eyes. He thinks he's a goldfish."

"Good!" She laughed. "They can survive eating garbage. They make do. I'm a goldfish, too." She made a swimming motion with her arms and puckered her mouth like a fish's. He noticed his gold link bracelet glinting on her wrist.

They walked through the park to the sailing pond, passing through the northern border of the Sheep Meadow on their way. Along the dirt access road were clumps of purple lilacs, the entire area smelling of their fragrance.

"I've never seen a rainbow in New York. Why is that?"

"I haven't the slightest idea, Jesse."

"In Minneapolis you could go to the Minnehaha Falls any day in the summer and there'd always be one hanging shimmering in the mist above the falls, one goddamn little rainbow. You could almost touch it. Rainbows are creatures of summer. The falls is ice in the winter, without its rainbow."

"Come to think of it, I've never seen one in Manhattan either."

"Perhaps they banned them."

"I'll buy you one." Enthusiastic.

She stopped and let go of his hand. She looked into his eyes, trying to understand his intentions. She had been playing, and she realized that he was serious.

"*Buy one?*"

"Yes. I'll have one made at Arpel's for you. Out of gold." He smiled, having decided he would do exactly that. His generosity was as great as his insecurity.

"Too easy, baby. *Make* me one. In the winter."

He laughed, not because the remark was especially humorous but because he was happy, and she was dear to him, and he took delight in her. He had fallen for her, and he knew it. He was courting her, and he had not courted in years, and every silly, nonsensical thing she uttered seemed gilded with charm. And he responded in kind.

Whenever Jaime was in New York, he took him to the sailing pond. In the summer people set their pet fish free in its waters where the fish darted about and grew fat until the winter's first freeze, when they rolled over on their backs and gave up the ghost, floating like capsized boats as dead and as white as snow.

In the summer Jaime loved to wade in the brown water and play at catching the slippery, lively fish. He never had any luck. McFarland bought a newspaper and constructed a paper boat and set it afloat on the water. Jaime stood in the water near the shore, bending his body and blowing hard at the paper boat, which never moved. It simply sat there obstinately absorbing water like a felt hat until it sank ignobly to the bottom to Jaime's intense delight.

McFarland found a newspaper and constructed a boat for Jesse, as he had often done for his son.

"There's your big ship, Jesse, coming into port."

She took a stick and threw it at the paper boat, sinking it. "And there it goes."

They returned to his apartment. Jesse had a drink, a large one. And then she walked about the place, giving him advice

104

on decor. "That's *got* to go . . . and that painting, good God! Unbearable. But the rugs are lovely. Did your wife decorate this place? Thought so. It's a little too artsy-fartsy Long Island City for me. . . ."

"Inwood. She's from Inwood."

"I like a place clean and trim and sparse. . . ."

"Like a jail cell?"

"Why not? Your apartment, frankly, looks like a very expensive bordello." It didn't, and she knew it. "Now I know where your wife picked up her wretched taste."

He laughed, thinking the remark indicated that she was jealous of Adele, competitive with her and, more important, that she was beginning to feel a proprietary sense about him and where he lived. It flattered him.

They went into the bedroom.

"Let me look at you," she said.

"Look." They lay on the bed together. They were dressed. She leaned on a pillow, looking down at his face. He crossed his eyes. He stuck out his tongue. He mugged for her.

She ran her fingers over his face. He closed his eyes. She touched his eyebrows and then moved her fingers down his nose and over his lips, playing with his lips, feeling his teeth and tongue, moving her fingers back and forth. "You're handsome, tough guy. But you're still a pushover."

"Then *push*."

"You don't even *need* a push. Ha-ha. Get up, baby. I want to see you."

"Look." He opened his eyes very wide. "See?"

"No. Take off your clothes. I want to see your body in the light."

"I'd better close the shades. The neighbors."

"Fuck the neighbors." She laughed. "Come to think of it, you probably have."

He undressed, turning his back to her as he stood at the far end of the room, by the windows, as she lay on the bed watching him intently. He felt oddly self-conscious, and he felt very white and pale and overweight. He was pale, not

105

having been in the sun since St. Thomas six months before. But he wasn't overweight.

"Nice ass, fella. Nice back. Small waist. Thighs are a little thin. Now turn around."

He did, clasping his hands in front of him.

She laughed. "You're like a little boy covering his wee-wee. Don't be so bashful."

He put his hands on his hips.

"And what a *wee-wee*. Ha-ha-ha. It's very pretty, baby."

"What's so funny?"

"'It's so *darling*. . . .'"

"It's big, you know."

"That, too."

"Shit."

"Come on, you shouldn't be so shy. I like *all* of you. I think you've made a sale."

He walked to her and turned full round, and she complimented him on his body. He felt like an object. He made a fist and flexed his arm muscles. She wasn't impressed.

"God, you men are so unbelievably *vain!*"

"Let's have sex." He was beginning to get an erection.

"See what I mean. Pure vanity."

"Let's."

"No, let's have dinner. My stomach's growling like a bear in a cage."

"Here?"

"Why not?"

"You have to cook it."

"I don't cook, baby. I'm not part of the house staff."

He cooked. Scrambled eggs and bacon. It was all he knew how to do.

After dinner they went up to the roof of the building, where they sat in two aluminum sun chairs, an ice bucket containing a bottle of white wine between them. It was a starless night. The sky above the park was clouded and pink-ish in color from the reflected lights of Manhattan, and the clouds were low, the skyscrapers of midtown disappearing into the low sky as if being eaten by cloud.

Below them, on Central Park West, hundreds of men cruised up and down the sidewalk, pairs of them disappearing over the wall into the bushes. Occasionally shouts could be heard from the park, and somewhere a phonograph was playing, Latin music carried and lost in waves on the weak breeze.

"Beautiful city. Such a cliché, but it is simply the most beautiful city in the world."

"Are you cold?" It was in the high sixties.

"No. I remember when I first came to New York. I had gone to the Hennepin Beauty Culture School. I went at nights after school. Do you believe it? Someone told me when I was sixteen that I looked like Alice Faye. I think my mother told me. I'd never *heard* of Alice Faye. But my mother said she was a gorgeous star, so I, of course, *had* to go to beauty school and become a model. All they taught me was how to do permanent waves and color rinses and to keep the hair dryers from setting fire to the client's hair. But I was determined to get to New York. That's where the famous Ford modeling agency is, in case you didn't know. I never got in the door. . . ."

"But I thought you were a model."

"For a time. Pour me more."

He filled her glass. "Nice and cold. I always dreamed of sitting overlooking Central Park, drinking champagne with a handsome man. Well, *white wine* with a handsome man. And here I *is*."

"Can I ask you something?"

"Shoot, baby. Get enough liquor in me, and I'll tell you state secrets."

"Why do you play that song so often?"

"What song?"

" 'The Dream's on Me.' "

She was quiet for a moment. "White wine gives me the hiccups—"

"Answer the question."

"—and gas. Well, I warned you, baby. . . . I like that song because when I first heard it, it was played by somebody I fell madly for, and it summed up my feelings for him. He also played a lot of Ruth Etting, 'Love Me or Leave Me,' 'Ten Cents a Dance,' 'Mean to Me.' I wasn't wild about Ruthie, but I did like 'The Dream's on Me.' And he was a real bastard, this guy. I was in love with a creep, for years, and he didn't give a damn about me. My life with him was a B movie, starring Ida Lupino. I mean, Alice Faye. I thought he loved me. Cross my heart I did. I *told* myself he did. Jesse, he *loves* you, I said. But he didn't. And I couldn't get out of love with him."

"Do you still love him?"

She patted his hand. "No, not really. He did have a magic to him. He wasn't that good-looking, but he was sex itself, if you can think of compulsive self-destruction as sexual. Haha. He knew exactly what to do. He was exciting, in every way. I . . . I don't know why. Anyway, I prefer not to talk about it."

"I'm sorry."

"You know, baby, I've had a miserable time of it with you men, more or less a lousy time. When I was little, about eleven, one of my father's friends got drunk and came at me. Nothing much happened. It was at the river playhouse in the summer, and they were playing cards and drinking beer inside the big house. I was sleeping outside alone in the summer playhouse because of the heat. We lived below the Mississippi bluffs, at the edge of the embankment, near the bridge. In the spring, every spring, the river rose and the basement flooded and sometimes the first floor, and my father would swear and slug whoever happened to be around, usually me, and he'd yell he was going to move out. He never did. But God, did he yell. . . . I loved him. And he didn't even *like* me. 'I don't like you, Jesse,' he used to say. 'You're a born tramp.' You couldn't trust him. His anger had no sense to it. You never really knew *why* he was angry. It came suddenly, I don't know, over something at work or my mother

108

or his paycheck was low that week. And he'd have a few drinks and rage. I got it a lot. He never laid a hand on my mother. He was wild about her, and I think a little bit scared of her. Now *she* was a *real* tramp. . . ."

"What happened in the summer house?"

"You really want to know?"

"Yes. Please."

"All right. I was lying there on the floor on a blanket in my Sears pajamas with sweet williams embroidered on the bodice. Strictly a class act. There was no light in the summer house. I remember the screens, it had walls of screen, and you could see the river and the barges passing up and down, from the Mesabi to New Orleans and back again, silently, dark except for small green and red lights at their corners. I pretended they were dragons with green and red eyes moving in the river. I lay there at night, watching the river and the barges and watching the fireflies play outside the screens above the damp grass. They were everywhere, swarms of them, in the cottonwoods and in the willows, in the sand grass beneath the high iron bridge. I loved them. They were like living stars you could trap in a Mason jar and they'd twinkle for you. . . ."

"And the man?"

"It was late, I don't know, and this friend of my father's, he must have been about thirty years old, I guess, he staggered outside while my father and the others stayed indoors playing poker. I could hear them yelling drunk at each other during the game. This man walked across the yard to the cottonwoods near the summer house. He stood there and peed against a tree. The moon was up, and I could see it sparkling silver, his urine like liquid silver in the light splashing against the tree trunk. . . . I must have coughed or something, because he turned suddenly and looked at the summer house, which was really one large room covered round in screens. I remember he was tall and dark, I think a Portuguese. He wore a mustache, and I thought that handsome. I was very naïve. I didn't know about sex or anything else

109

really. I was eleven, what did I know? I wore *pigtails*, for Christ's sake.

"He staggered toward the house, He hadn't bothered to put his thing back in his pants. It hung there shaking as he stumbled drunkenly across the wet grass toward the summer house, the fireflies blinking all about as he moved. He was about two feet away from me when he saw me, and he banged with his fist against the screen, and in a thick whisper, smelling of bourbon, he said, 'Girly, you like to watch, girly?' He pressed against the screen door, shoving his belly against it. And the door gave, and he sort of stumbled in. I was terrified and, I suppose, fascinated. Because he was hard. 'Girly, feel it, girly.' He made me reach out and touch it. He actually took my hand and put it on him there. 'Pet it,' he kept saying. 'Pet it.' And then he told me to kiss it, not to be afraid. I wouldn't do it. He put his hand around my neck and shoved my face toward it. He hurt me very much. I was choking. I was a small girl, and even then his hurting me, the attention, God knows, it excited me like a thunderstorm does, or a roller coaster. I have thought about it often, so goddamn often. When I told my father what happened, he called me a liar and said I was a tramp and he beat me. The man kept coming to the house, and when he'd see me, he'd rub himself down there and wet his lips and say, 'Hi, girly.' He must have known. . . ."

"Known what?"

"That I wanted it."

She spent the night at McFarland's. They did not have sex, although he asked her to. When he demanded why, she said that she couldn't have sex unless she was very drunk or stoned. "It embarrasses me."

"Why?"

"I don't know. Because that's all anybody wants from me, and if I'm at all sober, I don't want to put out. I don't want to give it. I'm self-conscious about it, and it makes me feel cheap. A lot of reasons."

"Do I make you feel cheap?"

"Sometimes. When you push too hard."

She looked at him, and she saw that he was unhappy. "It's not you, my angel. It's me." She knew he was frustrated; she resented his sad expression and his whining after sex. She did not want to feel guilty about not giving it to him whenever he wanted it. It seemed strange to her that when she was growing up, she was made to feel guilty for having sex and now, a few years later, guilty for not having it.

The following afternoon they went to a movie in Chelsea. Later they walked to the Village, where they had reservations for dinner in a garden restaurant on Bleecker Street, a few blocks from Sheridan Square. It was a warm night, and McFarland was dressed in summer whites and a tank top shirt. In the theater Jesse slipped her hand under his shirt, feeling his belly and chest, her hand coming to rest over his heart, its pounding exciting to her, like the thrusts of an ocean captive inside the chambers of his heart, its beat strong and constant. He placed his hand on top of hers, the shirt acting as a screen between them, pressing his hand down hard against hers, its heat and that of his chest, the thumping muscle . . . and it seemed her hand had pressed through his chest wall, become part of it, and with a grip of her fingers she could reach down into the heart itself and end its sound. It could belong to her.

After the movie, walking to the restaurant, she said he looked very young, dressed as he was. "You look a little like the actor in the movie."

"Did you find him sexy?" The actor was blond, although not as dark as McFarland.

"Too squeaky clean," she said of the actor, thinking it was also true of McFarland. "Too handsome. Men should be rougher than that." She paused and then said, "I never had sex with anybody handsome. . . ."

"You had sex with me."

"Sort of." She glanced at him and realized his feelings were hurt. Again she resented it. He was too sensitive about her

111

feelings toward him; he seemed constantly to make her feel guilty when she told the truth. She did not know if he did that intentionally or not. But it was obvious that the truth offended him. "It was good sex," she said, backtracking. It really hadn't been good, not when she had to tell him what to do. She thought he should have sensed what she wanted done. Why could he never perceive it?

"You think I whore around, don't you?"

"I never thought that. . . ." Said too loudly, protested too much. He had thought it from the beginning. He believed it now, and the idea intrigued and excited him, and he did not understand why. He hated promiscuity in any other woman, he hated it in his wife. But with Jesse, the idea that she had fucked a lot of men, strangers, that she'd been fucked up and down the Avenue until she met him, that notion, which he believed was true, excited him as it fueled his insecurity. She had told him little, and he imagined much, and his imaginings made her more desirable as they made her appear more intractably promiscuous. He would discipline her, break her, possess her, he would make her want only him.

"David must have said it. Or your buddy Tom. . . ."

"I never talk about you."

"Sure." She did not believe him. "The goddamn truth is that I don't have sex very often. When I do it's usually lousy. But when it's good, baby, I *explode*." She slugged him, laughing. "Pow!"

Moments before they reached the restaurant, as they turned off Christopher Street to walk down Bleecker, someone called Jesse's name. Jesse stopped, looking across the street at a furniture truck parked in a loading zone.

"Who is it?" McFarland asked.

"Wait here," she said, leaving him, and crossed the street.

A black man, about thirty, opened the cab door and stepped out of the truck. He kissed Jesse on the lips, laying his hands on her shoulders, grinning at her. She said a few words, turned and looked at McFarland; he saw her point toward him and say something to the black, who laughed. She left him and returned to McFarland.

"Who was that?"

"Some guy."

"I didn't like him kissing you like that."

She looked at him disgustedly. "Grow up, baby."

He was convinced she had fucked with the black; he pictured it in his mind, imagined them kissing and Jesse begging for it, her being drunk and naked and the black coming at her, begging for it, begging. He moved slightly away from her and was silent. She suspected what he was thinking, and it angered her.

During dinner he again brought up the question of sex, making indirect references to what he hoped would happen later. He was nervous and uncertain whether she would go to bed with him or not. He wasn't even sure she found him attractive. And the idea of her fucking with the black trucker was fixed in his mind, visualized, eating away. Tough luck all around.

She felt his insecurity and his jealousy and his insistence and gave over to it. It wasn't that Jesse did not want to have sex with McFarland; it was simply that she did not want to do it *because* it was expected, predictable, required and agreed upon like contract labor. She did not want to play his wife. The Late Show's off, so we ball. Yawn. She wanted him to take her suddenly, to come at her by surprise, preferably when she was drunk or stoned on drugs or in the morning when she was half awake and her self-consciousness was defeated before the act was begun, before the line between dream and wakefulness was bridged finally by his cock. Drunk or high, she could pretend he was someone else somewhere else or that she was responding to, helpless before a part of this man she did not know and was frightened of; she wanted him fiercer in sex, more intense, impolite, commanding, hurtful, in control.

Jesse was ashamed of sex, and yet she hungered for it. Her

113

hunger gave her guilt. She went for long periods without sex, renouncing her desire, refusing to touch herself or to be touched, telling herself she was asexual, that sex did not matter, that she was not a whore, an object, some fleshy, wet hole men filled as they liked, not something to be bought with a meal or a couple of drinks or the promise of affection. And yet when she had sex, it was good because during it, that was exactly how she saw herself, taken, raped, forced against her will, degraded, helpless. When it was finished, the guilt gathered over everything like snow across a landscape, and she felt cheated and used, and she resented the men who made her—so she thought—surrender to what she wanted and could not accept. She found it difficult having sex with men she admired or respected or had affection for, men whose respect she aspired to. So with them she would drink or drop pills until the embarrassment and fear were muffled and only the carnality, the empty availability remained. Drunk or stoned, she avoided responsibility for what occurred. Out of control, helpless, sex happened to her. She was an object broken from the branch and crushed. It was as simple as this: sex activated her self-loathing.

So she did not want to fuck with McFarland that night. Because, she thought, he doesn't want to *fuck*, he wants to *make love*. Love she distrusted. How could she believe someone loved her when she trembled with self-contempt? It wasn't in the cards.

She had considerable affection for him, distrusting his for her. The very things that drew her affection—his moral strength, his patience and assurance, his stated love for her, the decency of his instincts—were what made it difficult for her to be sexually aroused by him. He didn't turn her on, and there wasn't a goddamn thing to do about it. She would try to teach him, and she hated to teach. Teaching meant control. And she wanted to *be* controlled. She needed to be forceably taken, and his kindness disallowed it. He was too unthreatening to be her ticket. And yet . . . she loved him.

So she didn't want to hurt McFarland. She saw his self-

114

regard as vulnerable as her own. She understood his insecurity and his fear of sexual rejection, his blocked longing for her. So she decided to get drunk, what the hell, and make it work. Because he needed it. And she needed him.

"Did you sleep with the black?" he asked after dinner. He had ordered coffee. She had not touched hers.

"Order me another drink. Make it a double."

He called the waiter. When the drink came, he asked her again.

"What do you mean 'sleep'?"

"You know what I mean."

"Did I fuck that nigger, is that what you want to know?"

"Yes."

"No. I didn't. His name is Roy, by the way."

"I don't believe you."

"What can I say? When I was younger and still living at home, my father used to accuse me all the time, just like you're doing. I was a virgin, for Christ's sake, and he'd say, 'Did you fuck with so-and-so? Where were you last night? Isn't that a hickey on your shoulder? You been letting them in your pants, Jess?' On and fucking on until I began to believe it was true. Nagging at me, accusing me, insinuating things while my mother looked on, grinning and drinking two-dollar bourbon. Whenever my old man left town, and he did it practically every week in the winter because the lines were always coming down from the ice, our place became a regular cathouse. They didn't exactly line up in the driveway with their money in their left hand and their prick in their right, but they came by to see Ma. I never wanted to be like her. I hated her. I still do. I hate her. I always wanted my old man to love me, and he thought I was a whore because he needed to believe that. I don't know why. He beat me and talked dirty and yelled these obscene charges, and half the time I didn't know who he was talking about or what. That's how I learned about sex, by his screaming these detailed obscenities at me . . . you sucked his cock, Jess, didn't you, you little tart, you pulled it out of his pants and you. . . .

115

That's how I learned about it. He *had* to believe it, and I don't know why. I don't care why. I discovered that if I admitted whatever he said and even embellished it, he'd shake his head satisfied and say, 'I knew all along, you bitch, you tramp.' But he wouldn't beat me anymore. The truth was dangerous. The filthier the lie, the better he liked it, that perverse old man. I really loved him. Crazy. . . ."

"I'm sorry."

"You're *always* sorry. You should have cards printed: 'I'm so sorry.' Signed 'Paul McFarland.' "

"I. . . ."

"Listen, you wanted to know about Roy, right? Mike Rhodes, your college chum, pushed drugs on and off when I knew him. I was living with him. And dopers called all the time. Roy used to buy from Mike. One day he came by to get the stuff, and Mike wasn't there. I knew Roy wanted to go to bed with me, and Mike had arranged it so he could. Mike was a real bastard. So he could throw it in my face later. Mike was perverse, too. And poor Roy tried. But he didn't get anywhere. . . ."

"Son of a bitch!"

"Don't be an ass. I *wanted* to go to bed with Roy. I'd never been to bed with a black. I wanted to see what it was like. He was nice and attractive, and he was a laborer then. And I thought him sexy. But I wouldn't do it because I wouldn't give Mike Rhodes the satisfaction. . . ."

"Would you go to bed with him now?"

She stared at him, incensed. "What an obscene question!"

"Would you?" He had to know; his jealousy was too great.

"Would I fuck dat nigger buck? Yeah. Probably. If I didn't know you. . . ."

That pleased him. She loves me, he thought.

"You'd only throw it in my face for the next six months. Just like Mike Rhodes. Just like my old man."

When they returned to his apartment, Jesse was drunk. They sat on the sofa together and began to kiss. She felt nothing. Cared less.

116

"Do you have any downs?"

"I love kissing you," he said. "I love you, Jesse," his voice breaking.

"Downs?"

"No."

She pulled away. "Then go to bed." Petulant. "I want to go to the bathroom."

She staggered into the bathroom. She felt sick, as if she were going to vomit, full of disgust, felt cheap and used and trapped, wanting to be far away, lost, gone, never having to contend again with the importunings and the declared love of men whose love frightened her and whose importunings moved her not. The summer house. Before the Portuguese. Lying on the blanket hidden by screens, fireflies in the air, tiny spaceships, bodies of the barges unseen, only their lights bleeding color on the water. Alone.

She knelt by the toilet and tried to throw up. She couldn't. She lay down on the floor, feeling the cool tiles against her face. She felt feverish. Vulnerable. A child. She wanted to cry. Take me away. Nothing works, Papa, nothing ever works.

She heard him knock on the door. "Jesse?"

"I'm all . . . fine. I'm cleaning. I'm, uh, cleaning up." She started to giggle. And tears came as she giggled.

"Okay."

She got to her knees and, holding onto the washbasin, pulled herself to her feet. She wet a washcloth and rubbed it under her arms and then looked into the cabinets. She wanted to douche. There was no bag.

She staggered into the bedroom. The ceiling light was on. McFarland lay on his side on the bed, his eyes closed. At first all she noticed was how blond he was, the light shining on his hair, how long his body seemed, like a swimmer resting on poolside tiles. He wore white tapered boxer shorts. Then she saw his erection, saw his penis thrust through the fly of his shorts. . . . She was swaying, squinting, blurred, seeing his erection framed against the white cotton, the head of his

117

penis covered by his foreskin, the curled, flaccid tip pink, pinker than the white, thickly veined shaft. In Minneapolis, as a teenager, she and a boyfriend came home late one night in the winter. The house was quiet and dark. They went into the kitchen, and in the dark she got a beer for the boy. She did not like him. He wore glasses and had pimples, but he also had a convertible Chevrolet, and she liked that about him. She took his hand and led him through the living room toward the front door, the room dark except for the street-light that shone in through the frosted windows above the sofa, planning to take him out to the front porch, where they would cuddle under the blankets on the chair swing. She would kiss him and then watch the small portable heater, its coils glowing, and ask the boy to pretend it was a castle fireplace in the cold Alps and they were royal. She led the boy into the living room, and then she stopped. Her older brother, Daniel, lay asleep on the couch. The room was overheated, the sheets thrust off him, tangled over the side of the sofa to the floor, the room smelling of the beer Daniel had drunk. Daniel lay on his side, snoring, dressed in boxer shorts, his jutting penis erect and circumcised, shoved through the front of his shorts, its head purple, dark, throbbing with his heartbeat in his sleep, seeming large, too large: Daniel fragile, helpless, open to attack in his sleep, only his penis alert, endearing. . . She saw McFarland and she said, "Baby, turn out the lights."

"Jesse," he said, opening his eyes, smiling at her.

"Don't move!" She raised her hand like a traffic cop. "Don't open your eyes!" Don't ruin it. Don't intrude.

He closed his eyes. He lay expressionless on his side. She went to him and gently touched his penis, staring at it, running her index finger up and down its shaft, the organ throbbing, heaving in response; she drew her finger down the shaft and through the open fly to the base of his cock and then under to his taut balls. She withdrew her hand. "Turn out the lights," she slurred, closing her eyes so she would not see

118

him move. He got out of bed and turned out the lights. He returned, and she stood and pulled off her dress and panties. In the light from the window she saw him lying on his back, his hands behind his head, staring up at her as she undressed in the dim light. She moved and stood by the side of the bed, and spread her legs apart, and ran her hands along the inside of her thighs toward her sex, and bent forward, her breasts swaying toward him, and as he reached out, she kissed his hand. He began to pull down his white shorts. "Don't," she commanded. It baffled him. "Don't." Daniel. Why can't he perceive what I want? How can he ever, poor baby?

She lay on the bed beside him, and McFarland got to his knees and bent over her, kissing her deeply, and she groaned, reaching forward and lifting his balls out from inside his shorts so that his entire sex stood out, naked, surrounded by the white cotton covering his groin, bottom and upper thighs. And the idea of his sex having broken through the restraining material while the rest of him, his strong thighs, his muscular buttocks remained hidden from sight, prisoners of white, that excited her . . . he hadn't time to undress, he's too hot, he wants me too much, I don't know him, a stranger, a stranger forcing forcing forcing . . . she thrust her legs in the air and then let them fall wide, spread impossibly wide, and ran her fingers over her sex, parting it, as she felt his mouth on her cunt, his tongue against her clitoris . . . Daniel, Daniel . . . "Fuck me, baby. Fuck me. . . ." McFarland mounted her, and she wrapped her legs around the small of his back, pressing him against and into her as he kissed her, his tongue thrust deeply into her mouth with the same rhythm as his penis into her as his heart . . . gripping him with her legs, coming . . . rolling her head to the side, her body shuddering, his grabbing her hair and hurtfully, roughly gripping her and centering her head and mouth below his as he fucked her faster. . . . "Slowly, baby. Let me feel you inside me. I love you in me. Slowly, slowly, poor baby. . ." How would he ever know?

119

In the morning she complained about her hangover. "It's *never* worth it."

She wore his white terry-cloth bathrobe, with its angel cuffs.

"I think about you all the time."

"And I about you," she said quietly, looking down at her hands.

"You what?" He had heard. He simply wanted it repeated.

"I need a manicure." She rubbed at her nails. "I really do."

"If Adele were here, she could give you a dandy one. Her mother, the Archbitch, gave them professionally. She's still polishing cuticles in Inwood for all I know. A wop. She hated my guts, to put it mildly. She wanted Adele to marry an undertaker down the block. And when that fell through, the Archbitch tried to tie her up with the druggist. And when Adele married me, if she'd had the money she would've given her relatives a contract on my life. I had no money then, and to be a writer was to be unemployed."

"How long?"

"Eight years. And the whole family is sitting up in Inwood, arguing over how much the settlement will be. I wish I were broke, so there was nothing to split their way. But I'll get one good thing out of it. I won't have to pay her goddamn father's nursing home anymore."

"Vanity."

"What's wrong?" He touched her face, putting his knuckles under her chin and raising her face to him. "What'd I say wrong?" She suddenly seemed sad.

"You said you'd get one thing out of the divorce that was good. And I thought you'd say that one thing was me."

Later that day he asked Jesse to move in, saying he could not tolerate the idea of her living alone in the loft in Soho anymore. He told her that he loved her.

"Do you love me, too?"

"If you want me to."

"Then move in here. It's too empty now. I don't want you to be alone."

120

"I'm not alone. Durk lives with me. It's his place. And a Puerto Rican friend of his."

He had forgotten about Durk. "He's a fag." Contemptuous.

"Really?"

Because of the way she said it, he was immediately uncertain. Maybe they weren't, or not always; maybe they were bi or poly or whatever. You could be certain of nothing anymore. All the maps were out of date.

"Do you sleep with them?"

They were sitting in the bay window of his bedroom, the window overlooked the park. Jesse was smoking a cigarette, her face silhouetted against the window light, the smoke curling around her hair. She looked away, her eyes appearing very pale green, the circles under them darker now, as if buffed with gray clay. She glanced down at her small hands. "I did once with the Puerto Rican. I was stoned, and I was lonely. And a couple times with Durk," she said. "But I don't anymore." And then she looked up at him, impassively.

"You don't sleep with them now?" He did not know if he believed her, and it was important to him that he believe her absolutely because he knew he could not live with a doubt provoking his jealousy. He already felt possessive of her.

She rubbed her eyes with her hands, like a child rubbing sleep from her eyes, and then she sighed boredly. When she spoke, her voice was very flat and unfeeling. She did not care whether he believed her or not but regretted only that he had bothered to ask. Jesse never lied except by omission. She hated being interrogated.

"You remember that little mat in the corner of the loft? Where the dog was sleeping? That's where I sleep. The night you were there, the bed we slept in was Durk's. I sleep alone. On that mat. I have no money. I haven't had any for about six months. I used drugs for a long time. Downs. Anything. I would get stoned and trick. I wanted . . . I don't know. Durk was kind to me when nobody gave a damn. He took me in. That's why I'm there." She looked away. "That's why I

121

slept with him. Because he was kind to me, and I like him."

"One good deed deserves another."

"You're goddamn right. And don't *ever* ask me again."

"I had to know."

"Sure."

"I don't know why. But I did have to know."

"Do you still want me to move in?" She spoke passively, quietly. She always spoke that way when too much hung on an answer. Whatever the answer was she did not want him to be certain of its effect on her. She very badly wanted to live with McFarland because she loved him in her own way—she needed him and loved him in many ways, but not sexually, although she could not bring herself to admit that to him. She knew he was easily aroused by her, that sexually she was his ticket, but she was not as sure of his affection for her. She distrusted love when it was too easily declared, and he was continually declaring it. She did not believe in its words. If you asked her, "What is love?" she would have replied, Endurance. All expressions of love were to her bouquets one gave to another's vanity.

"Are you kidding?" He waved his arms in the air and shouted. "Hell, yes! Come live with me! Tomorrow. Tonight. *Now!*" He grinned, ecstatic that she might actually move in.

"All right." Cool. Unenthusiastic. "But don't change your mind. I don't want to be hurt."

"I won't."

"What I mean, Paul, is that I don't want to tell people I'm leaving, tell Durk, you know, and plan on it and everything and then have you change your mind. After so long a time and how I've lived"—she paused, her eyes tearing—"and then to have you change your mind."

"I won't. Never. I promise. I love you."

"You say too much. Always you promise too much."

"I do love you. You must know that?"

"I believe you. And don't worry about drugs. I'm clean."

He was worried about them, and she had sensed it.

122

He said he would rent a car to help her move, and that they would meet at her place in Soho at precisely noon of the following day.

She laughed. "Why the car?"

"For your stuff."

"Baby, I can get it all in one Food City shopping bag."

She decided to go home that night and pack. She was happy, and he knew it. He was happy, too. They went down in the elevator, and he got her a taxi. Before she stepped into the taxi, she unclasped the bracelet he had lent to her and handed it back to him.

"It's yours," she said, smiling. "I forgot to return it." He handed it back.

"Not anymore."

As she put the bracelet on, he saw the round scar on her right wrist, the size of a quarter. And with that hand she caressed his face and kissed him. Then she untied the white ribbon around her hair and, smiling, wound it around his wrist, tying it with a bow. "One good deed deserves another."

She grabbed his arm. "Listen to me, Paul." She spoke urgently. "Make sure you understand. If you want to back out of it, do it now. It won't affect my feelings for you. But do it now, if you're going to. Don't do it tomorrow or next week. . . ."

"I'll see you at noon tomorrow. I give you my word."

"Please don't leave me. Not for a while. I need you, baby." She was beginning to cry.

"I won't."

"Just give me half a chance. Don't walk out. I couldn't go through that again. . . ." She stopped speaking and gave over to tears.

He put his arms around her. "I won't, Jesse. Come on. It's all right. Everything'll be all right."

"I'm decent, Paul . . . I'm worth it. . . ."

"I won't ever leave you."

She moved out of his embrace. She entered the taxi. She

123

rolled down the window. She smiled at him. Her hand went to her lips, her fingers trembling. She threw him a kiss.

He put the white ribbon in his billfold in order not to lose it. He decided that for her birthday he would have a gold chain made for her with a jeweled pendant to hang from it. The pendant would be a rainbow. And when he gave it to her, he would tie the gift box with the white ribbon she had given him.

One good deed deserves another.

10

JESSE called him early that evening from Soho.

"Durk's taking me to dinner in the Village," she said. Her voice was excited. She seemed happy. McFarland felt a tinge of jealousy. He did not want her seeing Durk again. It could not be helped.

"*I'll* take you to dinner. . . ."

"It's already arranged. I can't cancel now."

"Why can't you move in tonight, now? To hell with waiting until tomorrow."

"I just can't walk out like I never knew him. I want to explain to Durk. I owe him that. Tomorrow, baby. . . ."

"Do you love me?" he demanded stridently. She was moving in with him in less than twenty-four hours, and he found himself nervous that it might not occur, impatient that it would. Loving her.

"Baby," quietly, nearly whispering it. "Don't you know?"

He didn't know. But he let it go.

He ate dinner at home that night and worked on the draft of the Nazi script. It was difficult to concentrate; his mind kept thinking of Jesse, drawn to her, jealousy and longing coloring his thoughts; only a few hours, and he missed her, wondering where she was now and what she was saying to Durk and if he was trying to keep her from her promise. He had lost his self-confidence in missing her.

About midnight he tried calling Jesse. There was no answer. It bothered him.

He had a couple of drinks and went to bed. She'll be with me tomorrow.

And then it happened: the phone rang and rang, and in his

125

sleep, fumbling for it, he knocked it off the bedside table onto the floor, and in the dark he bent over the bed and felt on the carpet for it, and picking it up, raising the receiver to his ear, he could hear the voice saying, "Paul McFarland? Western Union calling. . . . " and he knew before the smooth yellow plastic earpiece touched his ear, he knew— they were gone. Adele and Jaime wiped from the board in an automobile crash on Pacific Coast Highway in Santa Monica at six thirty Los Angeles time. The remains taken to Los Angeles County Hospital and from there to the Wooddruff Memorial Home, Malibu. And that was that.

He was asleep when the call came. The phone rang many times. And then the room was silent and dark again. He could not take it in. Dreamlike. His old lady. The boy of Warsaw. Now them. Easy come. Easy go. And you could die from all the dying. Here today. Gone tomorrow. Face it. You want to die from all the dying.

He lay in bed an hour. Stunned. Horrified. Too frightened to move. Lay in bed holding the yellow receiver in his hand, the constant warning bleep. . . . And then, around 3 A.M., he got out of bed and went into the bathroom and threw water on his face and looked at himself a moment in the mirror, and then, remembering Jaime spraying the shaving cream on the mirror, he cried.

He dressed to find Jesse, thinking that of all he loved she alone was left on the board. He had to get to her. He took a taxi to Soho and climbed the five flights to Durk's loft. He pounded on the door. No answer.

He then ran to the Bottoms Up Bar on West Street. It was a few minutes before closing, and the place was emptying out. There were several young men playing pool, and a couple slumped in a stupor on the floor by the jukebox. He asked the bartender if Jesse had been in the bar that night. He described how she looked and added, as if it were the determining evidence, "She wears lilac cologne."

"Listen, hundreds come in every goddamn night. How would I notice? It's last call, fella."

126

"What about Durk?"

"Who?"

"Durk, he plays pool. In his twenties, sort of a muscleboy, good-looking, cocky, oh, and a tattoo, a tattoo on his arm, here, with his name, his name is Durk, with his name written on his arm. . . ."

"Yeah. He was in earlier. About an hour ago. Just missed him. . . ."

"Was he alone?"

"Alone? Yeah, he played some pool. Met some guy, looked like a fag to me, you know how they look. Some guy he met and walked out with. Ain't seen him since. Maybe they went down to the pier. Wouldn't know. Last call."

McFarland walked down Hudson Street and then over to Eighth Avenue. He walked very fast, trying to keep from thinking of them colliding on the Pacific Coast Highway, trying to keep from thinking, counting the sidewalk sections, counting the parked cars, remembering words to songs, old hymns, anthems to keep from thinking of them erased from the board. When you coming home, Daddy? Screw it. Life. Screw it. No help for it.

You would die from all the dying.

Around five the eastern skirt of the city was weakly, pinkly light, the streets of Soho empty except for a lone sanitation truck spraying down the roadway, groaning as it chunked along. He again climbed the stairs of Durk's loft. He pounded on the steel fire door. All out of breath, feeling the blood pound inside his head. Pounding. Waiting. Finally the door opened.

"What d'ya want?" Durk stood at the door, a dirty bath towel wrapped around his waist.

"Jesse?"

Behind him, in the dark loft, a man's voice, "Who the fuck is it? It's goddamn dawn already."

Durk turned his head and yelled back into the room, "Fuck yourself, creep!"

"Where's Jesse?"

Durk turned back to McFarland, his jaw muscles rigid with irritation. He did not like being barged in on at dawn and demands made, particularly by an uptown type he did not especially like.

"Where *is* she?"

"What's wrong, man?" Durk eyed him, smiling contemptuously. Then he glanced down. "Man, you're wearing different colored shoes." He laughed.

McFarland looked. He was wearing one brown and one black half-boot.

"Tell me."

Durk yawned. McFarland wanted to strangle him. "Tell me, goddamn it!" He stepped toward him.

"What's the rush? You'll have her tomorrow. She don't want to see you tonight or she'd of seen you tonight, right?"

"Tell me!"

Durk sighed, losing interest. He tightened the towel around his waist, not looking at McFarland. "She ain't here. So shove off, huh?"

From the loft, the man's voice: "What the hell's going on? I got to get to work in two hours!"

"You're positive you don't know where she is?" McFarland asked again, convinced that Durk knew and would not tell him. He felt foolish and disconsolate and scared and angry and at a loss.

"Why'd I lie, man? What are you to me? She stayed out tonight. That's all I know." He smiled.

"Can you give her a message?"

"Why not?" He shrugged.

"Tell her that I have to leave for the Coast in a few hours. It's urgent. I'll call her when I arrive in LA. Tell her not to worry . . . tell her. . . ." He stopped. He could not bring himself to tell Durk about Adele and the kid, or that he loved Jesse.

"I got to go to bed, man. Okay?"

"*Please* tell her." He grabbed Durk's arm.

"Sure. Now go home." He shut the door.

McFarland stood for a moment outside the steel fire door as if he were waiting for it to open again. Go home? Home? His mind was blank. He could not remember how he got home, packed and taxied to the airport. He remembered facing the steel door and boarding the flight to Los Angeles still dressed in his mismatched shoes. And that was all.

He called Jesse as soon as he arrived at Los Angeles International Airport. Durk answered and said he had not seen her. She had not come home. No, he did not expect her. No, he didn't know where she was. Yes, he'd give her the message. Quit bugging me.

He rented a car at the airport and drove to the Wooddruff Memorial home, Malibu. It was a cream-colored stucco building built in the 1930s in a Spanish Mission style.

McFarland asked the woman at the desk where his wife and son were. She seemed confused. She asked him to wait a moment. She left the reception room.

He paced about the room, its floor carpeted in royal blue, the walls papered a darker blue, a large painting of the Good Shepherd gripping a lamb under His arm over the mantelpiece of the dead fireplace. Over the speaker system, seeming to come from the air-conditioning ducts, were Christian hymns played on a chime organ. The air was dead and smelled of carnation and something else, something bitter. His nose itched.

"Yes. We've . . . ah, we've been expecting you, dear man. . . . " The funeral director, a mortician named Wiggins, stood before McFarland, stretching for his hand, shaking his head, his face a combination of studied grief and sympathy, highlighted by the smallest and most insincere of smiles. "Your wife's brother, I believe, identified the beloved ones. . . ."

"Her brother?" McFarland thought, No, her lover. "Yes."

"I'm sorry to say that . . . well, they are not at rest in the slumber rooms as yet. . . . " He smiled, nodding. McFarland stared at Wiggins' face; there was something odd in its

129

coloration, the tan too even, the hairline too regular. He was in his late sixties, and he looked embalmed in his dark suit with its paper carnation, his gray tie. . . .

"Slumber room? I want to see them. . . ."

"Of course. In a moment. We are doing what is necessary, Mr. McFarland. Come this way. . . . "

He led him into the office and showed him a series of coffins and burial clothes and noted the various advantages and disadvantages of each, stressing the higher-priced commodities. McFarland sat listening to Wiggins speaking in his soft, low voice, a voice that reminded him of radio announcers in the late forties when he was a small boy and listened to the horror shows on the networks. He sat glancing at full-colored pictures of various funeral items being peddled, and he could not think what it had to do with his wife and son. Wiggins took his silence for interest.

"Are you the chief undertaker here?"

Wiggins flashed a very tight, disagreeable smile. "Sir, we prefer the term 'funeral director.' We don't like the word 'undertaker' at-*tall*. If you are interested, my specialization, as it were, is cosmetology and, er, plastic reconstruction of the face. The dermatological sciences. Ah, such advances we've made. . . . " Wiggins babbled on, leaning back in the high-backed swivel chair behind his desk. McFarland, who wasn't listening, looked around the room. The desk was absolutely clean of everything, an oak-veneer object with a glass top, the top bare except for a silver-plated pen set with the funeral parlor's logo imprinted on it. There were several quasi-religious pictures, several prints of birds, the windows heavily draped, four bouquets of artificial flowers in brass urns, indirect lighting. "Maybe we have to reconstruct the eyes, an area I am, sir, frankly proudest of, or the nose or mouth, or perhaps on occasion an ear or two. I learned that science in Shreveport. I would be happy to show you my diplomas and professional license. . . . " Wiggins leaned forward, the tight smile permanently fixed on his face as if he were a victim of his own cosmetology, as if his teeth were wired together, the mouth held in its tight grip by cotton and wax and nylon thread. "*More* than happy. . . . "

"What?" McFarland waved his hand. "No, just let me see them."

"In a moment. Why, we had a man the other day that stuck a gun to his left temple and blew the top of his head off, *just like that.* . . . " Wiggins giggled, pursing his lips, drawing his hands together at his chest. "And it happened that most of the scalp and hair was split and hanging and, er, we . . . most of the inside of the cranium, most of it was gone, and we used sterile cotton to remake the shape, and then we sutured, and, er, using a hidden stitch in suturing, and it comes down the forehead. . . . " Wiggins raised his hands to his face and, speaking intensely, compulsively, enthusiastically, illustrated with his hands the techniques they used to sew together a busted head while McFarland stared beyond him at the wall wondering in which direction lay the sea. "And we used wax to cover that and did cosmetics all over his face to give it all the same color. His hair, you understand, sir, was adequately *long* to cover the stitches there at the sides and at the neck. I know," he continued, trying to make a witticism, "people rail against hippie or beatnik hair, but in this case it wasn't *too* long!" He giggled again.

"About my family. . . . "

"Yes?" Wiggins sat up, raised his eyebrows and looked intently at him. "The late beloved?"

"I want no embalming. . . . "

"But. . . ."

"None. . . . "

"But I always *enjoy* taking someone that's been in a wreck and reconstructing their face so the family, *you*, sir, can come in and say, 'My, , that looks just *like* 'em!' So you don't have the horror of coming in and seeing, well, what nine times out of ten couldn't even have been shown, if you understand my meaning. . . . "

"I want them both cremated, as soon as possible." He said it laconically.

He felt nothing.

"Oh, I don't like burning up the body!" Wiggins announced dramatically, seeming genuinely alarmed. "After you do all your reconstruction and cosmetics, after all the love invested in your art and science, and then to see *all* your proud *work* going up in flames, why, in a few minutes destroyed. . . . I don't even like to make death calls on burned victims. . . . "

After McFarland signed the necessary papers and wrote the necessary check, a markedly subdued Wiggins walked him to the door, obviously unhappy about McFarland's unappreciative attitude toward the dermatological and cosmetological sciences. Wiggins shook his hand.

"The wind is coming up," he said as a gust blew into the stale reception room when the outer door was opened. He gave McFarland his tight, pursed smile. And then he whispered, "Pardon me, but you're wearing different colored *shoes.*"

"I know. I get twice the wear that way. "

Wiggins looked at him and then down at his shoes, and then up to McFarland again, not sure whether to believe him or not. Finally he shook his head, giggling. "How *wonderful*, how *heal*thy to keep your sense of humor so sharp in a moment such as this!"

11

THE HOUSE at the beach at Malibu was empty when he arrived. He never saw his wife's lover. He could not decide whether that was a sign of decency on the man's part or simply fear of involvement. Her lover left behind his health food and some clothes and his bowling bag which once carried his "stash" up Fifth Avenue. What could be given away was sent to the Good Will.

Jaime's baby shoes, which had hung from the mirror above the car's dashboard, he sent to Adele's mother with a note of sympathy.

It took him a week to handle what was necessary.

Their ashes were scattered on the Pacific within sight of the beach. There was no memorial service.

Every day during the first week he arrived in Los Angeles he tried calling Jesse. He spoke with Durk three times, and then the phone was no longer answered. So he wired her, telling her what had happened and asking her to come to the Coast, at least to call. Finally, about ten days after he left New York, the Puerto Rican man answered Durk's phone. He said that Jesse had left the city, but he did not know where she had gone. There was no forwarding address. McFarland gave the man his number in Malibu and asked him to call collect if he received any news of her. He considered explaining to him why he had left New York suddenly, but he knew that would sound as if he were appealing for pity, and he did not want that.

Knowing she had left New York, he gave up plans to return. He thought her lost to him. Crimson and clover. The worst always intruded against the best intents. He decided to

133

remain in Malibu for a time and finish the script. He was at a loss to know what else to do.

And so each day he would rise and make breakfast and sit out on the patio and read what he had written the night before and then begin to work. He worked until he was tired, until he could sleep. He worked to hide away.

The second week on the Coast David Rothenberg called. He was in Los Angeles. McFarland was not happy to hear from him. He regretted having answered the phone. But he had answered it on the unlikely possibility that somehow Jesse might be calling. Instead, it was Rothenberg.

"We're old friends, right?" He spoke very fast.

"Right." They weren't friends at all.

"I've got to come out to Malibu this afternoon to see Paul Newman."

"So?"

"He's staying up the Coast from you."

"So?"

"So I want to bring somebody by."

"I don't want anybody."

"I didn't say *any*body, kid. I said *some*body. That's a difference in nouns."

"Pronouns."

"Hold on." His voice adopted an executive tone. Rothenberg had once told him that he thought writers were children who had to be constantly supervised and then spanked if they did not keep on schedule, a point of view common enough among those who bought what writers produced. Children. He had never trusted Rothenberg after that. "We think it's bad for you to be alone. Christ, we've lost two goddamn weeks on this thing. We've been too lenient with you, Paul. . . . " He had fallen into the first person plural, something he had a tendency to do when he was on the Coast.

"I'll make it up." He wanted to get them off the phone.

"Don't you think we know, kid? But let us bring her by. A young girl. A nice Mexicano. What d'ya say, kid?" School chum's voice.

"I hate your guts, David. I always have."

134

Pause. He expected Rothenberg to fall into his Harry Cohn imitation: you'll never work this fucking town again. He didn't.

"Listen, Paul. Just for a day or two, okay? She can *type.*"

"I do my own typing."

"What do you want us to say? You know why she has to come. . . ."

He knew. If he stayed alone, they would cut him loose.

"Anyway, she's good with her mouth."

He wanted to say, so I hear is your wife, but it would have been a cheap shot, and it probably wouldn't have been true.

"I got a new one, Paul. What's the difference between a spik and a wetback?"

He didn't reply.

"A spik can't *swim!* Ha-ha-ha. . . . "

Rothenberg arrived that evening. With him was the Mexican girl. She was pretty, with large, soft eyes, the kind one sees painted on Latin madonnas. Her black hair was cut short and fell in little ringlets like those of a classic Greek youth. Rothenberg said she was eighteen, meaning she was legal, when in fact she looked younger, perhaps fifteen. She was healthy and shy and boyish in appearance. On her right cheek was a red birthmark, shaped like a crab. She spoke no English.

"She can't even speak English," McFarland said. "Take her back." He wanted to be alone. He had steeled himself against feeling, automatically. He felt detached and depersonalized, acting by rote through habit, emotionally numbed as if in shock. It was painful for him to think about Adele or Jaime, and it was painful to remember Jesse, who now was as lost to him as they were. And he knew the presence of the girl would act only to sensitize him to memory, her movements, gestures, the smell and look of her triggering longing for what was gone and could not be found again. He did not want to feel anymore. He wanted to be alone. He believed he had to move slowly, cautiously again into life, and work was the train and numbness the track carrying him back.

The three of them were sitting on the patio. Rothenberg

135

was drinking gin on the rocks. He wore a red Blass blazer, white cotton trousers and patent leather red Gucci shoes. He was suntanned. On his chest were several pounds of gold chains from which dangled various religious medals, tiny jade hands, a ruby heart, jewelry similar to that Jesse said the boys of Rome wear. There were no dog tags.

He shook his head no. "She cost us two hundred bucks, kid. That's just for starters. No way." He glanced down at his trouser leg. Water sweating off the glass had dripped on his pants. "Goddamn it! Fifty-five-dollar pants. Almighty shit. Don't you have napkins in this fucking hole?"

"I don't want her around."

"Listen, kid. She'll take your mind off things, you know?" He meant the dead. "We're on a tight schedule. . . ."

"Shove it."

"She stays. That's it." He glared at him, rubbing his trouser leg with his handkerchief.

"I'm not alone. Rafael's here." It was not true. Rafael was the part-time houseboy. He had fired him the week before.

Rothenberg popped his eyes. "Good Christ, you haven't gone over? There isn't a goddamn straight man left on the set. Poor Adele, did she know?"

"Rafael's the houseboy, David."

He laughed sardonically. "Sure, kid. I've heard them called a lot of things, secretaries, companions, cousins . . . never *houseboys* before. I guess I'm getting old, out of touch. I can't keep up with the camp lingo anymore."

McFarland blew him a kiss.

"Okay, but she stays. . . ." Rothenberg stared at his drink, and then he looked up at him. "I don't believe that houseboy stuff. Be a sport. Haven't I got enough worries with that insufferable bitch? She can even act in *bed*." He was referring to their probable star.

"I want to be by myself, David. Don't press it. What do you think, that I require a girl here, that I can't write unless I ball?" That is what he thought.

"You know what they say." He grinned at him and slapped

136

his hand very executive style against his knee, giving Mc-Farland his good-fellows-well-met wink, something he had picked up with cost accounting and the clap at City College. "Okay, kid. But keep her around. She'll come in handy."

He did not feel like arguing. He only wanted him out of the house. He would let the girl stay a couple of days and then send her packing. He stood up. Rothenberg looked up at McFarland, shrugged and then leaned forward and grabbed his cigarettes; as he did, his neck jewelry, dangling forward, clanked against his drink.

"You're a bell ringer."

"Come again?"

"Where'd you buy that junk? In Rome?"

Rothenberg stood up, pocketing his cigarettes. "What if I did? Who told you anyway?"

"That's the kind of stuff the boys of Rome wear."

"You've never *been* to Rome, kid. Anyway, it isn't *junk*. I bought most of it at Bulgari, and that's an expensive joint. I was over there last year seeing De Laurentiis. The deal fell through."

He thought of Jesse. "Did you go over alone?"

He grinned. "Do I ever?"

No, he never traveled alone.

He walked Rothenberg to the door. "Say, kid, have you thought about remarrying?" It was two weeks after Adele's death.

McFarland opened the door. It was raining. For a moment he panicked, thinking Rothenberg might insist on staying the night, walking around naked until morning to keep his fifty-five-dollar slacks from wrinkling.

"You'd better leave, David. In this rain the traffic will be murder."

"You ought to know," he said, chuckling. And then, seeing McFarland wince, he added, "I'm sorry. Jesus, that was thoughtless. " He patted his arm. He looked at him a minute while his facial muscles worked themselves toward an expression of bereavement.

"Where can I send some flowers?"

He never learned the Mexican girl's name.

He had her sleep on the sofa bed in the living room because he did not want her sleeping in Adele's bed. But Rothenberg was right. It was good having her around.

They went shopping in the morning together, at the A&P or farther up the Coast to the open vegetable markets. Once they stopped at McDonald's drive-in and McFarland walked inside. Lines of children with their parents stood in front of the counters. One small boy hopped around the floor, giggling singsong, his mother watching him delightedly. McFarland remembered, and turned away.

She cooked American food, hamburgers mainly, and she was kind to him. She never left his side until he was asleep, and he found that touching, and it occurred to him that Rothenberg, who spoke Spanish, had coached her about him, and that was why she stayed so close. She was to watch against suicide.

"*Quién?*"

She held up a photograph of Jaime.

He drew his hand across his neck in a slashing motion. "Dead. Dead. Lost. . . . " He knew no Spanish. "They erased him. Blanked him out. Dead. *Morte.* You know?" She did not understand. "In a car crash. Vrooom . . . bang!" He slapped his hands together. "Bang! Crash!" He fell to the floor and played dead. She understood.

She watched television in the evenings, and sometimes she repeated words that she had heard, and he made gestures to help her understand. For a time he considered buying a Spanish-English dictionary, and then he thought, what is the point?

One afternoon she stood out on the patio. He had given her one of his shirts to wear over her swimsuit. She stood, the sun dying, her shadow stretching through the glass doors and falling on the living-room floor. He stopped and gazed at her, immediately struck by how much like a boy she looked in

138

her oversized shirt, her small limbs, her short hair and tiny breasts. Like a boy, the way Jaime might have looked standing there as a youth.

One day he finally decided to go into Jaime's room and sort it out and close it up. Instead, he stood unmoving in the middle of the room and stared down at the carpet stained with chocolate milk and orange soda and crayons rubbed into the pale-blue turf. They had roughhoused there, at times both of them naked. He threw his son into the air and caught him; he laid him on his stomach and tickled him, feeling his feet pound and his giggling, screeching body. And sometimes McFarland got an erection, and his son played with it and seemed fascinated and unafraid, and Adele said, in deadly earnest, "Your son's a queer at two." He grabbed constantly at the gold chain his father wore around his neck, sometimes sucking on it as a baby or pulling it back and forth around his neck, leaving red marks there. And then Jaime broke it, clutching it suddenly when his father leaned over to lift him up, his small hands clutching it rigidly until it snapped from his small weight, two years before Jesse had asked for a necklace to wear.

One morning, several days after she came to him, the Mexican girl entered his bedroom when he was asleep. He woke when he felt her mouth on him. He looked down and watched a moment, and then he pushed her away, pushed too hard because she gave a small cry, like Jaime, and ran from the room.

Near the end of the first week the girl and he went walking along the beach at night. It was very dark, the moon gone. He took a flashlight, and they beachcombed for a while, collecting pieces of ocean glass, something the girl was fond of playing with. They lay on the cool sand. In the distance bonfires burned on the beach, and they heard music and laughter of the people gathered around the fires. Farther away the garish lights of the pier. It was cold on the sand. She shivered. He held her a moment, pressing her to him, her smallness and warmth reminding him of Jesse. Suddenly he was overcome

139

by loneliness, and he could not give its object a name: it was Jesse, but it was more.

"Come, it's cold . . ." he said, caressing her cheek with his hand.

She nestled closer to him. She did not want to go.

"No, no," tightening her thin arm against him.

He squeezed her tight, closing his eyes, "Jesse, Jesse," holding her, feeling the breeze from the ocean, its odor reminding him of the first time he held Jesse on the pier into the Hudson. He held the girl until she fell asleep in his arms, and then he stood and lifted her, carrying her across the sand into the house and put her gently down on the sofa and covered her with a blanket.

He made himself a drink. He could not sleep. He thought of Jesse and wondered how he was ever to find her, and he dwelled on that as he drank, considered it for hours although he knew he never would.

He fell asleep in the armchair in the living room opposite the sofa. The sun rose high, and its light came through the glass doors and woke him; it fell on her face, her Indian cheekbones casting shadows on her cheeks, the red birthmark seeming very bright against her dark skin. Her features were more Indian than European, and her expression when asleep was stoical. He wondered what her dreams were like, and what poverty had driven her north, and who had first bought her and at what age. What did it matter?

A few hours later she stood on the patio, looking at the sea, and then she started down to the beach. He called out to her that breakfast was ready. She turned and looked toward the house, facing into the late-morning sun. She squinted in the sunlight, her left hand placed on her brow, like a sailor saluting, a common enough gesture but one characteristic of Jaime.

He made breakfast for them in the kitchen, something he had habitually done when he was with Adele. He was coming to terms with what had happened to her and to his son. He had tormented himself with guilt over their dying, as if he were the force that sent them careening into death, as if there were some intimate and ineluctable, irrefrangible connection between their personal separation and the collision, and thus he reproached himself for not being conscious of her unhappiness early enough, for not having acted stronger, more decisively. Their marital crackup now seemed to have come through an accumulation of small gestures, words insufficiently precise, petty misunderstandings, inattentions, half-conscious acts that came naturally from them and whose entirety was what they were. He knew he could no more have controlled the character of those gestures—his reaction to small things, smiling or not smiling, listening when listening did not seem required, using a voice too hard or too soft, not remembering when remembering was important—than he could will his hair from blond to black or his son to life again. He had finally concluded that a life that welcomed regret was untrue. Regret implied an essential freedom and therefore a consequent responsibility for the totality of one's acts, for their hapless consequences. And he did not understand anymore what a pickup truck swerving blindly onto the Pacific Coast Highway and into his wife's automobile had to do with his freedom and its consequences, with a marriage broken, with whether he wore cuffs or not on his trousers. So he refused to accept the guilt he suffered. He denied it. He couldn't do anything else. But the denial didn't hold water. Renounced or not, the guilt remained and gradually bled into romance, cheapening itself. Two weeks after their death he had forgotten or refused to remember what had hurt him about Adele, and instead, only the goodness and the erratic beauty remained. To contend with grief and the guilt emanating from it, he had to repudiate the anger and hatred he had often felt for his wife. If he had always and only loved her, then he could not have wished her death. He was not accountable. Therefore, in coping with guilt, he murdered her memory in his mind. Adele became a secular, if overweight, saint, the perfect mother and wife. And her lover? A figment in passing, an episode, a forgivable indul-

141

gence. Lucky McFarland, lucky that such blatantly banal revision of past experience worked. The shoe fitted. And Jaime? He remained true. He had never once hated his son.

He made breakfast in the kitchen. Eggs and bacon and toast. As he stood at the counter squeezing oranges, the Mexican girl came from behind and put her arms around him and hugged him for a moment. McFarland turned around and smiled at her, and with his hands wet with orange juice he took her head in his hands, cupping it in back, his wet fingers pressed against her hair. He smiled at her and kissed her.

An hour later he called David Rothenberg to come and take her away.

"What's wrong? Won't the bitch put out?"

"She's fine. Beautiful. But I have to work." That was not the reason. Her being there had helped him through the worst, and he did not want to hurt her. He did not want to take the chance.

"I knew you'd like her. Those Mexicano chicks. I tell you, they sure know how to use the hot mouth. *Mmmmm.*"

"This afternoon?"

"Sure. . . ." Rothenberg started to cough. He had taken up smoking again. He'd given it up in New York and went back to it when he returned to the Coast. Nerves, he said. "You know why those wetbacks are so good? It's from all those hot peppers those taco-heads eat! Hell, it's damn lucky for us!"

McFarland started to tell him that they had not had sex. He stopped. Rothenberg would not have believed him.

Before she left, he went into his bedroom and took from the bureau drawer the gold chain Jaime had broken. He had intended to have the clasp repaired. He had thought about it in New York, to have it repaired and to give it to Jesse . . . he gave it to the girl instead. She smiled broadly, tying it around her neck with a piece of kitchen string. It glittered against her brown skin. She smelled of orange.

While they waited for Rothenberg, he sat with her on the patio, on one of the chaise longues, holding her, his arms around her, clasping her hands in his. He was having her

142

leave because there was no life to be made with her. More, because he knew if they had sex—and he was certain that she wanted it; he was convinced of it in the kitchen when she hugged him from behind—if they had had it in the kitchen, if he had thrust himself inside her, rage would have overcome him, and he would have hurt her, as if she were someone connected to the grief and to the loss he had sustained. And there was no connection to it anywhere except in his heart, and he knew it. But in him there was the need to strike out, to level the balances, to bring to account. And sexually, with her, something would trigger that rage. He felt it when he saw her birthmark close to her mouth, that red, crablike, woundlike disfigurement on her brown skin inches from her mouth. Her helplessness and her youth, her disfigurement, her openness to sex, an openness that seemed obscene and too insistent for her age, her ability to ignite memories of Jaime and the others, all of it or maybe none of it, he did not know, something there in her or in the room or in the smell or texture of orange or in the possibility of the act released a fugitive anger come home to him, an unfocused anger deeper than any he had known since a boy when his father brought that anger, powerless, to him. He did not understand it. It was irrational to him. It was new. He wanted no part of it. It scared him. She had to leave.

She kissed McFarland before she entered Rothenberg's car. He winked conspiratorially from behind the driver's seat. McFarland ignored the wink, not liking it.

"I'll get the bitch on the way back to LA. Taxi fare," he said, grinning.

He leaned out the car window. "Oh, I forgot to tell you. Priscilla's definitely getting a divorce. But she has no grounds. Still, it'll probably cost an arm and a leg. I hope she goes after irreconcilable differences. Shit, if she goes for adultery, it'll be a mess. I'll have to contest. In any event, she's entitled to some of the ball of wax. She'll file in the New York, the bitch, so it'll have to go to trial, whatever the grounds. She's nuts."

"You're certain about the divorce?"

143

"Pretty certain. What the hell. You lose them one way or another." He slapped his hand against his forehead. He actually blushed. "Christ, I'm sorry, Paul. It must be Freudian."

"It's all right."

"Your Adele was one sweet chick. Sorry she isn't around anymore."

When they were gone, he had several more drinks and grew despondent. He went into the bathroom and took out a vial of Ritalin and a syringe. It was a stimulant Adele used when she felt depressed. And then he put it aside. He went to bed instead.

At three in the morning Priscilla called.

"I'm committing *suicide,*" she wailed. "Come at once!"

12

WHEN Priscilla and McFarland had last seen each other in Los Angeles a year before, she told him that she would never see him again, hinting without too much subtlety at disasters likely to overtake her, kidnapping, suicide, the loss of credit cards, old age, divorce. But then she always parted from him as if it were the last time. Priscilla was like an alky constantly taking the pledge only to break it, and when she broke it—when she was unfaithful to Rothenberg, as she had been since the second night of their marriage—she would berate herself in front of McFarland or whichever male friend was handy. He was the only male friend she had with whom she had not had sex, and contradictorily, she saw that sad in both ways: sad that she hadn't, and sad that he was the only one with whom she hadn't. She would condemn herself for being a no-good whore and drunk and unfaithful wife and declare her sexual incontinence was ended and that she was going back to David come hell or high water and never part her legs for strangers again. "They aren't Moses, Paul. And I'm not the Red Sea." Usually several weeks later he received a call from her in the British or Chinese or Italian accent she used to disguise her voice because she knew Adele hated her. And Adele, exasperated, would say, handing the phone to him, "It's lamebrain Priscilla disguising her voice again," and the woman would pour out over the phone some desperate story, some lament of her despair, her being jilted, abused, suicidal, lonely, languished, disconsolate, deprived, put-upon, misused, at the end of her rope, wits, road, money, strength, powers, happiness, life, helpless, distraught and out of gas.

McFarland always went to her because he cared for her, broken down and peering transfixed at what she thought was madness—it was loneliness—poking at it, dizzy on the edge. She was the kind of person whose physical salvation resided in the lack of physical courage. Therefore, she could never bring herself to complete her life. She was always hauling the plank over the railing and then never walking it. And her irresolution increased her self-loathing and humiliation, because how many times can you threaten suicide and not carry it off without looking silly? She could find no way out of her situation or out of herself. She was trapped, and that was that.

Priscilla loved men passionately, and she was bored by women. She loved men too much because of what she remembered of them in her youth. Rothenberg she loved and grew to despise, still liking him. And McFarland? She had once been sexually attracted to him, and that had passed, and what remained was the residue of the affection and pride she deposited with him. Her respect for him and her pride in him came from the fact that he had never given in to her importunings for sex; he had never two-timed Adele with her. She liked that, despite her complaints. She trusted that. He was okay.

Since he backstopped her, acting as a first-aid station, an emergency ward, their relationship was self-dramatic and erratic, depending on her need for solace and conspirators. She was also exhausting to be around for very long. So their friendship was on again, off again, and each time she called and each time he saw her she was a little more frayed and busted somewhere new inside and, crying, repeated to him her old story with new players: Ah, betrayed again. And so it didn't go.

It was after 4 A.M. when he reached Priscilla's motel on Sunset Boulevard. It was a third-rate motor court built in the early fifties, its detached bungalows in disrepair. He parked the car in the lot and went inside the front office.

The desk clerk was asleep at the switchboard. He was an

146

old man, bent over the board, his head on his arms, his false teeth in a glass of water beside him.

McFarland pounded on the desk. He didn't move.

"Pardon me!" he shouted at the clerk.

He awoke, startled. "Yeah?"

"I was wondering. . . ."

"We're full up." He gestured toward the door. "Close it when you leave. The latch is broke." He dropped his head and arms back onto the switchboard counter and closed his eyes.

"What room is Mrs. Rothenberg in?" Priscilla had not given him the room number.

"One oh six. But she ain't there. Wait a damn minute." He took a slip of paper off the desk, read it to himself and said, "She's at Barney's."

"Barney's?"

He drummed his fingers impatiently. "Bar down the road. On Hollywood." He slumped back into his chair and dropped his head on the counter. "Close the door behind ya. The latch is broke."

Barney's was an all-night saloon-restaurant on Hollywood Boulevard near Las Palmas, or between Ruby Keeler's and George M. Cohan's brass stars in the sidewalk, however you cared to place it.

Priscilla was sitting in a booth in the middle of the large room. The decor was Texan—longhorns mounted on the walls and wagon-wheel chandeliers and plastic imitation rawhide covering the banquettes. The place was filled with Hollywood Boulevard trade: hustlers in worn Levi's, hungry vacant eyes; and street angelics nodding, blurred on counterfeit pharmaceuticals; and johns, cash-register faces, ill-fitting suits; and two drags in blue and silver wigs chattering madly. Death row.

Priscilla was staring down at her coffee, her chin resting on her hand. She looked terrible, her hair undone, her face flushed and damp with sweat.

Priscilla was a large woman. Her most striking feature was

her eyes because they were the one section of her face not completely overrun with makeup. They were large and black and shimmering and seemingly immune to the wreckage all about her. And that was what her life had become, its needle pointing to empty. The only love Priscilla could believe in was love gone. She could never believe in the love there was around her—it wasn't much because she was difficult to love; he did not believe he loved her, although he really did not know—and she came to accept worry in its place. She was self-destructive, and her body was the map on which she marked the series of wrong shots, losses and embarrassments that counted for a life. Men always did her wrong.

She stared at her cup, her mind God knows where. McFarland slipped into the booth beside her and kissed her. She looked up, her initial expression fright, and then relief and maybe love came in its place. She leaned against him, thrusting her hands between her thighs. "Darling," she whispered, "I thought you wouldn't come."

He reached down and took her left hand in his and raised it to kiss.

"Don't," she said, "please don't," shoving it back between her thighs, like a rodent burrowing.

He did not have to see. He could feel the bandage around her wrist.

"What do I have, darling? David? You? Oh, Paul, poor darling, how horrible what happened to them, to your poor child. . . ."

"Drink up, Priscilla. It comes with the lease."

At the motel. The dawn light was coming up. They stood for a moment on Sunset and looked over the Los Angeles basin to the east where the pinkish gray light filtered through the mist over the city like a valley of Gehenna beneath which a fire smoldered.

They lay on the double bed next to each other.

"It started with another bitchy fight with David. God, how've I lived with that egomaniac for twenty years? I was certain he had another woman after promising me. . . . What the hell, screw it. Give me a cigarette."

He handed Priscilla a cigarette.

"I don't mind his fucking around so much. Yes, I *do* mind it, but I'll let it go by. But I won't tolerate for one goddamn minute his supporting some goddamn whore somewhere. I'm sure he's doing that, the little prick. . . . So I ran out. I was *sick* with jealousy. I told him I was leaving him, no tears, no screams, very calm and gentle, ladylike. I took the car and started to drink from a bottle I bought at the Seven Eleven on La Cienega. Have prices gone up! And about two in the morning I was driving down Hollywood Boulevard, so fucking depressed, darling. . . ." She stopped speaking and stared down at her wrist. "Just *talking* about liquor makes me thirsty. Pour me another."

He reached for her glass and poured her another.

"Soooo . . . I was driving down and around the Huntington Hartford Theater, very lonely and unhappy, and then I saw him!" She rolled on her side, her enormous breasts sliding under her dress as she did. She sipped her drink, enjoying what she thought was nearly theatrical tension. He didn't give a damn whom she saw.

"Aren't you interested, for Pete's sake!" She tapped his leg.

"Shit!" She raised her bandaged wrist to her lips and kissed herself. "At least Mama will never leave Mama," she cooed to herself. The first few times she made that self-pitying gesture of kissing herself and pledging fidelity, years before, it had broken him up, sent him laughing. It bored him now.

"Whom did you see?" He smiled, encouraging her to continue. He wasn't interested at all.

"Paul, please don't nod *off* when I'm telling you about Heartbreak City. I live there."

"Go on." She would anyway.

"I saw this boy, about seventeen, a baby. He was leaning against the hurricane fence, so very young, young enough to be my son if I had a son he could be . . . oh, darling, I'm sorry. About Jaime."

"I know."

She was. She had no kids, and she had wanted them. And now moving, or rather sliding helplessly toward middle age,

149

she felt the alarms of its panic and knew she would have to face it alone. No kids. And nearly out of gas.

"So I swallowed my pride, darling, admittingly not difficult to do since I have swallowed so many larger things, and I pulled over to the curb and called him to the car. . . ."

"When did pride ever have anything to do with it?"

"Ha! In Kentucky. . . ." She gave up. "To hell with it. He got into the car, and we went to Barney's café, and I'm driving, and I keep looking at his crotch because he keeps scratching it, you know, working it with his fingers. And I am dying to know what it looks like. If it's . . . well, it wasn't. But it was passable, all things considered. We drove to Barney's café, and I bought him a huge breakfast. Lord, could that boy *eat*. He was from the Valley. I asked him his name. 'Leslie,' he said. 'Leslie what?' I inquired." Priscilla did an imitation of the boy's voice. She was terrible at it. "'Leslie Leslie!' Ha-ha. Get it?" Priscilla nudged him, and he jerked his leg in reflex, knocking over the vodka bottle resting against his thigh on the bed and spilling some of it on the sheet.

"Both names are the very same identical name," she explained. "Isn't it fascinating? I asked him what his friends call him. I mean you cannot call a boy by *two* first names."

"What do they call him?"

"Lee. They call him Lee."

"Sara Lee, you mean." He laughed. He found it funny because he knew that all the boys who worked Hollywood Boulevard were homosexual hookers, and everyone, including Priscilla, knew it, too; only Priscilla did not want to have to admit the truth.

"He wasn't queer!" She smacked him.

"On Hollywood Boulevard? Come off it."

"Not with me, anyway. Not with me. He had beautiful eyelashes. Lord, lashes so long and silky, like awnings on a super deli, and such a body! He spent the night with me. In this very room. In this very bed. He was very good at it. He could go all night. . . .

"And in the morning he lay beside me, and I loved the

150

smell of him. He was sweaty, but nice. And those long, long, furry eyelashes, like ebony feathers, like stage fans, closed like flowers in sleep. . . ." Priscilla was off on the romance that always came to her on the heels of loss, like a sweeper following horses in a parade. She rocked back and forth as she spoke, her arms wrapped around her, the smoke from the cigarette held in her bandaged hand rising in the dead air.

"Get on with it. I have to get home."

"In the morning I said to Leslie, 'We'll have breakfast in the room. But first we need a drinkie.'" She glanced around the room. "It *is* tacky as hell, isn't it? I mean, the *room*. It didn't look this bad in the dark. Ha-ha. But then, neither do I! Ha-ha. Anyway, I gave him thirty dollars and told him to go promptly to the supermarket and buy a quart of vodka and some vermouth. I planned to *live* in this motel room, move in permanently, grow *old* with Leslie!" She giggled with pleasure, rocking back and forth on the bed. He wanted to tell her that he could hear the loose screws rolling around in her head. He didn't. He never would.

"He never came back with the vodka, right?"

She looked reproachfully at him. "How did you know?" He had unintentionally spoiled her story.

"I was making a joke. I didn't think anyone . . . why the *cad*, the little bugger. . . ."

"*He wasn't queer!*"

"Of course not!"

"No, he never came back, the faggot." She was deflated. "I got into the car and drove around, looking for him. I saw him on Sunset by French's bookstore. I pulled over. He stood staring at me like I wasn't even *there*, like we hadn't made *love* only hours before, like he hadn't fucking *robbed* me. I got out of the car. I screamed, '*Take anything you want, but come back!*' I was desperately unhappy. He said, 'Go away. You're old.' *Old?* Since when is forty *old?*" She was eight years from forty. "I screamed and threw dollar bills at him. '*If you don't come back in ten minutes, I am cutting my wrists. I mean it. I am not a frivolous woman!*'"

"And you did," he noted sadly.

151

"Excuse me?" Her mind had wandered.

"Cut your wrists."

"No, wrist. Only one. I came back to this rat's hole, and I didn't want to do it. But I sat on the bed, thinking Leslie might come back, it wasn't impossible, and I'd look like an old fool, some sort of aging hysteric. So I slashed one, just to be on the safe side."

McFarland went to the bathroom, and when he returned, she was stripped to her slip, and she lay on the bed, the sheet pulled up to her waist. He opened the window curtain, and the noon light brightened the dim room, and Priscilla shrieked, and he closed them again. Rothenberg was right. She laid her makeup on with a trowel. She looked like a mess.

"One more drink," she said.

He made them a final round. He brought the drink and sat next to her on the bed, both of them leaning on pillows against the headboard.

"I stopped having sex with David the second week of our marriage. . . ."

"You've told me that before. . . ." Many times.

"And now I've become window dressing. He's sick. A *sadist*. . . ."

He laughed. "I know. I work for him."

"That, too. I mean in bed, Paul. He hates *women*. He likes to abuse them. He tried it with me once . . . tried to burn me with a cigarette. God, did I let him have it. I knocked him one. Threw the phone at him, glasses, even a chair. Oh, you should have seen it! The rat! My finest hour . . . and since then, darling, he buys these poor tramps. They really must be on the sick side, really on the *skids* to put up with that bastard. How could anybody need money so bad? He has pimps that he employs. . . ."

"You're talking drunk talk, Priscilla."

She pulled her hand away. "Don't patronize me! It's *true*. You think I'm lying? I'm goddamn not! One is a Chicano pimp named Gomanez who lives on Ashland. He even has a

152

pimpmobile. It's rather nice really, in a vivid way. Another one is named Rhodes. Don't know where he lives. They both provide my sick husband with whores."

"Come off it, Priscilla." McFarland could picture Mike Rhodes doing many things, but pimping for Rothenberg was not one of them.

"I've seen them, at the house, I've seen them arrive with their chippies. And leave alone. Rhodes was up to the house a few days ago, very late. David thinks I'm a dummy, but I know every goddamn thing he does. He used the maid's room. Tacky, isn't it? The maid's room. I chose not to mention it. I chose to wait. But I remember." She tapped the side of her head. "It'll all come out in court!"

"Bullshit. Rhodes is a writer, Priscilla."

"So was *Hitler!*"

"He was a painter, dear, a much lower order. Rhodes has even done a script for David."

"Bullshit, yourself. He's a sniveling pimp, as sick as my husband, who's as sickie as they make them. I was in East Hampton when your Mr. Rhodes and one of his girls came by. It disgusts me. I took the next train back to the city. I died of *heat* on that crummy Long Island car. But it was better than staying. I told David I wouldn't be under the same roof with trash, regardless of how large the house. And the three of them spent the week together, cozy as buns in the oven. And when I returned to the house, I had to open the windows for a *week* to clear out the stench of that cheap lilac perfume that rent-a-wench wore—"

"Lilac?" He knew. Jesse.

"I don't know what it cost David, but it was sure as hell more than he ever—"

"What was her name, do you know?"

"—spent on me."

"Her name. What was it?"

"Whose?"

"The girl Rhodes brought?" He grabbed Priscilla's arm and shook it to get her attention.

"You're hurting me." She glanced at him, narrowing her eyes. He had asked too eagerly, and she was suspicious, and by her expression he understood she knew and she would not tell him.

"I never asked her name. Why should I? I don't speak with my husband's whores."

"I think you're fibbing." He laughed. He did not believe her. Lilac perfume. It was common enough. And what if Jesse was there? She was close to Rhodes then. She would hardly have gone to bed with Rothenberg with Mike Rhodes there. And, too, Tom Stein had said they had not done it, although Rothenberg had tried. She was clean of it. Priscilla was paranoid.

"Fibbing? The other night, Mr. Smartass, I went to the fucking maid's room, and there was a goddamn mess. He's keeping somebody, and I don't know who the hell it is. He's waiting around for the divorce, thinking I don't know. Well, I'll find out who she is, and I'll break his head, the son of a bitch. I don't give a damn about the tramps, but that son of a bitch isn't going to have a wife-in-training. I mean, in-waiting. Up with that crap I will not put!"

McFarland got up to leave. He kissed her.

"You know something?" she said as he stood at the open door silently. She held her hands over her face to hide it from the light.

"What?"

"I hate life."

When he was gone, she would have to choose between the vodka and the last wrist. He knew she would always choose the vodka, as would he.

154

13

SEVERAL weeks later, after Priscilla's suicide attempt, she drove from Beverly Hills to Malibu and arrived unannounced at his house. McFarland was sitting out on the patio, late evening, having a drink. He had spent the day working, and he felt good since the script was at most two weeks from completion.

Priscilla walked around the house, having tried the front door and finding it locked, and burst in on him.

"I caught the son of a bitch!" she shouted.

McFarland looked at her. She was some distance away, yelling that she had caught the son of a bitch, marching toward him across the beach. She was dressed in a black dress, high heels and a large sun hat. It was late dusk; the sun was a blood-red, copper sliver above the horizon of the Pacific. There was a silk scarf wrapped around her injured wrist. She had difficulty maneuvering through the sand in her high heels.

"Whom did you catch?" he yelled out.

"Wait a damn minute. Why don't you asphalt this goddamn beach so a person can walk?"

She finally stepped from the beach up onto the wooden deck of the patio. She pulled her shoes off, dumping sand dramatically on the floor, giving him a look of disgust, as if the beach's sand were a result of shoddy housekeeping.

"Again, whom have you caught?"

"*David*, of course." Priscilla was mildly hysterical, her mood a combination of triumph, the taste of coming revenge, self-righteousness and sheer bitchy delight in having the cat in the bag. "I know *where* he keeps his woman."

"Where?" He couldn't have cared if Rothenberg kept the Los Angeles Rams. He wanted to go back to his drink, to be alone, maybe to watch some television or read a book, and go to bed. He did not want to spend the night listening to Priscilla telling him the latest installment of her personal world war.

"I can't possibly tell you until I am properly fortified." She wanted a drink.

She put her shoes back on, and they went through the house into the kitchen. "When was this place last cleaned? It looks like SRO housing."

"Vodka?"

"No, scotch. And water. With a trifle of ice."

She sat down at the kitchen table, the week's dishes cluttering the room. She looked around disapprovingly, lighting a cigarette, using a coffee saucer as an ashtray. He made her a drink. He sat down opposite her.

"You're tanned," she remarked, obviously displeased. "It ages the skin."

"Really?" He had heard it before. "Tell me what you came to say."

"Take Merle Oberon—"

"Priscilla. . . ."

"—She's got skin like a baby's ass. And she's sixty going on eighty." She was feeling very cocky.

"Is that right?" He gave up. There was no stopping her.

"She *never* goes into the sun. She's no fool."

"Surgery," he said, bored. Priscilla was in one of her onward and upward moods, and he sensed she was about to roll into her self-improvement sermon. Priscilla swung like a cow's udder between self-loathing and optimism.

"What?"

"Surgery. They do it with knives."

She eyed him unamused. "Perhaps." She touched her face. "Who cares? Anyway, they say Merle's face is pulled so tight she can't open her mouth and eyes at the same time! When

156

she yawns, her belly button rides to her chest! Ha-ha." Priscilla laughed, tugging at the sides of her eyelids Chineselike. "See what I mean?"

He didn't laugh, so she dropped the mugging. Instead, she patted her face exploringly, like an adolescent searching for zits. "It's starting to fall." Starting?

"What is?" He knew.

"Not the rain. *This*." She slapped her cheeks. "See? Like the stock market on Black Monday. . . ."

"London Bridge. . . ."

"No, Rome. No, ha-ha-ha, like my tits, an inch a year." Priscilla groaned. "Soon I'll have to tuck them under my belt when I drive! God, do I need an overhaul." She felt her breasts in false alarm as if checking to see if they had slid inches as they spoke. "The first thing I'm doing with the settlement money is going to the Greenhouse this year if it kills me. They do wonders for the skin."

She looked at McFarland, really for the first time since she had barged in on him. "You should work out, darling. Your body's beginning to go."

McFarland looked down at himself. He was wearing denim shorts and sneakers. He thought he looked all right.

"Paul, your face is beginning to slide. . . ."

"Why did you come by tonight?"

She reached across the table and felt his face with her fingers, sighing like a doctor giving the word to a terminal patient. "Circles under the eyes. You're getting puffy here, and see these tiny lines. . . ."

"Priscilla, I'm hung over, it's—"

"Paul"—she nodded slowly, patronizingly at the wreckage before her—"you want to age *gracefully*, naturally, naturally, and that takes *concentrated effort*. Discipline, Paul. *Fortitude*."

He smiled at her. She was never aware of the irony of her remark. Her house was a veritable warehouse of whatever Charles Revson, Lauder, Rubinstein, Factor, Von Fursten-

157

berg, Cover Girl, Fabergé, Arden pushed that month in the women's mags promising Priscilla immortality from a bottle.

He gave up. "Want dinner?" he asked, concluding she had forgotten the reason for her rush to his house. Or there had been no reason beyond loneliness, and that was reason enough.

"I can't," she said. "I've an appointment. I'm meeting somebody."

"*Meeting* somebody. Since I've been in town, the only somebody you've met is Leslie Longlashes, and the doc for a shot. What a crock, Priscilla."

Her eyes lit up. "Hey, that *rhymes*. Doc. Shot. Crock."

"Stay for dinner." He felt bad about his remark.

She sat deciding a moment and then reached over and patted his hand, lowering her voice. "All right, I know how important it is to you."

"Important?"

"Yes"—gripping—"they're *dead*, Paul."

"I know."

After dinner she sat with her back to the kitchen windows. The yard lights were on. Outside the trees in the courtyard were covered with white flowers. Priscilla was chain-smoking cigarettes. He imagined she had spent the day drinking in her house, thinking about getting older, her mind fixed narcissistically on her body, her appearance, as if it were all that stood between her and the gallows, musing anxiously over whether her husband had found someone younger to replace her, hoping he had, so she had the consolation of a just hatred, and hoping not, so she was not alone. But the anxiety was reality enough, sufficient anyway to cause her to greet him, when he came home, with accusatory glances and bitchery. She was a great lone hater, Priscilla. That is, she could sit alone seething for hours, mulling over in her mind her favorite dislikes—at one time or another they included every woman she knew, including Adele. What was unforgivable to her was that they had more than she had and less

158

than she thought she deserved: Adele had had McFarland and a son. And what did she have? A husband who feared her and cheated on her, no children; worse, nothing to do because Weight Watcher sessions and charity bored her sick and the brain could stand only so much television, and she hated going to the movies alone, and she played no sport and had little capacity for friendship, and she was an atheist, so church was out, and apolitical, so politics was out, and too afraid of losing Rothenberg seriously to play around. She settled for cruising the streets in her Cadillac, picking up stray boys and paying them to pretend it was love. Because she had no real sense of the tragic or because there was no real tragedy in her life, she had bitterness and contempt in place of sorrow. So she sat and drank and watched it go to waste, cherishing her bitterness. And because she knew panic and no security, she made wisecracks instead of conversation.

"Why do you stay with him?" He didn't know why he asked. He felt sorry for her; perhaps that was why.

She glanced suspiciously at him and then shrugged it off. "I won't when I catch him. But I can't just walk out without a reason. It's been too long for that. Anyway, I'm running out of batters. He tries to be good to me. But I can't stand his planning to leave me. I've got to know. Hell, he tries. It's all a game anyway. God knows David's not the bitch your Adele was—"

"Lay off."

"You know," she continued, holding up her glass for more scotch. He took it, filling it full.

"You know what?"

"Thanks." She sipped her drink. "When I was younger in Santa Monica, I mean very younger, I used to go to the beauty parlor by Bullock's in Westwood and have my hair done. All these women sat there under the dryers complaining about their husbands and kids and how it had all gone bad, you know, nothing had turned out like it was supposed to. They married some lug they thought was so handsome and romantic, sexy, and now the romance was gone, and they

159

were bored silly and stuck with the kids, and the biggest thing in their lives was when they got new slipcovers for the convertible sofa and paid the phone bill. And despite all this women's liberation talk, they're still sitting there, millions and millions, and nothing's changed. I would sit there, paging through *McCall's* and listening to them and thinking, those poor old bags, those losers, they got what they deserved, but *me?* I was going to marry some rich guy and live happily ever. . . . And I married him. And now I sit in Jean Marie's hair dump on Beverly, the third chair over, and complain to that pansy about David playing around on the side and how it's killing me under my heart, knowing it's only a matter of time and inches, Paul, until he opens the door the last time. I think he's there now, I think the handle's turning. I think. . . ."

"You're wrong," he said, suspecting she was right.

"Maybe. I'll know tonight. But I don't want him to get *away* with it! If he leaves, I want him to *pay*, and I want the pay honest. . . ."

"Priscilla, come on." She was getting bathetic, and it made him uncomfortable.

"You know"—she was still on the same jag, and it was serious what she was saying, only he had heard her say it so often before—"Adele was *lucky*. No, really."

"I don't want to hear. . . ."

"Listen to me." She slapped his hand for attention. "I'm talking to you. Lucky. *Really*. Young when she went, before the goddamn rot really set in for sure."

"Shut up, Priscilla."

She smiled. "Okay." She finished her drink.

He started clearing away the dishes, piling them in the sink and on the counter, thinking he would have to get someone over tomorrow to clean the place up. She was right. It looked like a dump.

"Oh, I forgot to tell you," she said. "How could I forget? There's a package for you on the front steps."

"Why didn't you bring it in?" Your mind is gone, that's why.

160

"Your front door was locked, or I would have brought it in."

"Come off it."

"Well, I wasn't going to carry it across the *sand* dunes. Not in high *heels*." Priscilla stood up, groaning dramatically, acting as if she were going to the wall for him. "I'll get the thing."

She left the kitchen. He heard the front door open and then slam shut. She returned carrying a small parcel post package.

"Who's it from?" he asked.

"Who do you think?" she smiled wickedly. She knew all about him.

"How would I know?"

By way of a clue, she wrinkled her nose in disgust.

"Daphne?" That was the least likely person he could think of. Daphne Bernier was an older actress who, at fifty, had had an affair with Rothenberg. It was fifteen years before, and Priscilla had neither forgotten nor forgiven. She never tired of attacking Daphne.

"*Daphne?* Ha-ha-ha. Dream on." She dropped the box with a thud on the table, clattering the flatware. "When did anybody last get anything from her? That is, anything that couldn't be cured with a *triple shot* of penicillin. Every time she thinks of me she remembers how truly *ancient* she is. I don't even know where the old hamette is or if she's still tottering among the living—"

"In London, I think. David said—"

"David!" She snorted in contempt, grabbing her drink and raising it mockingly in salute. "Up his!"

"—she's living with some guy in South Kensington."

"Not bloody likely. South Kensington indeed."

"True."

"Imagine. . . ." Priscilla rolled her head in disbelief. "Still getting the field plowed at her age. It's obscene. . . ."

He picked up the package. "It's from—"

"It shouldn't be *legal* at her age."

"—my mother-in-law."

"*Former.*"

"I concede the point."

He put the package down. He did not want to open it in front of Priscilla. Instead, he took a glass from the dishwasher and poured himself a drink. Priscilla held her glass up, waving it in the air. "Refresh me, please."

"You've had enough."

"Can it."

He refused to refill her glass. He wanted her to leave.

Priscilla reached across the table and took the package. "Are you going to? Or should I?"

"I will." McFarland opened the cardboard carton.

"So what is it?" She dropped her cigarette on the kitchen floor and ground it out. She reached eagerly for the box, her face full of mischief.

"Some of Jaime's stuff," he said, closing the box. He did not want her to see.

"Let me look already." She stood and moved somewhat unsteadily toward him. She grabbed the box from his hands. She sat down again, holding the package in her lap, and removed Jaime's baby shoes. She held them up with her fingertips in front of her. "Isn't that cutesypoo? Little biddy baby booties all in bronze!" She dropped them back into the box. "What're you going to do with them? They're too light for doorstops." She snickered.

"I don't know."

"Why don't you use them for planters? It's all the rage in the Valley. Très *chick*. Plant cactus in them . . . *yum*sie."

"Fuck off."

She threw him a look of pretended shock, slapping her hands to her face. "My, my! Such language. I bet Adele never let you talk that naughty around her. Always little Paula Pure, your Adele, like her mother, your former in-law." Priscilla laughed bitterly, off on a number. "Little Paula Pure"—she singsonged it—"Little Paula Pure. Darling, it's enough to make snakes cry."

"You better leave, Priscilla." He was angry. She never knew when the hell to let up. He took the box from her.

162

"Wait a minute. Listen, you know what I gave Rodney?"
Rodney was the first romance Priscilla had, a bush-league baseball player she knew in Kentucky before she met and married Rothenberg. She lived with him for a year, and one day he wired her from training camp in Pensacola to tell her that he had married someone else on the road and would she mind returning her Keepsake engagement diamond since he still owed payments on it. She never forgave him.

McFarland shook his head no. "Time to go, Prissy."

"Hold it a minute. I want to tell you a funny."

She stood and walked to the kitchen counter and poured herself more scotch. Her voice acquired its familiar, irritating, whining edge. No wonder she drove Rothenberg bananas.

"Hot Rod, remember him? For God's sake, Paul, I've told you about him fifty times. The baseball player? The one who wore a beanie through four years of college because no one let him in on the secret?"

"Yeah. So what?"

"Do you know what I gave him for his second wedding anniversary to that dumb besotted slut from Pensacola? God, wasn't she a sight with her Mary Pickford ribbons yet and little bow mouth?" Priscilla lit a cigarette, smirking at him. "Come on, Paul. *Guess.*"

"I don't know. A dildo?" He had no idea.

"Close. *Very* close. . . . I had my famous diaphragm bronzed, the one that carried Hot Rod and me through a year together babyless? Had the thing bronzed and gave it to him. Ha-ha. And you know what he told her it was?"

"What?"

"An *ashtray!* Ha-ha-ha. . . ." Priscilla spilled her drink. "Damn it," she said, brushing against the front of her dress.

"There's a towel behind you."

"To hell with it. We have to go."

"Pris. . . ."

"Come on." She took his hand and started pulling him to the door. He jerked his hand away.

163

"Wait a minute."

"We haven't a minute. It's after eleven. He'll be there by now."

"Who?"

"David. Out in Venice. Oh, the *idiot!* Why must he make it so *easy?* Has he no cleverness left? He's been giving personal checks to that trollop made out to her address. Can you beat that? He's terrified of using her name. Thirty-three Church Street. They're *signed* that way. That's where he is, with that befouled chippie, Miss Thirty-three Church Street. And we're going to catch them in the act—"

"What do you mean, *we?*"

"—climactus interruptus!"

"Priscilla!"

"Can't wait to see the schlemiel's face!"

They were out the door.

14

McFarland sat in the front seat of Priscilla's yellow Cadillac Seville. He was dressed in his denim shorts and tennis shoes, shirtless. She had not given him time to change.

Priscilla leaned forward in the driver's seat, her body pressed aggressively against the steering wheel, her hands gripping it tightly, her sun hat shoved back on her head as she squinted myopically at the road, seeing a white line surrounded by a moving gray blur. They roared down the Pacific Coast Highway toward Venice.

"Tell me when you see a sign that says Santa Monica Canyon Drive. We turn left there."

"Look for it yourself." Disgruntled, unwilling to cooperate, angry with her and himself for getting trapped on her chase to catch her husband, his boss, in the clutches of some two-bit benighted prostitute who might or might not exist in actuality but who lived with biting bile and petty vengeance in Priscilla's mind. She needed to believe the worst to justify what she had decided to do in any event: punish David.

"I can't see, you fool. I'm nearsighted as hell."

"You're what?"

"*Blind.*" She laughed. She abruptly swerved the car into the left lane, nearly sideswiping a red Volkswagen bus with an IF YOU LOVE MY JESUS, HONK! sticker on its rear fender. She blared the horn, yelling, "Son of a bitch, get out of the way!" The driver, a young woman with a beatific smile on her Midwestern face, mistaking the honking horn as a sign of coreligionist greeting, raised her fingers in a V sign and tooted her horn in reply. McFarland smiled at the driver. Though your sins be as scarlet. . . . Priscilla shouted obscenities.

165

"How can you see to drive?"

"Road hogs!"

"Priscilla. . . ."

"So I'm a little bombed. I just keep my eyes on the white line. That's why they paint it. Couldn't read a road sign if my life depended on it."

"That's reassuring."

They turned left off the ramp onto Santa Monica Drive.

"Now look for Lincoln Boulevard, darling."

"Slow down, for Christ's sake." She was traveling twenty miles an hour over the limit, and doing it badly, the car swinging erratically between the center line and the lane strips, occasionally dipping momentarily into the wrong lane.

"I should've married Rod. The only vices he had were a partiality for beer on the rocks, if you can believe it, and sleeping in his socks and jockstrap. I never knew a man so attached to white socks. He'd wear them to the beach—"

"You're slurring your words."

"—white socks and white shorts. He looked like a Nassau traffic cop. Ha-ha."

"Next intersection."

"Thanks." They turned right onto Lincoln Boulevard, running the red light.

"The light, Pris. . . ."

"What light?"

They drove slowly through Venice, trying to locate Church Street amid the used car lots, taco stands, commercial blood banks, pizza huts, saloons, parking lots, porno stores and massage parlors, run-down motels. McFarland did the looking since Priscilla's eyes were sewn to that endless white line.

"There it is. Pull over."

They parked the car in the lot of an empty Exxon station. He reached over and took the key from the ignition. "I'm driving on the way back." She hiccuped.

There was no vehicular access to Church Street from Lincoln Boulevard. They walked the block to the beachfront, hand in hand, Priscilla somewhat wobbly on her heels. The moon was up and high and small, and it gave a faint mercury light to the promenade under the date palms; winos asleep and junkies nodding on the public benches, runaways and others without accommodations asleep on the sand or gathered in small noisy groups around small fires built with broken sand fences. In the distance, hulking into the water, dark and ominous, like some great wounded beast, some great structure in ruin, was the Venice Pier, abandoned and broken, falling piecemeal into the ocean.

They walked to Church Street and then up it to Number 33. The street was narrow and lined with small bungalows and six-unit apartment houses, dating from the twenties, built when Venice was developing from a fishing village into a middle-class suburb; now, decades later, the rot grew, and the area was populated by dopers and rummies and welfare Chicanos and blacks and illegal aliens and ersatz "artists" and "poets" living on pushing and panhandling and an occasional hustle out of the life, their visas expired. So the atmosphere was one of decay and misuse, semi-abandonment, disrepair, startling because the California climate, the temperance of it, the benignity of the beach was in contradiction to the deteriorating housing and humanity.

Number 33 Church was at the far side of the dead-end street. It was a small one-story gray frame bungalow with a green tar-shingle roof; its front lawn was paved in green asphalt which clumps of crab grass broke through. At the yard's center there was a birdbath formed of three concrete swans supporting a basin on their heads, and around it, stuck in the green tar, were rigid plastic tulips in need of a wash. Priscilla pointed at the birdbath. "*Charmant*," she said.

They climbed the four cement steps to the front porch, opened the rusted screen door and stepped inside. The porch smelled of mildew and urine. It was dark. The only light came from the curtained window that overlooked the porch.

"He keeps his lady in style," Priscilla said.

They heard voices inside. She tried the front door. It was locked. She slapped her hand hard against the door.

"Open up, you bastard!"

"Shut up, Priscilla."

They waited. The voices stopped talking. She slapped her hand against the door again. Then she began to kick at it. The door opened.

Mike Rhodes stood on the other side smiling coolly. McFarland, who had not seen him since their days at college fourteen years before, recognized him at once. Still the smile, aloof, detached, haughty; still the uplifted chin, the narrow patrician look of him; still the arrogance of his pose, the condescension, the curiously relaxed physical grace; the ambiguity of sexual identity overlaid like a fractured porcelain with a glaze of genuine and consistent hauteur. McFarland did not trust Rhodes, and upon seeing him again, he instinctively felt what he had always known before in his presence: a desire to both avoid and attack him. He felt threatened by him, that he was perverse and evil, that in a crucial way Rhodes was disconnected from the moral limits that bound other men. He could not be reached.

"I've been expecting you." He continued to smile, his tall body lounging against the door frame.

Priscilla rushed past him. "Where is he?" she demanded, marching around the living room, throwing pillows off the sofa, checking the ashtrays, glaring around the room, looking for evidence of Rothenberg's presence.

"Who?" Rhodes moved from the door, smiling disingenuously. McFarland followed him inside. The back door slammed. Priscilla yelled, "Bastard!" and, half toppling on her high heels, rushed out of the room, down the hallway, through the kitchen and out the back door.

"Sit down," Rhodes said. "It's been a long time."

McFarland sat on a blue canvas director's chair. Behind him, on the soiled waterstained wall, were travel posters, one showing the Spanish steps, another the Temple of Apollo at Delphi, a third a photograph of two round apartment

168

towers in Chicago. The room's three windows were nailed shut, the air stale. On a side table by the corduroy-upholstered sofa were large brandy sniffers filled with various colored pills.

"Did Jesse ever mention me?" Rhodes asked, smirking.

"How did you know?" Suspicious.

"That you're seeing her? Ha-ha. David told me."

"We never discuss you." He did not want to talk with Rhodes about her.

Rhodes unbuttoned his sleeves and rolled them up. "I'm sweating. Forgive me. I haven't changed my clothes as yet. I always dress for business, and it's been a profitable day." He stared at McFarland, maintaining his patronizing smile.

Rhodes had aged extremely. His hair was prematurely gray; deep laugh lines were channeled around his eyes, forehead, and mouth. His skin was pale and unhealthy in appearance, like that of someone never in the sun. And yet he looked boyish, despite the fact his nose was broken, the damage recent, and the repair badly done. It gave to his face what it had never possessed before, an expression of strength. Yet his eyes remained young and alert and even playful, touched with cynicism and mischief. Oddly, despite his grayness and his aged skin, he appeared as young as or younger than McFarland. He was older by a year.

"Cigarette?" he asked McFarland.

"Please."

Rhodes went to the sofa and lifted his white linen suit jacket off it and took from its inside pocket a gold cigarette case. He offered him a cigarette. McFarland took it.

"I've seen that before."

"This?" Rhodes held up the case before he placed it back in his jacket pocket. "Good memory. I had it at Columbia. It was the only thing I ever got worth keeping."

Rhodes then pulled a lighter, also gold, from his white trouser pocket and lit his cigarette. During the entire episode his eyes remained fixed on McFarland. It made him uncomfortable.

169

"You're right to go without a shirt. It is hot in here." He lifted his jacket off the sofa and laid it carefully over the sofa's arm. And in that gesture McFarland knew it was he who had been in St. Thomas with Jesse and had beaten her there. He hated him.

The net and the wire.

Rhodes sat down, crossing his long legs at the knee.

He continued to stare at McFarland, smiling, holding the small gold lighter between his thumb and fingers, his hand resting on his crotch, rubbing the gold lighter slowly in his hand, the motion deliberate and patently sexual.

The net and the wire.

"I should go find Priscilla. . . ." McFarland moved to get up.

"Sit down. She'll be back. I presume it's David she's after."

"Of course."

"Too late, poor pussy. He's over the fence and gone. She ought to leave him be. He's terrified of her. I remember in East Hampton, about a year ago, she created this enormously ugly scene over nothing, really. She claimed David was sleeping with a girlfriend of mine, not that it mattered, but it was simply untrue. Not that weekend, at any rate."

"She gets hysterical. She's afraid of losing him."

"She goes about keeping him in a strange way. I mean, the week before she threw the scene she fucked with me. Twice. I think she was jealous, not of David, but because the girl was with me. Perhaps I flatter myself. . . . "

"Please stop it."

"Stop what?"

"Rubbing that thing."

Rhodes laughed, putting the lighter in his pocket. "So touchy, Paul. Too touchy." He laughed at McFarland, bending forward and laying his hand playfully on his leg, squeezing him at the knee. McFarland shoved his hand away.

"See what I mean? Touchy. Ha-ha. . . ." Rhodes sat back, continuing to stare at him. He unbuttoned his shirt with his left hand. "It *is* warm," he said, running his hand under his

170

open shirt, "and I'm afraid the windows can't be opened. . . ." smiling at him, rubbing the left side of his chest.

"You're crazy as ever, Mike."

Rhodes made a dismissing gesture with his left hand, the skin covered with thick pinkish white scar tissue. "Yes, like a fox."

McFarland saw the scar tissue. And he remembered.

Finals week, fourteen years ago, about half a dozen male undergraduates got together in Tom Stein's room at Livingston Hall at Columbia. Rhodes was among them, as was McFarland. They were all drinking Rheingold beer, except Rhodes, who was drinking straight vodka from a bottle because he was two classes ahead of them, which gave him certain prerogatives, and because he said beer made him vomit. They did not know why it made him vomit because he never explained why. But they suspected it was because of the downs, mainly Quaaludes, that he bragged about taking. McFarland didn't think beer really made him vomit, believing it was merely an affectation similar to Rhodes' refusal to ride in airplanes. But you could never be sure with a screwball. Rhodes was twenty years old at the time, and all McFarland knew about him was that he was head of some student organization and that he was involved in campus politics in a decidedly muddled way. Curious, because he did not think then that Rhodes gave a damn about politics, although it was a highly political age; no, it was the psychological drama and soon the chances of engaging in violence that drew him to it. Rhodes had a deep restlessness in him, joined by a resentment against the world.

So, fourteen years ago, one of the students put water on to make coffee since some of them had to stay up to cram for exams. He boiled the water on a one-burner hot plate on top of the desk. At that point in the discussion Rhodes fell silent. He had been talking jokingly, yet earnestly, about all of them being the terminal generation, mankind's last act, that all the bombs and gases and biological weapons and radiation meant that life was about to hand them a bill they couldn't pay and the lights would go out: worlds, galaxies, universes colliding, all of it coming to a head like an overripe pimple waiting for some kid to come along and explode it with a touch. That was how Rhodes talked then. He talked like McFarland's mother; only he left out Jesus and the rapture. It was very subversive blather because the thrust of his argument about planets falling into stars falling into black holes falling into oblivion as empty and as wide and as blind and as final as the eye of God, the ringer to it, what made it breathtakingly impressive to their sophomore minds, was that the honest-to-God end of things, the withering away of creation, justified *anything*. There was no law or limit. It was simpleminded stuff; nevertheless, it seemed to cojoin in a vague, imprecise way with the equally simpleminded existential nonsense ground into McFarland's mind by Columbia's Humanities Department. In short, Rhodes seemed brilliant to McFarland and the others, and he gave them hope of being as brilliant as he when they hit twenty.

At Columbia, Mike Rhodes abruptly stopped speaking, and a distant, passive expression came over him as if he were remembering something urgent and out of reach. It was similar to the blank look that came over McFarland's mother moments before the plug was pulled and her mind went into its recurrent brownout. McFarland had seen him fall into like moods, so he was convinced Rhodes had some screws loose somewhere. The effect of the mood was to make one concerned about him and a little frightened, a sense that he stood in peril and the most insignificant false gesture would send him tumbling over the line. It was finally that consciousness of peril and his apparent indifference to it that caused everyone he then knew to excuse him so goddamn much and to tread carefully around him, as though he were a field set with mines.

Rhodes was also excused because he had a charm that was effortless and beguiling. He cast a spell. He was handsome in a patrician way and naturally elegant and gracious. Despite his violent talk and his apocalyptic ravings, he radiated vulnerability. He would lose that in time, toughen in time, grow jaded and, to McFarland's mind, decadent in time. . . but when he knew him in college, he was magnetic and threatening and highly stimulating.

It was winter. Rhodes wore very tight brown corduroy trousers—he was partial to corduroy—and a pale-blue shirt unbuttoned to his navel, showing off his darkly tanned skin. He played with a heavy gold chain around his neck. His gesture irritated McFarland because he did not own a heavy gold chain, and if he did, he would not have the nerve to wear it, and he certainly would not play with it as flirtatiously as Rhodes did. He curled the gold links around his fingers and rubbed the fingered gold slowly over his chest, left to right, and as he did he caressed his nipples like a woman playing with her breasts, a whore exciting a john. He looked like a joyboy, well kept. Rhodes' movements, his pose and poise, had to them a self-consciously sultry quality. Sex, his bearing said, was too easy a matter for him, carelessly so.

McFarland envied him that ease. He was reduced to Barnard mixers where he made small talk with eighteen-year-old zitzed intellectual princesses from the Chicago suburbs whose sole interest in sex seemed to be defensively conversational, while Rhodes would appear at night in the Columbia haunts with midtown women on his arm, always treating them with ballsy disregard, a disregard McFarland could never muster.

So that night at Columbia, fourteen years ago, Rhodes said, "*I* saw a niggerboy killed yesterday."

McFarland knew he used the "niggerboy" to get a reaction out of his listeners. He used it comfortably. Rhodes called the others self-righteous, snot-nosed liberals. And they were. And most stayed that way, long after Columbia, not because most of them believed it anymore; they stayed that way because they did not know how to be anything else. And Rhodes? A communist-anarchist. Small *c*, naturally.

"Please don't use that word," Tom Stein said.

"Niggerboy dark as the ace of spades."

"Where did you see him killed?" McFarland asked.

Rhodes told many bizarre stories, and most of them turned out to be true.

"In Washington Square."

"No shit." Stein was hooked. He shared with Rhodes an interest in violence. Both of them spent much of their free time watching gangster movies and reading crime novels. Only Rhodes went a step farther, he usually did—he kept a scrapbook full of newspaper clippings of criminals and their victims. He carried an old yellowed clipping in his billfold from the *National Enquirer:* COUPLE AXED TO DEATH!!! THEIR BODIES FED TO DOGS!!! He claimed the dog food was his parents. He lied. He also boasted that he had pulled off various petty felonies. Crime was a sexual act to him.

"In Washington Square. . . . I was on downs, and I was sitting on a park bench, and a young cop and this niggerboy moved down the street—" Rhodes had a high, thin voice which would not deepen with the years and a Connecticut accent. And he never raised it.

"*Black*, you mean." Stein was still trying. His father was on the board of the Westport Chapter of the Anti-Defamation League. He never forgot.

"—He moved very, very slowly. The cop had a gun in his hand, pointed at the niggerboy, and the niggerboy kept glancing back and waving away the cop, like this—" Rhodes made a graceful wave, indifferently, aristocratically, like a man waving off a page.

"—dismissing him. Leave me alone, boss. They went on like that for three or four minutes, moving down the street, the cop several feet behind, the niggerboy turning around occasionally and waving him away, taking their sweet time about it. Then, near the end of the block, when they were no more than three feet from each other, the cop shot the niggerboy. *Bang!*"

Rhodes slapped his hand hard against the desk top. It star-

174

tled them. The boiling water bounced slightly on the hot plate. Rhodes glanced at it, noticing the steaming pot for the first time.

"It was a street ballet they were having, something choreographed by Balanchine . . . in slow motion. The bullet hit the niggerboy here, in the throat, left of his Adam's Apple"— Rhodes ground his long fingers into his throat—"right below the chin, and the niggerboy looked astonished, baffled, in *dig*-nant. He couldn't fucking *believe*, see, that the cop would actually shoot him dead. He couldn't believe he was ten seconds from being one dead nigger. A torrent of blood spurted out of his throat, and it made this enormous slow motion arc in the air. It was like a long scarlet piece of silk suddenly blown out and wafted down in the breeze. The niggerboy fell down one way, and his blood shot out the other, so that the motion of his falling and the flying blood was like two monarch wings opening in a red sunset. . . . "

Pause.

"So?"

"So it was beautiful, klutz." Rhodes smiled. "And the worst of it was that that niggerboy had no *gratitude* for it."

"It was murder," Tom Stein observed mordantly. He was right, of course. "Racist murder." This was during the last, unhappy days of the civil rights struggle in Dixie, about the time CORE and SNCC were throwing out whites and publishing anti-Semitic distribes. They all were very touchy about racist murder back then, way back then.

Rhodes shrugged. He had lost interest. He fell silent, and the rest of them sat there embarrassed, McFarland staring at his hands. What was embarrassing to McFarland was Rhodes' tone of voice, the sensuality he brought to the telling.

Someone changed the subject by asking if anyone knew where good grass could be gotten. . . those were also the days when Timothy Leary was telling the young that grass and acid were better than Jesus Christ.

Rhodes, again withdrawing into his thoughts, stared down

at his body, watching his hand move down his chest and stomach and over his navel, coming to rest on his lower stomach where he played with the line of hair that ran up to his navel. McFarland watched him, fascinated by his quick changes in mood and by his unpredictability and his unvarnished narcissism. Rhodes was continually touching himself as if to assure himself that he was still alive.

His expression blank again. No, not blank. Immobile. That numbness people sometimes see in the face of some unlucky bastard upon whom it has just dawned that the person he loves most will never love him in return. It is the presentiment of hell, to know relentless desire for what you will never possess.

Mike Rhodes owned some dirty secret that kept madly whispering away at him, something only he heard, like a guest in a dilapidated boardinghouse futilely complaining to the half-deaf landlady about the mice he alone hears scratching inside the walls. McFarland knew he had received some kind of traumatic hurt when he was about seventeen—so what? Who hadn't—but he was never clear as to the nature of the hurt. Rhodes' close friends, and there were many of them, camp followers trailing around him like snobs around a slightly batty prince, his friends, whenever he fell into one of his despondencies, would vaguely refer to the teenage trauma, hinting at apologies.

So Rhodes sat perched on top of the desk beside the boiling water, his face a blank slate, his dark hair glinting, his large mouth hung slightly open. . . . Rhodes sat on the desk and raised his hand and easily lowered his fingers into the boiling water, submerging them gently, slowly, with exquisite deliberation, with the movement of a person languidly testing tepid bath water. He said nothing, good old insane *Wasp* self-control, not a sound, expressionless.

It was such an absurd, unaccountable gesture that it was for a moment unreal. McFarland couldn't take it in. It was funny. Several of the boys laughed. McFarland had not a clue to what he was attempting to prove. He had not a clue to why his mother painted all the living-room funiture white, using a roller to slide the shiny white enamel over the brocade sofa and chairs, or why she started calling him Henry when his name was Paul, or why she really said Merry Christmas in August. He hadn't a clue.

He responded to Rhodes' gesture the same way he responded to his mother the very first and every following time she fell to pieces, the same way he immediately reacted when Adele and Jaime fell to pieces, the way he responded to calamities and disasters and wars overtaking other people suddenly making them fall to pieces; he looked on helplessly, numbed, depersonalized.

So years later in California, seeing the scarred hand, he remembered when and how but never why it had happened.

"Do you still see Tom Stein? It's been a long time," Rhodes asked, staring at McFarland, his smile tight on his face.

"On occasion."

"Pathetic little Jew. Full of dirty, tiresome habits. . . . "

"I like him."

"More the pity. He is absolutely without taste. Do you remember how he used to dress? Ha-ha. Boringly. And his ideas, or lack of them. Hell." Rhodes clapped his hands together. "They want to bind the earth, see?"

"They?"

"You swam, didn't you? I can see. You have the body for it still, truly. I used to watch you swim. . . ." McFarland remembered Rhodes coming in the afternoons and sitting in the bleachers in the pool room, dressed in a jacket and tie, schoolbooks beside him, sitting in the hot, steaming Columbia pavilion, an arrogant smile on his face, watching McFarland and the other undergraduates swim and dive naked in front of him, acting as though the swim practice were a command performance done for his benefit.

"I remember."

"Yes," Rhodes said, his hand playing with his chest, "I

kept waiting for someone to drown. Ha-ha. . . . Really. And you know, of the several hundred in our two classes, thirty-one are dead. Think of it. I *know*. I read the alumni bulletins and the obits in the *Times*. I keep track. One hanged himself. Two murdered. One lost in Kenya. Auto accidents. Overdoses. . . . Thirty-one, most before they *were* thirty-one. . . . "

"The war. . . . "

"Only eleven got it in the war! We were an *officer* class. I never believed in death until I was seventeen, and then it was the only thing I was ever sure of again. Ha-ha. Funny. I think of it sneaking in on one at night like a cat burglar in tennis shoes, and there it meets one alone. After all, Paul, we're of the generation born during or immediately after or slightly before the Great Patriotic War, and therefore, we're privileged to number among our classmates and sometime lovers, think of it, a score plus eleven, all of whom dropped *alone*. . . . "

"We're no different," McFarland said, knowing it wasn't true. They were infected, all of them, and so few chose to resist it.

"Ah, but we are." Rhodes leaned forward smiling, his voice as passive as always, his intensity expressed by his eyes. "If only he or she hadn't been *alone*. . . . if only I had seen him or her that night. . . . *That's* the guilt coda we sing after each not quite unexpected demise."

"I feel no guilt."

"You lie, Paul. The clock ticks, and we've grown used to watching the hands beat toward our number. Ha-ha. . . . Suffice it to say"—he fell back languidly against the sofa—"I have known them hanged, shot, self-poisoned, drowned, slashed, car-crashed and one, ha-ha, electrocuted by the wires of his Panasonic portable color television set during an afternoon showing of *The Gang's All Here*. Weinbaum, remember? At Jones Beach. Your senior year. Ha-ha. Tico. Tico. . . . "

"Where does the difference lie?"

"Shit. Others ran from it. We run toward it. . . . "

178

Bang! Priscilla clomped back inside, her nylon stockings torn, her left knee scrapped. "You ought to clean that goddamn yard. It's a menace to the public health."

Rhodes stood as she entered, nodding at her, his hands cupped behind his back, a headwaiter listening to a customer's complaint. "It's a rental," he explained.

Priscilla glared at him. "*Look* at me. I practically broke my goddamn back. You said you'd keep him here. You said eleven o'clock."

"You were late. Nearly an hour, in fact."

"Well, I'm not paying. Not until I catch him in the act."

Rhodes smiled. "Bitch."

Priscilla laughed. "We're some pair, aren't we, Michael? Ha-ha. . . . "

"The game's not over. . . . "

"But the quail's escaped the net. . . . Do you have some grass, darling?"

"In my jacket pocket. . . . "

Priscilla went fumbling through the jacket. She found several joints and offered them around. They were thick and strong. She lit up, inhaling deeply. Rhodes followed suit. McFarland refused. It was just becoming clear to him that Rhodes and Priscilla were collaborators in it together to get David. Perhaps blackmail was the goal.

"Paul, I'm sorry," she said. "You'll have to make the trip out here again. We were late. My fault."

"No way."

"Darling, I need you. Why do you think I brought you? For the conversation?" she asked. Rhodes laughed. "I need a witness. Someone of impeccable reputation. And, excuse me, Michael. . . ." She made a small bow toward Rhodes and, doing so, sucked on the joint. "*Mar*velous stuff. . . . " She began to cough.

"Sit down, Priscilla, before you fall down," Rhodes said.

She sat and began to giggle. "You should have seen David run. I think he believed I was a cop. I saw him throw a package in the alley. . . ."

"Small, about this size?" Rhodes illustrated.

179

"Right."

"It was the coke he bought tonight."

"What was I saying? Oh, Paul, you see, darling, Mr. Rhodes' reputation wouldn't do me much good, not with several drug arrests, although no convictions, thank God. It would be useless in a divorce proceeding or the threat of a divorce procee—" She burst into laughter. "I forgot what I was saying."

"Divorce," Rhodes said, and then turned, smiling, toward McFarland. "You see, Mrs. Rothenberg—"

"Prissy, *please*—"

"—Prissy cannot forgive him because she loved him once. And she's only loved twice in her life, and so she's used up her credit in that area and has none left. So he'll have to pay."

"Fucking right. Call me Prissy—"

"—And I empathize with that. When I was, well, seventeen, the only person I was ever *in* love with died on me quite deliberately, planned it, and I know this will sound mad to you, but I've never forgiven. I have never loved anyone since. Why take the chance?"

McFarland stood. "I'm leaving."

"But *why?*" Priscilla asked, alarmed.

He started toward the door, wanting to get out, feeling foolish and taken, badly used by Rhodes and her. He did not care how desperate she was or how much she hated Rothenberg.

"Wait, Paul." Priscilla stood somewhat unsteadily. "I want to show you something. I'm not crazy. I'm not a frivolous woman. . . ."

She weaved into the hallway.

"Follow me, Paul."

"What is it?" Irritated. He wanted it over with.

Priscilla walked down the hall, staggering slightly, the grass beginning to marry with the liquor and render her stoned. She stopped at a door on the right, near the kitchen. "I think this is it." She opened the door and reached in and

180

turned on the ceiling light. She grinned at McFarland, who stood several feet away. She was proud, triumphant, justified. "In there," she said, gesturing into the room.

McFarland hesitated.

"Come on. . . . "

From the ceiling hung a brass chandelier with blue and red lights. On the floor were two mattresses laid side by side. An open suitcase lay in the corner, and scattered about were clothes, phonograph records, magazines. The room smelled of sweat and grass and amyl nitrate and faintly of vomit. Its one window was closed, its black shade nailed shut.

"*That's* what he's giving me up for," Priscilla said drunkenly. "Do you believe it?" She pointed to the bed. On it lay a woman with her back to the door. She was covered with a sheet. They stood ten feet away, and for a moment they were quiet, listening to her deep, irregular breathing. Then Priscilla staggered forward. She reached down and awkwardly yanked the sheet away.

"Get out!" McFarland yelled at Priscilla, grabbing her arm. "Get the fuck out!"

She tried to pull herself free of his grip. "You're hurting me, Paul."

He let go. She staggered backward toward the door. He stepped toward her and shoved her farther back, his face flushed with rage. "Out!" She turned and stumbled out the bedroom. He slammed the door after her, falling hard against it.

He leaned against it a moment. He took a deep breath and then turned and looked back at the bed. He felt dizzy and relieved and frightened.

He knelt on the mattress and looked down at her for a time and then cautiously, shyly, hesitantly, reached out and touched Jesse's shoulder. "Love," he whispered, laying his hand on her head, caressing her hair. Her breathing was labored, her body unusually cool and damp. She made deep, stressful sounds when she inhaled. "Jesse," he whispered. He gently turned her on her back, and then, out of an instinctive

181

sense of modesty, he drew the sheet up to cover her breasts. He looked at her a moment, touching her face with his hands, running his fingers tenderly under her eyes, along the dark circles there, the skirts of shadow, and down to her mouth, over her lips, along the side of her mouth where saliva ran to her chin. Then he kissed her. She did not wake. He lay down beside her, putting his arm across her chest, and then, turning on his side, he drew her to him, holding her tightly against his bare chest, saying her name softly again and again . . . his face against her hair. Lilac. He held her for about twenty minutes, afraid to leave, never wanting to leave her, complete again. Everything in him marshaled now to protect her and keep her beside him.

And then she moved and groaned and moved and shoved against him. "Don't hurt me," she mumbled, opening her eyes partway. She did not recognize him. He was alarmed. She's drugged, he thought. He felt her wrist. Her pulse was weak and slow. He kissed her and moved carefully away.

He left the room, shutting the door quietly behind him. He went into the living room. Priscilla was sprawled on the sofa next to Rhodes, sharing another joint of grass with him. She was giggling over nothing.

McFarland stood a moment watching them, letting his anger rise inside him until it was almost palpable, until he could feel it inside him like another body, feel it and come to terms with it and use it. He took several deep breaths, and then he said, "What have you done to her?"

Rhodes smiled, glancing up. "Who?"

"Whooo whooo whooo. . . ." Priscilla giggled, mimicking an owl's call, falling laughing against Rhodes' shoulder. "Whoooooo. . . ."

Rhodes laughed, pushing her away. "She's stoned, dear Mrs. Rothenberg—"

"Call me Prissysissy—"

"—Quite, quite stoned."

"Tell me!" He moved closer to the sofa where they sat. He

182

held his fists against his body, trying to keep it under control, to hold it until he knew what he had to know, to bank it until then and then to let it go.

Rhodes continued to smile, looking up at McFarland, his chin held high, his eyebrows raised, his face breathing condescension and contempt as if the question were too stupid and impertinent to deserve reply but, being old school chums, he would indulge him with an answer he already should have known. "Downs. Barbiturate. Eats them like candy. A very expensive candy indeed. . . ." He stared at McFarland. And then he laughed. He appeared relaxed and passive, feeling perfectly safe. And it was the arrogance of that sense of security, the feeling of powerlessness it produced in McFarland, that lit the fuse.

"Son of a bitch." Quietly. Between the grinding teeth. He let go. He kicked over the coffee table with his foot and flung himself at Rhodes, who made no attempt to protect himself. He struck Rhodes in the face, aiming hard for his contemptuously smiling mouth; he hit him again and again, breaking Rhodes' lips, knocking out teeth, cutting his own knuckles on Rhodes' teeth as he beat into him.

Rhodes lurched back against Priscilla, who looked confusedly stoned and somewhat amused, a delightful game, these roughhousing boys. McFarland hit him again, tearing his ear, and Rhodes' head banged against Priscilla's shoulder, knocking the joint of grass from her hand.

"What's going on? You'll burn my dress, darlings. . . ." She giggled, as she felt on her lap for the fallen joint.

McFarland, raging, grabbed Rhodes by his shoulders and pulled him to his feet. He slapped his face. "Don't go out on me now," he said coolly, not wanting to stop, not wanting Rhodes unconscious until he had punished him enough for Jesse and the rest.

Rhodes staggered back against the wall, opening his eyes momentarily. He felt his torn mouth with his hand, and then he stared at McFarland, a semblance of a grin returning to his

183

face. He seemed confident and unafraid, beyond the power of McFarland to damage him. It enraged McFarland. He wanted Rhodes to cry out in pain, to plead with him to stop.

The two men stood a moment, looking into each other's eyes, McFarland's anger still unsatisfied, Rhodes balanced against the wall, held there by McFarland's hands pressed against his shoulders, his shirt and trousers splattered with blood, grinning grotesquely, benignly, passively, welcomingly at McFarland, who hated him, McFarland, whose knuckles were torn and bloodied, whose chest and stomach were wet with sweat and wet from Rhodes' pounded face.

McFarland stepped back a foot, and with his left hand, he reached out and raised Rhodes' head by the chin and stepping forward, pressed it back against the wall. He slowly raised his clenched fist up and back and waited a moment while he centered Rhodes' head exactly, like an artist arranging a model's pose. Rhodes glanced at him and blinked slowly, and then with a modest gesture, cautionary and futile, caressed McFarland's raised fist and then dropped his hand.

McFarland slammed his fist into Rhodes' face, feeling the nose crack under the blow. Rhodes toppled onto the floor, blood gushing from ear and nose across his cheek and down onto his scarred hand, the hand with which he had caressed McFarland's fist. Unconscious.

"Do you have a light, darling?" Priscilla asked, stumbling from the sofa to her feet. "This is the most mar . . . mar . . . greatest grass. . . ."

McFarland, his anger spent, watched her approach him. His eyes teared, and suddenly he regretted what he had done. There was no help for it.

She stumbled forward, grinning idiotically at him. "Baby got a light for Mama?"

15

HE WRAPPED Jesse in the sheet and carried her through the house past Rhodes' busted body and Priscilla's manic giggling and carried her to the car and laid her, heavy with drugged sleep, on the front seat, and then he slid behind the wheel, lifting her head gently and resting it on his lap, caressing her face with his hand as he drove to Malibu, as his mother had caressed him in the winter the day the room went white;

carried her to the house like a child carried, someone precious and lost and found again, someone necessary to life, loved more than life, she, whom he now held in his arms and could not comprehend how he had survived her absence, gone it alone, how he had done and done it again;

he laid her in his bed and then took lukewarm water and a cloth and wiped her body in the unlighted room, only the hall light, indirect and dim there as he played his hand tenderly over her body, washing all of her as he whispered her name, her presence unreal to him;

he spent the night in an armchair by her bed, the room silent except for her hard breathing;

and then he heard her groan and gasp for breath;

then he saw her half rise, lurch forward and saw her tumble off the bed;

and he rushed to her, pulling her to him, as he saw her face go rigid, distorted, felt her head slam back against his chest;

and then her body went rigid, boardlike, and her eyes rolled back into her head, only the whites visible as she went stiff and wailed loudly, gutturally, painfully like a woman in unassisted childbirth;

and then the first wracking convulsion hit and broke over her and her body bolted madly off him as she shot forward, shaking horribly, the convulsions waving over her while he gripped her, shouting her name, frightened;

her head swung back sharply, her skin turned bluish, her teeth began to grind;

and he forced open her mouth with his hands, frightened for her, frightened, and shoved his rolled belt into her mouth to prevent her teeth from biting through her lips, to keep her tongue from being swallowed;

and then she went unconscious, limp, and masses of sweat broke forth all over her body and froth bubbled from her mouth, the white foam pouring out of her and dripping on to his hands that held her head;

and then she slept deeply, unmoving;

and then she vomited, sobbing;

and then she slept once more as he washed her down again and waited for the doctor;

and he arrived and examined her and he said, she's suffering barbiturate withdrawal, mild case really, not unusual really, in this time in this place;

he gave her an injection, and he said, she is dehydrated, probably hasn't eaten in a few days, that's the pattern of it, they're all the same, so she'll sleep a day yet or more, and then she'll be herself again, but watch her pulse every now and again, if it speeds or grows too weak, faint, if it fades and fades then call, but tell me, why the hell do they do it?

He sat up the night and morning by her and never once did she speak or look at him knowingly or sense where or who she was.

About five o'clock the following afternoon Priscilla arrived by taxi at the beach house. McFarland heard her pounding at the door. He waited a moment, hoping that she would go away. Finally, he opened the door.

"I want my goddamn . . ." she started to yell at the sight of him, and then she stopped and looked him up and down, and an expression of concern and mild amusement came

186

over her. "Well, don't you look like the shit that hit the fan?"

"You look like the fan."

"Shove it!"

"I've been up all night. What do you want?" He was impatient for her to leave. He was not going to get involved in her lamebrain schemes again.

"At the moment, a drink. . . ." She stepped inside the doorway. He put his arm across it to prevent her from entering his house.

"You can't come in. She's asleep. And lower your voice, damn it."

"Where are my keys?" she demanded, gesturing broadly toward her Cadillac parked in his driveway. She was irritated that he would not give her a drink and further irritated that Jesse was with him. She knew very little about Jesse, other than that she had discovered her in East Hampton with Rhodes and her husband, and now she was with McFarland. She thought her a prostitute and a gold digger. The fact that men fell for Jesse, or so she thought, only convinced her of the shallowness and lack of discrimination on the part of most males. Still, she was surprised that McFarland would be infatuated. She had always thought better of him.

"They're in the ignition. . . . Okay?" He smiled at her. "I've got to get some sleep. It's been a tough night. . . ."

"You've had a night!" She snorted sarcastically. "What about me? God, I've been through the lower, least desirable reaches of hell where, I assure you, darling, my husband will end quite alone. He's the one responsible for last night's calamity. None of us would have been there if that bastard. . . ." She trailed off, winded.

McFarland laughed. He felt giddily happy with Jesse back, and the comparison between his luck and Priscilla's luck struck him as extraordinary and made him laugh. He was tired and full of joy.

Priscilla stood on the welcome mat in front of his house, dressed exactly as she had been the night before; only her hair was wildly mussed, her dress wrinkled, stockings torn, and her makeup smeared across her face. She looked like a carnival reveler the morning after.

"What's so funny?" she demanded, stamping her foot. "Me?"

He smiled, his affection for her returning. Silly, pathetic, unlucky, unhappy woman, he thought, caught in steel and still scheming to free herself from the trap that was her life.

"Everything's funny." He laughed again, throwing his head back, taken by the absurdity of their lives.

"Shhhh!" Priscilla put her finger to her lips. It only made him laugh more.

He stepped outside and closed the door behind him, laughing, enjoying it.

Priscilla stared at him, perplexed and offended. "You've no marbles left in your bag, darling. You're as insane as the rest of them."

"Kiss me, beautiful lady!" He embraced her in mock passion, pecking her on her heavily powdered cheeks.

He put his arm around her shoulders. They walked toward her car.

"After you left with what's-her-name—" Priscilla began.

"Jesse?"

"—I had to take charge. It took me some time to recover my faculties sufficiently to get that wrecked punching bag to the hospital. . . ."

"How is he?" McFarland asked, not really caring. He was of two minds about what he had done to Rhodes: he felt the violence had been wrong, his loss of control; still, he felt good about it because in attacking Rhodes, he had finally fought back. Once, just once, he had ended his passivity, his detachment, and lashed out. It had accomplished very little beyond sending Rhodes to hospital, and yet in some curious way the fight had broken his irresolution. Enraged and fighting, he had felt freer, more autonomous, more in command, manlier, more *himself* than ever before.

She stopped walking. She eyed him, her expression ironical and indulgent.

"He's terrible, thank you very much. He wouldn't let me call an ambulance until I flushed tons of pills and powders and blocks of grass and whatnot down the toilet. The fish must have had quite a night! Ha-ha. . . . He lay on the floor, where you dropped him, seeping blood from his mouth and nose, unable to move and mumbling orders to me like I was a stock clerk in Katmandu. Decidedly déclassé. Do you know he had packets of cocaine sealed in the door casings? Ingenious man. . . ."

"So how is he?"

"Broken nose. Five teeth gone, including three caps. A broken jaw. Rather nasty of you, Paul. What does it matter to him? Poor sick man. . . ." She said the last piteously.

McFarland took her hand, and they continued down the driveway in the lessening sunlight to the car. "You're not falling for Rhodes?" he asked facetiously.

"Me?"

"You seem to bleed with pity for him."

"Falling for him? It's a little late for that, darling. He has cancer. . . ."

"No. . . ."

"Didn't you know?"

"How would I've known?" And then he laughed. It was too much. One too many. His old lady. His wife. His son. And now this number. That'd make it an even thirty-two. All out of gas. It was ridiculous. Excessive. Carried away. It was *funny.*

Priscilla ignored his laughter. He's nuts, she thought. "He's had it for about a year, apparently. When I took him to Cedars of Lebanon, I had to sit there signing forms, or rather signing David's name to forms. . . . Rhodes had no insurance. Maybe that's why he pushed drugs. Cancer is wondrously expensive. . . ." She stopped at the car and opened the door. She stood by it a moment. "So at the hospital, sometime this morning, the doctors told me. Who would've guessed?"

He said nothing. He had not known, yet it did not surprise

189

him. Rhodes had always been obsessed with death, and now he had finally coaxed it in and given it a home. He wondered if Jesse knew.

Priscilla entered the car. She closed the door and started the motor.

"Oh, I forgot," she said. McFarland leaned down by the window. "I found some of what's-her-name's stuff—"

"Jesse?"

"—Yes. A pocketbook and a dress, rather soiled, and that was it. I had them mailed to you here. I didn't know what else to do since I wasn't sure you'd see me again. At least not for a while. And since you, well, carried her out last night I assumed you'd know where. . . ."

"Thanks."

"Rhodes can't or won't go back to the house. He's afraid of the cops. I'd have your girlfriend stay away, too." She smiled and reached out the window and touched his face. "Darling, the truth is that I didn't know you *knew* what's-her-name. Or I never would've set you up last night. I only wanted to catch David. Not to hurt you."

"I know."

"How is she?"

"She had convulsions early this morning. I called a doctor. Barbiturate withdrawal. He gave her a shot. . . ."

"Will she be all right?" She seemed genuinely concerned.

"Yes. By tomorrow. She'll probably sleep straight through."

Priscilla nodded. "We do go on, don't we, darling? While the others drop from heat exhaustion. . . ."

"I don't know."

"Sure you do." She smiled. "You're a good man, Paul. Once and always."

"Rise and shine, baby. Come on. Another day, another dollar. The early bird. . . ."

He opened his eyes. Jesse stood by the sofa, smiling down at him. Her hair was damp from a shower, and tiny beads of water glistened on her shoulders and back and on her upper

190

chest above the top of the white beach towel she had wrapped around herself.

"Hi," he said, smiling up at her.

"Do you always sleep in your white shorts?" She sat down next to him on the sofa, absentmindedly rubbing his chest with her cool fingers. She smelled of Bendel's soap, like Adele.

"Why not? It worked once. It might work again. . . ." He put his hand on her shoulder and tried to tug her toward him. "Give me a kiss."

She kissed his nose. Then she stood up and said, "Shower. Shave. Brush your teeth. And make me a *huge* breakfast. I'm *fa*mished."

He did as she asked.

When he was dressed, he found her in the kitchen, sitting at the table, drinking coffee and smoking a cigarette. In front of her was a used bowl. She had eaten cereal.

She was dressed in a pair of his blue jeans, the cuffs rolled up, a red scarf serving as a belt. She wore one of his T-shirts. She had no clothes of her own. All she had worn when she came from New York to Rhodes was a dress and shoes. She had left the rest behind.

"I'm starving. I couldn't wait."

He kissed her. "You still hungry?"

"Yeah." She laughed. "I haven't eaten in days."

"You want some scrambled eggs?"

"Yeah."

"Bacon?"

"Yeah."

"English muffins?"

"Yeah."

"Vanilla yogurt?"

"Yeah."

"Orange juice?"

"Yeah."

"Grits? I have canned grits I can fry."

"Yeah."

"Melon?"

191

"Yeah."

"Me?"

"Later."

They ate. He told her about Rhode's hospitalization, although he did not mention the cancer.

"I want to see him. May I borrow your car?"

Is there no end to it? he thought. Why must she ask?

"I do not want you ever to see him again, Jesse. Promise me that."

She looked down at her hands and then slowly raised her head, brushing her hair back. Her eyes seemed very deeply green and liquid.

"You're jealous. You'll always be. So I'm going to tell you and get it over with. . . ."

"Can't it wait?" His stomach tightened. He was afraid of what she might say. "Please," he said, taking her hand in his.

She sat back in a kind of slouch, withdrawing her hand; he looked at her, hoping she would not tell him what was hurtful and necessary to know: that she loved Rhodes. She rubbed her left cheek, dark circles under her eyes, her face thinner than he remembered. Curiously, she looked younger than before. Perhaps it was the fact that her small body swam in his oversized clothes. Or that her hair was cut shorter. Or that she had been sick and now was better, and whatever it was she was recovering from, not the drugs but the reasons for her taking them, still lay drawn over her face. She looked fatigued and vulnerable.

She lit a cigarette. "This is how it was. The last day I saw you, the night before I was to move in with you, that night I had dinner with Durk at Emilio's in the garden. It was pleasant, although Durk doesn't like you or trust you. He thinks you're a bit of a phony. That was after I told him I was going to live with you. I think he already knew. He wanted me to stay the night, for old times' sake, and he was hurt when I refused. Instead I stayed at Howard Johnson's Motor Lodge on Eighth Avenue. Durk lent me the money. . . ."

"Why didn't you come to me?"

"Why? Because we had made a plan, the two of us, and I

didn't want to fuck it up. I wanted to keep it to the goddamn letter. Because I trusted you. Because it was late and I knew you were working. Because, okay, I wanted to be alone the last time. That's a scream. A lot of reasons. . . ." She spoke quietly, not looking at him, her voice cold.

"What are the other reasons?" He had to know.

"You bastard. . . ." She looked up at him, slowly raising her head. She dragged on her cigarette. "I stayed in a hotel because I didn't want you throwing it in my face. . . ."

"What?"

"The fact that I spent the last night at Durk's. If I had, no matter what I said, you'd always believe I'd been disloyal after loving you. So I got a room and a receipt for that room, and the next day when I went to Durk's to get my stuff and to meet you, you never arrived."

"But I told Durk. . . ."

"Your phone never answered. I tried for two days. And then I knew it was a brushoff. And I didn't care."

"But I saw Durk that night! I *told* him. . . ." He leaned across the table, hitting it with his fist, feeling panic, sensing she might still leave him, that she did not love him anymore.

"I never saw Durk. What did you tell him?"

"That my . . . that Adele, *Christ!* That she and Jaime had been . . . they had been killed and I had to leave."

She stared at him for a long time. And then tears came to her eyes, and she stood abruptly and went to him and kissed the top of his head. "I'm sorry," and she went into the bedroom and cried. Until that moment she had not known. Until that moment she had hated him.

Later that afternoon, as they left the house to get in his car, McFarland picked up the package Priscilla had mailed.

"What is it?"

"It's some of your stuff Priscilla found."

He handed the package to Jesse. In it was a torn jumper and Jesse's pocketbook. She threw the dress in the garbage and tossed the pocketbook in the back seat.

They drove to Beverly Hills and parked the car in the garage at the Beverly Wilshire Hotel. Then the two of them walked hand in hand to Saks, swinging their arms as they went. Happy.

Into Saks. McFarland was dressed in a cotton sports jacket and cotton slacks and loafers, Jesse small beside him in the borrowed baggy jeans and T-shirt and bare feet.

"I'm terribly sorry." The saleswoman approached them. "You *must* wear shoes in Saks Fifth Avenue."

"That's what we're here to buy."

Saks Fifth. Gucci. I. Magnim. Yves Saint Laurent. Bonwit Teller. Lord and Taylor. At Saks he bought her a cotton day-dress, black in a subdued rose pattern by Giorgio di Sant Angelo. McFarland, breaking another store rule, went into the dressing room with Jesse.

"Watch," she said, giggling, a little embarrassed to find him sitting on the bench under the dress hooks, grinning up at her. It reminded her of school, ninth grade, in the cloakrooms at Cooper High School in Minneapolis, in the winter in the afternoon after classes, after most of the students had scattered, the boys to metal shop or wood shop or to gym, and the girls to home economics or personal hygiene or to the Lutheran released time classes. She stayed behind in the cloakroom waiting for her brother Daniel's friend, Jack, one of the few she loved and could not forget so long ago, big, tough, monosyllabic, boastful, crude, handsome Jack, whose father was a cop and he the hockey captain, he who had seen it all, so he claimed, and talked about it, bragged on it, the prostitutes and gangsters and brawling drunks and marauding Indians, those blanketasses crowded steeped in their own deserved, miserable, they-asked-for-it poverty in the Northside slums. . . . She waited for Jack, who told her months before of a gang rape that he boasted, at seventeen, he had been a party to—one drunken, ginchy broad and nine high school toughs over the state line in Hudson, Wisconsin, on the Minnesota River by the miller's dock; high on styte when they cornered her, and the bitch didn't even put up a fight, she shoved her hands a little and fell down, the dumb old bitch, and we had her there, gave her slivers in the ass from those old dock boards, and I tell you, Jess, she loved it, she couldn't get enough . . . cunts are all the same . . . without love it's rape, Jack, it's dirty, it's wrong. . . . But she loved him and so she waited for Jack to come. How is love possible in such a world? She waited for Jack to come with his large hands, each one of which could crush a beer can between its fingers, yes, she had seen it done; waited for him in the musty cloakroom, the still snow-damp woolens jammed together on too few hooks, the room dark, overshoes and rubbers standing in spreading puddles of now-warming slush. It was exciting waiting in the humid darkness for him, for the quickly opened door, the light flashing in and then shut out again, the blackness complete and safe again. In the dark she heard Jack come toward her, swear as he kicked some overshoes out of the way, closer, her heart throbbing, her nipples erect, getting wet, wet, warm as the steaming coats, as itchy . . . the odor of it, and his mouth suddenly on her lips, the taste of Sen-Sen, her collapsing against him in the dark, her heart beating so hard he felt it against his chest . . . his hands running down her stomach to her skirt, lifting up her skirt, his strong, thick fingers thrust under the leg band of her panties and in one rough jerk tearing them down her thighs, goose pimples all over, shuddering, his tongue deep in her mouth, pushing her against the hanging thick, damp woolly coats . . . say you love me, say it please, Jack, so it's all right, so we can do it, so it isn't wrong to do it, say you love me forever, will marry me, want me, never leave me, say it . . . as her hands rushed over his back and down the small of it to his butt, pulling him to her, and then over his strong muscular haunches that made her think of horses thundering along the flatlands, thunder over me, crush me, love, love me . . . one of his hands free now, the other bracing her head, one hand free and in her clumsily, hurtfully; she makes a small cry, don't, please, and then his hand, those thick fingers, were off her and onto himself. She could hear the zipper slip, hear it scratching down. His hand

195

reached in and yanked his cock out and against her and she could smell his sweat, the funk, the bitter unwashed stink, it made her dizzy . . . no, no, not here, do you love me? then it's okay . . . and later, what? Later, what? If not her brother, Daniel, whom she loved, the only one always kind to her, if not her brother and his friends coming at her late as she waited for Jack, late, and nearly, *almost* raping her. Worse, at sixteen, to have your blouse torn and your breasts exposed and the grinning pimply boys, except for Jack and Daniel, grinning at you, laughing because you were too small there as they pinched and pulled and hurt your too small breasts . . . until your brother, seeing what he had done, said urgently, "It's the Teach!" And down she sagged alone, despairing, hot, wrapping her arms around herself, hot, yet shivering among the woolens and the wet shoes. And Jack? He no longer wanted any part of damaged goods.

"Watch," she said. "When I worked the fashion shows, I could change in under a minute. Time me."

She laughed, and McFarland raised his wrist, staring at his watch, and then, when the second hand hit twelve, said, "Go!" But the second she began to unzip her borrowed blue jeans his eyes went from his wristwatch to her body. She noticed immediately and turned the undressing into an exaggerated strip, enjoying the tease because she felt safe with him, and that feeling of safety was why being with him was unsensual, nonerotic. It was children at play. She pulled the blue jeans slowly off, puckering her lips and fluttering her eyelashes, giving him a come-hither look. She drew the trousers down, and stood a moment standing on them, one hand resting on her crotch. She slowly pulled her hand away, tugging at her pubic hair as she drew her hand up toward her stomach, smiling as she touched her body in her parody of a striptease. Next she pulled off her T-shirt, slowly, very slowly stretching her arms high in the air as she took it off. She flung it at his face and stood naked before him, laughing unself-consciously.

She put on her new dress.

196

"What do you think of it?" she asked, falling into her model's pose, turning gracefully around the small dressing room.

"It's crackjack."

"Let's buy it."

They did. They also bought a beige jersey Bonnie Cashin outfit of silk jersey slacks and sweater. A white wool Halston cardigan sweater. A Rudi Gernreich dress with pale Art Nouveau stripping. Panty hose. An Indian silk coat and matching Indian cotton batik dress. Four pairs of Delman shoes. A white satin blouse and a black skirt by Anne Klein. A knobby bouclé wheat-colored Chanel suit. Three pairs of Jax blue jeans and T-shirts and Jax turtleneck pullovers. Black patent leather high heel sandals from I. Miller. A Hermès clutch bag and a Gucci shoulder bag. Three Yves Saint Laurent scarves and two blouses. Two J. Kenneth Lane bracelets, two necklaces and two sets of earrings. Two Dior belts. Two thin wool Korrigan sweaters, again from Jax.

From there they trooped to Schwab's Drugstore, where Jesse had McFarland buy for her a Max Factor Hi-Fi base powder; a Revlon blush and lipsticks in pale pinks; a powder puff; eyebrow pencils; Mary Quant mascara; Eyelure eyelashes; tweezers; Pond's cream; a toothbrush; two tortoiseshell combs; a hairbrush; Luriderm lotion; disposable douches; a Conair Pro Style hair dryer; a Clairol Kindness Deluxe 3-Way Hair Setter; Leslie Blanchard Maintain shampoo; Ultima Perfumed Body Velvet; Love's Fresh Cleaning Lotion; Lip Service lip gloss; Miners Butterfleyes eye shadow; Tampax; Borghese Moisturizing Facial Soufflé, cucumber base; Vaseline Intensive Care Lotion; Mary Quant Facial Crayons.

McFarland bought himself a new razor and a bottle of English Leather cologne. He didn't need them. He just got carried away.

Finally, at Bonwit Teller, Jesse bought perfume.

"It's called Rivière. Do you know what it means?" she asked, dabbing some on her finger and rubbing it on the back of his hand. "Smell it? Do you remember?"

Lilac.

"It means river? As in Mississippi?"

"Pretty good guess. It means stream. It means a stream of diamonds. Or a necklace of diamonds, or stars. Lovely word. . . . It reminds me of fireflies, of the river and the fireflies. . . ."

From one store to the next Jesse dressed, until by seven o'clock she was wearing her Bonnie Cashin slacks and sweater, an Yves Saint Laurent scarf, her panty hose and Delman Spanish leather pumps, with her J. Kenneth Lane bracelet and gold necklace.

They walked back to the Wilshire Hotel, their fifth trip, and locked more packages in the car. Then Jesse took her pocketbook and dumped its contents into her Hermès bag and threw in lipstick, a comb, eyebrow pencil, eyelashes set and powder and blush.

He waited in the hotel's lobby for her while she made up in the toilet. When he saw her coming across the lobby toward him, walking lightly, briskly, her head held high, smiling at him, her eyes bright and full of play, her clothes elegant and beautifully tailored, looking more beautiful than he had ever seen her look before, more elegant, healthier, his response was openmouthed. He was dazzled. Lost.

They walked into the bar in the Beverly Wilshire, an oak-paneled room of black leather banquettes and red walls, highlighted by a large, crudely painted portrait of the hotel's owner, dressed in Spanish costume, which dominated one wall. The bar was a gathering place for Beverly Hills celebrities. It had the one prerequisite needed by them all: table phones connecting them to their careers.

As they entered, they stopped at a table where the actress Rothenberg wanted for the Nazi script sat with Frank Sinatra and several other men. McFarland introduced Jesse. Jesse was not impressed.

They took a table in the far corner, opposite the bar. They ordered drinks.

"You look so beautiful, Jesse. I'm still not used to seeing you. I'm so goddamn proud you're mine."

"Yours?" She smiled. "Because you brought me some dresses?"

"I didn't mean it that way." He hadn't.

"When I make money again, I'll repay you."

"What do you think this is? A business proposition? I *enjoy* giving you things. It gives me pleasure." That was all he had meant. However, she had sensed what he knew but would not admit, that in buying her things, in taking care of her, in loving her unequally, he sought to bind her increasingly to him. And she did not want to be bound. She wanted to be free. And the more he did for her, the more he heightened her awareness of her dependency. She wanted to be self-supporting. She wanted to pay her own way in order for *both* of them to know that she was with him because she desired to be, not because she had no other choice.

"I tried to tell you about myself today. . . ."

"At breakfast?"

"Yes. You don't know much about me."

"I know I love you. That's enough."

She laughed. "You think that's enough? You're very naïve."

"Well, I know you're from Minneapolis and your father is a lineman and you were a model. . . ."

"I *am* a model. I want to work again. I want—"

"Okay." He raised his hand to silence her. "I want you to do what makes you happy."

"No, it's what I *must* do."

"Okay."

"Listen to me, Paul. I love you. And you believe you love me, and you don't *know* me."

"I don't need to know anything more." He said it firmly. He did not want her telling him things that would activate his jealousy.

"We're going to be living together a long time, right?"

He grinned. "Hell, yes!"

And thus she began to tell him about what had taken her from Minneapolis to him.

"When I first came to New York, it was in the winter, I couldn't get work as a model, and that was what I wanted to be. I didn't know anybody. I had no money. I didn't know how to go about doing it. I had a room at the Barbizon Hotel. I took a job at Bloomingdale's, in the coffee shop, to pay the rent. Each morning a man named Hilary usually came in for coffee and a cheese danish. We'd make small talk. I told him I wanted to model. He thought I wasn't tall enough. But he liked me and called a friend of his, a photographer, who took pictures of me and made up a minimum portfolio for me. I was very ignorant. I thought the photographer loved me. He kept saying he did, God knows. I lived with him a couple months, until he got bored. . . . I did some work for Hilary's agency, and one thing led to another, and in a few years I started making a lot of money, well, it was a lot to me. But, you see, the photographer I lived with, that bastard had a big mouth and a bigger imagination, like Tom Stein and David Rothenberg, and after a while, a year or so, every time I showed up for a casting call some asshole would make a clumsy pass at me. Why not? There were thousands of models and very little work. So when I had to, I put out. Sooner or later they would say they loved me, when they didn't. I didn't love them either. I felt cheap because I knew they were throwing me work because of sex. I don't know. Maybe not. I never understood why sex was such an issue with men. I never understood its importance. It didn't matter to me. If they wanted it, why not? And then I met Mike Rhodes—"

"When was that, Jesse?"

"About three years ago. He was living high on the money from his only book. He was exciting, Paul. He knew everybody, and I was very impressed by famous names then. He was invited everywhere. He enjoyed having beautiful wom-

200

en with him. He liked being seen with them. He was greatly charming. I was in love with him—"

"Don't go on. I don't want to know about it." He reached across the table and touched her hand.

"I want you to know. Listen, at that time, I would have died just to be near him. I was crazy for him. He was terrific sex because he had no feeling for me. Do you understand? Nothing was at stake. It wasn't me he fucked; he just fucked. It meant *nothing* to him. I could never possess Mike. I could never get a commitment from him. Nobody owned his heart, except his sister, except her, and that was a long time ago. He loved nobody, not me or anyone. And that was hard on me, because I desperately wanted him to love me. And the more he said he didn't love me, Paul, the more he said the question bored him, the more he laughed when I asked him to say it, the more wildly I loved him. It's insane, isn't it? I suppose if he'd fallen in love with me in the beginning, I never would have looked at him twice. But he never did. He was honest. He never lied. He never said what he didn't mean. He never badgered me or cared what I did or with whom. You see, baby, all anybody ever wanted from me was sex. I felt like meat. And Mike never pressed me to have it with him. I had to initiate it. He always acted bored when we started, like it was a great effort he was making, but once into it. . . . He knew sex embarrassed me. That I didn't like being pawed. He let me be the aggressor. Sure, and I was relaxed in sex with him because I knew it meant nothing to him, so whether I was good or bad didn't matter two pins. And also, every time we had sex we were stoned. . . ."

"Bastard." McFarland twisted the napkin between his hands, trying to keep his expression noncommittal but interested. And interested he was. But he knew, the more she spoke, the longer it would be until he had absorbed and come to terms with what she was telling him, the longer it would be until he would no longer helplessly do what he was doing now—picturing masochistically in his mind her having sex

201

with Rhodes. "He was the son of a bitch that got you on drugs. I'd like to kill the bastard."

"You tried once. Why be redundant?" She smiled. "Let me go on. The drugs became more important in his life, correct. Because he could not work. He could not write. And what he wrote wasn't any good, and he knew it. And we traveled to the Coast and back, to the Midwest and through the South and to the islands, trying to find the *place* where he would find the words. More and more he used drugs, and he got stranger, and then I realized what everyone else knew except me, that Mike wanted to die. He collapsed several times in restaurants. Once in the men's room of a movie theater. From drugs. He was so self-destructive and so wonderful. He made me laugh. We laughed all the time. Over nothing really. He just enjoyed laughing. One night in Chicago he told me not to worry about his dying of an overdose. He wouldn't die accidentally. He wanted someone, a person, to kill him. He said that was an act of love. To kill someone. . . . Every time he was in a situation of peril, he said, where he thought he might be killed, he fell in love with the person threatening him. . . ."

"Shit." McFarland thought it disgusting. "It's a lot of doper bullshit he was shoveling. Bathetic, self-indulgent, self-dramatic. . . ." He called the waiter. "You want to order dinner or you want another round?" He ordered them another round.

"A year or so ago he was told he had cancer. . . ."

"I know."

"He had radiation treatments, and they arrested it for a time. He ran out of money paying for them, and that's when he began to push drugs, grass, cocaine, uppers and downs. Then he had chemotherapy and went gray. He ran out of money again. The son of a bitch doctors were bleeding him when they knew he had nothing. And when he couldn't pay, the treatments stopped. Then I started supporting him. But I didn't have enough. . . .

202

"Last year we were certain he was going to die. He loved the islands. We took the money we had and went on a cruise through the Caribbean, and he was in great pain. The Phenaphen didn't stop it. We left the ship at St. Thomas and stayed there for a week. He screamed one night in the room from the pain. And then he drank and drank to kill it. A doctor on the island, some bastard alky, gave him Demerol, but it wasn't strong enough. From the time we arrived in the islands Mike was in a constant stupor, half conscious, sometimes delirious with pain. . . .

"And then he found his pusher and got heroin, and it did not hurt him anymore. . . .

"I was terrified of heroin. The syringe, the spoon, the rubber tube—all of it frightened me. He had promised me one night, when we first arrived, that if the pain got too great, he would fly to Miami and be hospitalized. . . ."

"How did you plan to pay for it?"

"I had good credit. We were going to get married, that way I'd be liable for the bills." She laughed. "Weren't we innocent, though? But, as I told you, he found his pusher, his connection, the candy man. I knew he would die if he stayed on St. Thomas, and I knew he would stay as long as he had access to heroin. . . .

"One night we went to a bar, called Katie's. And I told him I had made reservations on a plane to Miami the next morning and that we were leaving. He said you can't take heroin on a plane. And I told him I had thrown his junk into the harbor, and if he tried to buy more, I would call in the police. I was terrified he would die. I loved him too much to let him die. . . ."

"Did you go to Miami?"

"Ha-ha. Dream on, dreamboy. Hell, no. He slugged me in the bar. He stood and hit me very hard and screamed at me that I was killing him. I wanted him to suffer, he said. I had broken the rules of our game, and he wanted me out of his life. He would never see me again, he said, and he knocked

203

me to the floor and left. He didn't go back to the hotel. I never saw him again on the island. Each night I went to Katie's bar, thinking he would come back. I played the song he loved. . . ."

" 'This Time the Dream's on Me'?"

She looked down at her hands. "Yes."

"And he never came back?"

"He never came back. I had done wrong, and I knew it. He had raged at me and struck me because he knew in hours the pain would return to him, and he'd have to spend the night in the bars on the docks and in niggertown looking for his candy man."

"Why wouldn't he go to the hospital? I don't understand that." McFarland had always thought Rhodes crazy. Nothing Jesse told him had altered his opinion.

"Because he didn't want to die in a public room in an institution, not in a terminal ward, and he knew once the bastards got him inside, they wouldn't let him go until they saw him die on their terms."

"When did you see him again?"

"I didn't see him again until I came here, until the week you never showed up to take me to live with you. I pawned your bracelet, the gold link chain bracelet you gave me. I'm sorry, but I pawned it to buy a plane ticket to come here. I had nowhere else to go. I located Mike in Venice and flew to him. I was so lonely, Paul, so unhappy after you left. I had nothing to live for anymore."

"You must promise me not to see Rhodes again."

"Mike's on heroin, and he's really only months from the end." She said it quietly, sadly. She still loved Rhodes.

"Then why did you come back to him?"

"Where was I to go? I couldn't get work in New York because Mike or I had insulted everybody in the industry. And even if I could, I didn't want to put out anymore. I was down and nearly out, baby. And just when I thought you loved me, you walked away without kissing me good-bye."

"You know why."

"Yes. And even knowing it, baby, I'll never again be certain you won't walk away once more."

They ordered dinner. And during it he asked her what had happened to Rhodes when he was seventeen. "I've heard stories about it, and he referred to it the other night."

"His sister committed suicide. They were twins. He was in love with her. I think she was the only woman he was ever in love with. I know he never loved me."

That night they walked hand in hand along the beach in front of McFarland's house. It was a cool November night. There was a full moon. McFarland was happy and content. He felt complete. He loved this woman, and he believed that she loved him.

"My son used to play here. He'd dig holes in the sand, and I'd help him fill them with water. And then he'd sit splashing in them—"

"A goldfish."

"Yes. You remember." He kissed her. "Never leave me."

When they returned to the house, she unpacked her clothes and tried on various items for him, parading around the bedroom as he sat naked on the bed, admiring her. She was trying to postpone going to bed as long as possible because she had no physical feeling for him. She loved him, and she needed him, but sexually he did not arouse her. It was baffling to her, and it made her feel guilty, as if there were something wrong with her that she did not physically want the man she loved. She was cold sober, and there wasn't time enough to get smashed, and there were no drugs, and when they hit the sack, she'd have to fake it cold. How could she tell him that he did not excite her sexually, how could she when she knew the telling would wreck him, cut him irreparably? She comforted herself by thinking that in time it would change. In time.

"This is what I'll wear tomorrow."

"To what?"

"When I go looking for a job."

Later he said, as they sat together on the terrace having a nightcap, "May I ask you something?"

"Shoot."

"I'm only asking because I'll have to deliver the script to David soon, and I want to know. Did you ever sleep with him?"

She said nothing.

"Hell, I'm sorry. You don't have to answer." He regretted the question.

"I'll answer. I was trying to remember. I don't think I ever did."

Later she was unaroused. They used a lubricant. She had no orgasm.

She landed a job as an assistant buyer at Bullocks in Westwood. She was delighted, since she enjoyed the work, and it promised travel to New York and even Paris to scout the collections next season. She opened a checking account with her first salary, and she announced to McFarland that from that point on she was paying for their groceries.

He bought her a car. It was her birthday.

He finished the script and sent it to San Francisco, where Rothenberg was having meetings. He and Priscilla had officially separated, and Rothenberg had taken an apartment at the Beverly Hills Hotel. The script was accepted, and McFarland flew to San Francisco, where he stayed at the Mark Hopkins Hotel, where Rothenberg was also in residence. He spent three days in script conferences and casting conferences with Rothenberg and the two associate producers. While there, he signed to write another picture for Paramount, this one based on the double suicide in New Orleans. It would pay him one hundred thousand dollars.

While he was in San Francisco, Jesse stayed alone in Los Angeles.

When he returned home, he sensed something was wrong.

Jesse greeted him happily. She had restyled her hair. He was delighted to be home. They had a late dinner, and they both got very drunk, and they had sex, and it was good. Good, because she was too stoned to know what was happening.

The following morning when he went into the bathroom to shave he noticed that the new unused razor lay in the cabinet. It had been used in his absence. And the English Leather cologne had been opened. He said nothing to Jesse.

The following day, looking for his shoes under the bed, he found a bottle of Seconal. He asked Jesse about it.

"I couldn't sleep with you gone. I went to a doctor, and he gave me some pills."

"Then why is there no pharmacy label on the bottle?"

She tensed and took the bottle from him. She walked into the bathroom and poured it down the toilet. "Satisfied?" she asked, and then walked angrily out of the house.

She came back in time for dinner. She showed him the hotel receipt from Howard Johnson's in New York that had been in the pocketbook Priscilla had sent. "See, I wasn't lying. And this. . . ." She handed him a worn slip of paper. It was the note he had left on her bed at Durk's the morning after they first slept together. She had carried it with her ever since.

A week later, when she came home from work, she was wearing his gold link bracelet. She had sent the pawn ticket to New York with a check, and the bracelet had been returned.

After dinner that night, they drank. Later he asked her to marry him.

"I'll think it over," she said. "You're the tenth this week." She laughed. But she was worried. She had missed her period that month, and she did not know whether or not to tell him. She decided to wait.

McFarland was very high, as was she. And sometime that

207

night she ran into the bathroom and soaked a towel with cold water and came up behind him, as he sat in the kitchen having a beer, and threw the towel in his face, laughing as she did. He followed suit. And for several hours they ran around the house, naked as savages, throwing wet towels at each other, laughing, the mock fight finally degenerating into a pillow war in the bedroom, a snowstorm of pillow down whirling about the room as they ripped the pillows and dumped the white stuffing over each other, hurling handfuls of it at each other. And on the bed covered with piles of feathers, they lay sweating, the feathers sticking to them, coating them until they resembled snowpeople embracing on a white, white field. They made love.

In the first week in December he left alone for New Orleans to research on the picture. He would be gone for ten days. Jesse stayed behind since she could not get a leave from work.

Jesse drove him to the airport in her new car. They had a drink in the airport bar as they waited for his flight to be called.

"Tell me something." He pointed to the small round scar on her right wrist. "How did you get that?"

"I was about to say I had a mole removed, but that would be a lie. And I've never lied to you. If I tell you, it'll upset you. . . ."

"Tell me anyway."

"Mike Rhòdes . . ." she began.

"Shit!"

"You asked. Mike and I were stoned on board ship one night. I thought he was dying. He kept saying over and over, 'Remember me.' I said, 'I love you, Mike,' over and over. And suddenly he sat up abruptly, we were lying on the bed. I was smoking a cigarette. He took it from my fingers and held the burning end of it about an inch above my wrist. 'How much do you love me?' he asked. 'This much?' . . . and he moved

208

it closer to my skin . . . .'This much?' . . . closer still. I was stoned, and I didn't really feel it, not very much. He finally broke off the end of it, the burning part, and let it burn out on my wrist. We just stared at it, like two loonies. 'Now you'll remember me,' he said, 'every goddamn time you look at your wrist.' "

"I hope he dies slow. I hope it's a horrible dying."

"Life means little to him, Paul. Death even less."

16

IT WAS unusually warm in New Orleans. The temperature was in the low seventies, and the sun was intense. The newspapers were full of theories explaining the curious heat wave. It had not been as warm in New Orleans in December in fifty-odd years.

The second day in the city McFarland called Jesse from his hotel. He described the heat, and he said he missed her. Then he went to the jeweler's and ordered a necklace made for her with a pendant designed like a rainbow with precious stones inlaid to simulate the bands of color. It would be ready in a week.

He strolled about the French Quarter, telling himself that he was actually working, scouting locations as it were, for the movie he was about to begin writing. He went into Jackson Square, a small fenced park opposite the St. Louis Cathedral near the banks of the Mississippi. It was a warm day, an uncomfortable one because of the stifling humidity.

He took off his shirt and sprawled on the grass beneath a tulip tree. Across the park that day, as most days, by the fountain a number of teenage runaways, hippies, lay in the sunshine on the grass or sat on the sidewalks, some of them smoking joints and drinking pop wines, many of them obviously high on speed or downs. One of the girls was about seventeen years old. She was dressed in torn Levi's and wore a tight white T-shirt. She had small breasts. She lounged on the sidewalk by the fountain, manically tapping a steel spoon against her jaw as if she were keeping time to music. But there was no music.

She stared across the way to the cathedral, rocking her body, her mind traveling blown past what contentment or grief? Wrapped around her ankle was the end of a long clothesline, and tied to the other end of it was a small boy, with Negroid features and curly yellow hair, who crawled happily near the base of the fountain, splashing his hands in the water spilled on the sidewalk, ignoring dogs and litter and other children who competed for the puddle.

McFarland lay on the grass with his elbow up and watched him, and it is obvious: he thought of Jaime on the beach below the house at Malibu; of Adele running on the sand, carrying him in her arms; of his digging with his son in the sand or building delicate sand structures and surrounding them by moats through which he marched like Alexander across the Euphrates to level Susa, his laughter high and curiously strained as if a hand were pressed against his tiny windpipe, more a screech than a child's laugh, resembling the shrill calls of terrified crows above a field, only much higher in pitch. It was always when Jaime laughed that his desire to protect him was most urgent, for even his laughter sounded of peril. It was too late now.

He walked across the square and stood at a distance and watched the boy play in the water. Near him was an empty pint bottle of wine. He crawled to it and grabbed it and started to put it in his mouth. McFarland looked at the woman at the other end of the rope. She was indifferent to the child. He went over and squatted by him.

"Give it to me, son. It's filthy."

He tentatively lowered the bottle. He looked at McFarland with an expression of wary bewilderment. The skin around the boy's mouth was marked by a rash, and on his tiny chest, below his collarbone, was a dark yellow bruise. He had a small gold earring in his left ear. His ear was pierced.

"It's dirty, son. *Ugh.* . . ." He took the bottle from him.

The boy stared at him, his eyes very wide, startled at losing his toy. He looked down at his tiny hand, double-checking the theft, and then up at McFarland again.

He smiled and touched the child's cheek. The boy began to cry, his cry quickly turning into a loud wail.

"It's okay. . . ." He mussed his curly hair, adopting the

212

gestures he remembered having taken with Jaime, trying to comfort the boy, and the more he caressed him, the more he screamed. He wanted to lift him up and hold him, but he was afraid to, and so, finally, the boy began to crawl sobbingly away uncomforted along the limp clothesline to the young woman sitting nodding in the sun.

"What the hell are you doing?"

"What?" McFarland was still squatting. He glanced up and the sun hit his eyes and he squinted, trying to see who was speaking. The man angrily repeated himself. "What the hell do you think you're doing?"

He stood. The man was a tall, heavily built black man, about twenty-five years old, apparently the child's father.

"Pardon?" McFarland smiled. It was difficult to see the man's face because his back was to the sun. "Listen," he explained, "he was putting that wine bottle in his mouth. It was very dirty, you know, and I—" He was embarrassed, and he did not know the reason. He had an impulse to bend down and retrieve the bottle and show it as evidence of his good faith. He felt dizzy and glanced down. The man's hand was shoved in his trouser pocket. He thought, he's packing a knife; if I argue, he'll kill me. And then he saw his penis outlined against his trouser leg. The boy's father. His *father*. He had an urge to touch it.

"Leave my kid alone."

"I'm sorry. Really . . . *awfully* sorry." McFarland smiled, blinking in the sun, nodding absurdly at him like a theater goer who had stepped on someone's toes in reaching his seat.

"Too many white faggots in this honky town." The black bit his lower lip and glared at McFarland. He outweighed McFarland. But it was not his size that was intimidating; it was his fatherhood, it was the recollections and the similarities between the boy and his lost boy that paralyzed and confused him suddenly.

"You're absolutely correct," he said, feeling on the man's side. "The situation's becoming impossible." He spoke too agreeably, too politely, going on in a kind of cocktail chatter tone as if he were at a party at Century City, babbling inanely about runaway productions. "Something has to be done." It was the wrong tone to take.

As McFarland turned to go, the black grabbed him by the shoulder and swung him around and shoved him toward the cathedral exit from the square.

"Get the hell out!"

It humiliated him. For a moment he almost struck the man. Then he saw the boy, and the man's blackness, and his guilt over the loss of his son, and his guilt over being white, his guilt stopped him.

He left. It was the boy's father, after all. And his child was still alive, after all. McFarland wondered if the man had sensed it about him, if he knew simply by looking at him that his son had perished, if knowing that the black had acted instinctively to protect his son. He wondered if he knew.

He was drawn to Jackson Square because there were many small children there. In the afternoons nuns brought groups of children from the cathedral school into the park. The little boys wore short pants and blue blazers with the school emblem on a patch on the jacket pocket. The girls wore skirts and white blouses with blue vests, also sporting the school patch.

McFarland started writing children's stories. He found it difficult to concentrate on the script. He did not know why.

He liked to sit by the bandstand near St. Anne Street. The trees were very old and the shade deep, and on the other side of the iron fence artists laid badly painted pictures against the railings which they sold to tourists. The tourists put the paintings under their arms and climbed aboard horse-drawn hansom carriages and rode off, looking very pleased with themselves.

214

At the end of the school's fall semester, just before the beginning of the holiday vacation, various high school bands performed free concerts in the park.

The third day in New Orleans McFarland spent the morning at the clippings morgue at the *Times-Picayune*, reading through piles of material on the double suicide. He got the names of several people who knew the families. He intended to interview them.

That afternoon he sat on a bench in front of the bandstand, listening to the music. A few minutes after the concert started, a boy, about fifteen years old, came into the park leading a large sheep dog on the end of a heavy chain, a shag dog whose front and rear looked very much alike. The boy sat down next to him on the bench and throughout the concert fought heroically to keep his dog seated at his feet, the animal clearly suffering from the heat, restless, frightened by the band; every so often the dog would lurch mightily, and the boy would be yanked off the bench to grapple with dog and chain, like a trainer with a grouchy dancing bear. When he would finally succeed in momentarily subduing the animal, when he had resumed his place, the boy would nudge McFarland with his elbow, smile proudly, manfully, and say, "I'm just watching him for a friend."

"What's your name?" McFarland asked. He liked the boy. He liked his cockiness, his forward manner. The boy looked physically delicate, but he was outgoing and unafraid.

The boy stood and turned and bent over slightly, showing his backside to McFarland. On his blue jeans, on each cheek of his butt, were patches. One said CLOSED FOR REPAIRS, the other, SLIPPERY WHEN WET. And written in silver sequins on one bun was BARTHO, and on the other LOMEW. Bartholomew.

He sat down again. "I did it myself."

"Did what?"

"I sewed that. I don't have easy fingers for nothing." He grinned.

"Are you hot?" he asked. He touched McFarland's hand, a

gesture he found embarrassing. He moved slightly away from the boy. It was a small bench.

"Are you?" he inquired again.

"Yes. Why?"

He shrugged, smiling sweetly as he did. He pulled off his sweat shirt and threw it under the bench. He stretched, yawning.

"It's cooler now, right?" he said, and then he leaned over and in a loud whisper confided, "I tan easy," and as he spoke, he rubbed his bare chest delicately, as one would feel the surface of a painting. McFarland's stomach tightened. He had a sense of *déjà vu*, and a sense of boreboding. He could not account for it.

He turned back to the band, who played nothing other than marches, each sounding like "Stars and Stripes Forever."

The band struck up another march, "Washington Post," and in the middle of it the boy was yanked off the bench by his dog and fell to his knees and with a barage of Southern-accented obscenities fought to bring the dog under control. It was a funny scene, the boy grabbing the dog, his arm around the animal's massive head, and half pulling, half being pulled, the two of them floundered their way out of the square, as they moved the boy turning twice to look at McFarland, who was laughing with delight, the boy's face a combination of happiness and consternation. McFarland suddenly realized that he had been staring at the boy, especially at the movement of the muscles in his back as he struggled in the sunlight with the dog, the sun setting low and falling at a critical angle, emphasizing the play of flesh.

On the way out of the park he passed the bench where he had been sitting. He saw the boy's sweat shirt lying on the grass. He picked it up and draped it over his shoulders. Tying its white arms in front of him, he went out of the square and got a drink.

17

THAT night he tried calling Jesse. It was late. There was no answer in Malibu. He assumed she was asleep.

He called her the next day at work.

"Make it quick, baby. I have to be on the floor. It's busy as hell here, and half the girls are out."

"What would you say to moving here for a few months? I'm going to take an apartment. There are a number of people I have to interview, and I'd like to get the hell out of LA. New Orleans is lovely, Jesse. You'll be happy here. . . ."

"But my job—"

"You can get one here. . . ."

"Let me think about it. I have to run, really." She was anxious to get off the phone.

"Okay. But I'll take the place anyway. I hate the hotel. I can always *commute.*" He laughed.

"I have to run. Bye, baby. . . ."

"Jesse?"

"Yes?"

"I love you," he said softly. He missed her very much.

"I love you, too."

He spent the day walking around the Quarter, looking at furnished apartments. He wanted one that Jesse would like. He missed her, wanted her with him, and so he thought to find a place congenial to her, and then, once it was accomplished, to talk her into coming to New Orleans. When she did, he decided, he would rent out or maybe sell the house at Malibu. It was Adele's house, after all. He wanted territory now that belonged only to Jesse and him.

He found a sublet on Dumaine in a cooperative building.

217

Two bedrooms, a large living room, a study, and a gallery, a kitchen and two baths. It was in the top floor of a slave quarters behind a converted town house. The apartment opened onto a gallery that overlooked a large red-brick courtyard and a swimming pool and a lot of plantings. In the corner of the yard was a sandbox in which sat several children and a dog, all of them digging furiously in the pile, and several feet away a set of children's swings. Near the pool a children's slide that overlapped the water. It was all very handsome and very Southern. It would be a nice place to raise kids, he thought. In signing the sublet, he paid out an extra thousand and purchased an option to buy.

That afternoon he signed the lease and then moved his things from the hotel to the new apartment. He called Jesse at work and told her about the apartment and gave her his new phone number. He then called Rothenberg's office and gave it to them.

He spent the next day in Algiers, on the other side of the Mississippi, interviewing a close friend of the dead girl. She said she was the only one who had known it was coming. She took a perverse pride in that fact. She had masses of letters from the girl. McFarland bought them from her for a hundred dollars. He would use some of the material in the new script.

He slept that night in his new apartment, the french doors open, the breeze cooling and sweet. He was happy with the place, and he fantasized what it would be like living her with Jesse. And so he called her. It was late. She sounded very tired.

"I had a hard day. On my feet all day. We're having a pre-Christmas sale and the store is jammed. . . ." She was slurring her words.

"Have you been drinking?"

"What?" She seemed distracted. He could hear a kind of ruffling noise as if she were holding her hand over the receiver. He sensed someone was with her.

"Are you—" He was about to ask if she was alone. He decided not to. "Nothing. I just wanted to hear your voice."

218

Silence.

"Jesse?"

"I've got to hang up. I'm so tired, baby."

"Sleep well."

"Paul, when are you coming home?"

"In about three days."

It was late morning when he came down the steps of the slave quarters from his apartment and out into the courtyard. It was a warm morning.

By the time McFarland returned from Algiers it was late afternoon. He had seen the parents of the suicide and had been shown pictures of the two victims. It had depressed him.

McFarland sat on the gallery outside his living room. Several youths lounged by the pool below, a radio playing. The sky had darkened. The wind was now very strong. The palms slapped against themselves in the breeze. It would rain.

He tried to work and could not. He tried to read, the letters he had purchased from the girl in Algiers. Adolescent protests of love, excessive sentiments, hopeless schemes. He found the letters both depressing and irritating. Too much love expressed too badly, childish and self-indulgent.

He was restless. He walked inside. The apartment was dark. He put a call through to Jesse. There was no answer. He thought, she hasn't come home from work yet. He missed her very much.

He went into the dark bedroom. He lay on the bed. He felt Bartholomew's sweat shirt on top of the covers, where he had thrown it that morning. He wondered where the boy was. He put the sweat shirt to his face. It smelled of Noczema.

It was after seven o'clock when he awoke from his nap. He put another call through to the Coast. Again no answer.

He showered and changed and then sat out on his gallery and had a martini. The wind was very strong. He heard thunder in the distance. A storm riding toward the city from the gulf.

219

Below him, at the pool, a young man, in his twenties, lay asleep on the tiles, a beach towel thrown over him, his hands folded on his chest, the ends of the towel flapping in the wind. After a while he stood up, draping the towel over his massive shoulders. He was naked. It suddenly occurred to him that if Jesse had been sitting on the gallery with him and that man had risen naked, he would have been angry and jealous, even knowing her indifference.

The young man glanced up at him and then looked startled. He apparently thought he had been alone. McFarland found himself embarrassed that he had been watching the young man, who now waved at him and smiled.

"You better get inside. It's going to rain," he shouted down, and then realized the absurdity of his remark. The man was naked. Why would he care if it rained?

He yelled something back, but he could not hear, the remark lost to the wind. He stood a moment, smiling up at McFarland, undecided or expectant. McFarland then had the unsettling suspicion that the man was waiting for him to invite him up. McFarland looked down at his martini. When he glanced up again, the young man was gone.

He tried Jesse once more. No answer. He was worried. What the hell, I'll go back to LA. It was two days before he was expected to return.

He called the airport and made a reservation on the next flight. He then ordered a taxi.

He went downstairs to wait for the taxi on Dumaine. The wind had died down, the storm turning from the city for the bayou country to the east. A light rain was falling. The air had grown chill.

Standing outside was Bartholomew, the boy he had seen with the dog in the park. McFarland was startled to see him. The boy came up to him as the taxi appeared.

As McFarland flagged the cab down, the boy's face changed from delight to disappointment.

"Where are you goin'?"

"To Los Angeles. What are you doing here?" He could not

220

account for the boy's presence, and he suspected that Bartholomew had deliberately come there and waited for him. He wondered why.

"Nothing."

He looked down at the boy's shoes. They were badly scuffed, the sole of one clearly broken away from the toe. The boy was wet and chilled. It moved him to pity and guilt. He didn't know why he should feel guilty, and yet he did.

"I'll be back in a few days. I'll see you then."

"They locked the church," Bartholomew whined.

"They did?" He did not know what the hell he was talking about.

"I got no place to go."

On impulse, because he cared and yet did not, because he did not want to travel with the guilt of the boy in the rain with no place to go, whether true or not, because in the most real sense it meant nothing to him one way or the other, he took a twenty-dollar bill from his pocket and handed it to Bartholomew.

"Pay someone to walk the dog. Take some time off."

The boy grinned. McFarland patted him on the shoulder. Bartholomew seemed both delighted and abashed, speechless.

"Be good, son."

He arrived in Los Angeles shortly after 10 P.M. He called Malibu. Nothing.

Since he had left the car at home, he took a taxi to the beach house. He kept urging the driver to go faster. He was anxious to see Jesse. He was feeling horny and high, happy that he had decided to return early.

The house lights were on when he arrived. But there was no one about. Still, he was relieved. For a moment, when coming into the house, he had the premonition that she had walked out on him. But her stuff was scattered about, the bathroom cabinet stuffed with her things.

Around eleven thirty he heard a car drive into the drive-

221

way. He went to the window. He was on his third drink. Because of Jesse's absence, he had become nervous and fretful, and then he heard the car in the driveway and felt great relief and expectation, a kind of joy. He pulled open the curtain. It was Jesse. Thank God, he mumbled, ecstatic at seeing her car.

He went to the door, and as he pulled it open, as he was about to step outside and call her name, he saw a Volkswagen bus pull into the driveway behind Jesse's car. He saw Jesse step out of her car, not looking back at the house, where he stood waiting for her, but rather she turned and watched the Volkswagen come into the drive. Jesse was dressed in blue jeans and a white T-shirt, dressed as she had been the night he first met her in the Village bar. It struck him as wrong, a kind of warning, as if she were again what she had been before she met him, almost as if he had never existed in her life.

She moved away from her car and started walking toward the Volkswagen. Its door opened, and a man began to get out. McFarland yelled, "Jesse!" Suddenly he was terrified for her.

She abruptly stopped and turned toward the house, looking startled and somewhat frightened. She raised her hand to shield her eyes from the light coming from the house, and then her hand moved to her lips.

She turned and waved the man back. He ran a few steps to the Volkswagen bus and backed it hurriedly out of the driveway onto the Pacific Coast Highway. Then Jesse continued up to the house.

"Jesse."

"So now you know."

And that was when he knew.

18

"EXPLAIN! Explain yourself!" he shouted. She walked past him and into the living room to the bar.

"There's no ice," she said, taking the ice bucket off the counter and carrying it into the kitchen.

McFarland stood in the center of the living room, tense with jealousy and anger. He stood unmoving, fearful of what she would tell him, his stomach tight with anticipation. He listened to the refrigerator door open, the ice trays pulled from the freezer, the water turned on in the sink, the trays held under the water, the cracking of the aluminum ice jam, the rocky tumble of the cubes into the silver bucket, the trays being refilled with water and replaced in the refrigerator, the door slammed shut.

He waited several minutes for Jesse to return to the living room, concentrating on the noise, visualizing her hands reaching into the white frostness of the freezer, her hands gripping the cold trays, minutely visualizing all that, obsessively focusing on it to keep from thinking of other hands upon her, of what she must have done in his absence, of her disloyalty and his jealousy and defeat. Less than a week alone, and she cats it up, whores, puts out, spreads it, gives it away. . . .

"Martini?" she asked, returning to the living room, acting as if nothing untoward had occurred, as if it were the most ordinary of nights.

"Vodka," he said. He immediately became cool and detached, removed, as though he were outside himself watching himself watching her. Depersonalized. Disconnected. Calm.

"You're tan. You look so healthy, baby. Weather must have been nice," she said, dropping the ice into two glasses, making them drinks.

"It was pleasant enough, although it rained tonight." He remembered Bartholomew in the rain.

She carried the drinks toward him, smiling politely. She wasn't nervous. She was tired, worn of combat and argument and self-defense, tired of not being trusted, of interrogation and accusation. So very tired. "I'm surprised to see you, Paul," she said without irony. "But very pleased you're here. We never did decide. We should decide now."

"Decide what?" He expected her to bring up marriage.

"Where we're spending Christmas. I'd like to go south, maybe Mexico. For a few days. Just the two of us. I hear it's wonderful there on the holidays."

McFarland took his drink. He stared at her. "Are you mad? I catch you practically in bed with some man and you want to know about *Christmas?*"

She continued, ignoring him. She would not be drawn into it. She would not be made to answer. He did not own her. She would not let him force guilt on her. "I know you have the script to do in New Orleans, but what's a few days in Mexico more or less?"

"Priscilla's right. You're crazy."

Jesse sat down on the sofa. She patted the cushion next to her. "Sit by me, baby. I miss the feel of you."

"I don't goddamn *want* to sit." He began to pace the room, his frustration building, her equanimity driving him up the wall. They said nothing for a time, Jesse sitting too casually on the sofa, staring down at her glass, turning it in her hand, the ice tinkling against the glass; she avoided his eyes now, sensing that anger was building up in him and not wanting to provide the occasion for it to explode. She thought if she could just get through the night without a fight, if she could somehow get his mind off the man who followed her home, if she could make him laugh or talk of other things, plan the

224

future . . . if she could make it through the night without a break between them, then in the morning, after sex . . . but if not, then it would fall to pieces and where would she go, whom did she have to go to without him, without him what was there worth going to, worth going on . . . she would get drunk, yes, very drunk, and he would fuck her and that would make him feel secure, and that would convince him that she loved him, and he would forget, even though he would trust her less, in time he would forget and they would go on.

"Funny what you remember. I heard a bit of 'Ave Maria' on the car radio driving here—"

"*Who was the man?*"

"—driving here tonight, driving *home.* I don't especially like that song, I'm a Lutheran, you see—" she laughed quietly—"but I remember in high school I went to an afternoon elective assembly, that's where the students can go or not as they like. It was a concert by a violinist. There were very few kids in the school auditorium, and the place was large and full of echo. I was fifteen years old. I remember every day I wore to school a pair of penny loafers my brother, Daniel, had given me for my birthday, and in them were two shining pennies my boyfriend, Jack, put in the shoes. For luck. The violinist played 'Ave Maria.' He stood by the piano at the far left side of the auditorium, not on the stage but on the orchestra level by the wall. He was about sixty years old, grayhaired, with eyes that stared ahead unmoving. I thought he played beautifully. There were only about fifty kids in the auditorium. The place sat two thousand. All of us sat grouped together in the center section. When he stopped playing, we applauded very loudly, and the applause echoed through the auditorium as if the place were packed with students. The violinist was blind, and he bowed blindly again and again to the empty seats in front of him. Some of the kids started laughing and yelling bravos and making fun of him because he thought we were sitting in front of him, and he kept bowing to the empty seats and throwing little kisses. Smiling foolishly and throwing kisses to empty seats. I cried for him. . . ."

"Jesse." Mad, he thought, what is she telling me?

She looked up at him. "Funny as hell, isn't it? That I'd remember that? He played so well and bowed to empty seats. Every time I was ever good, listen to me, every time I thought I had been decent and tried to take a bow for it there was nothing but goddamn empty seats. Listen, you bastard, I haven't cheated on you."

"No, then who was the man tonight?"

She sighed and stared down at her drink. What's the use? He came to the sofa and stood in front of her. Without looking up, she could see his tight trousers, the outline of his thighs, the slight mound at his crotch, his large, long-fingered hands at rest at his sides. She wanted to reach out and lay her hands against his strong thighs and drop her head against his groin and cry, waiting for those hands to touch and caress her head and shoulders and for him to say, It's all right, Jesse, everything's all right and good. What's the use?

He reached down and cupped her chin in his hand and raised her face. She looked at him. The green eyes, the circles beneath them as if eyes could cast shadows . . . her lovely mouth. He smiled helplessly at her, and for a moment he simply gazed at her face, once more taken by his sense of luck, the amazement of it, that this woman whom he loved was there on his sofa in his house in his presence, her chin cradled in his fingers, soft as snow. For a moment, then, he decided to forget the man, to hold it off, suppress the jealously. Let it go.

Too late. "Okay. You want to know?"

He said nothing. He did, and he did not.

"I picked him up," she said, twisting her head out of his hand. "I was lonely. I was horny. I was tired of being alone."

"Alone? Christ! Can't you go one week without fucking? I'm gone a few goddamn days and you've got to get your—"

226

He stopped. He couldn't say it. After all, he loved her. After all.

"Say it! Got to get my what?"

"You have to have it? You're supposed to love *me*. Me! To belong to me! You filthy whore!" The image, picture it, of men he did not know and, not knowing, hated, fucking her. He clenched his fists, for a moment feeling dizzy, the blood rushing to his head. "Goddamn son of a bitch bastards! How can you let them touch you!" He raised his hand to strike her. Instead, he threw his drink against the wall, smashing the glass, the ice and glass clattering along the floor.

"Go ahead, baby. You're so tough, aren't you? So butch. So manly. You can't even control your own jealousy. You have too much pride, my angel. I did not fuck him. I didn't. What the hell are you angry about?" His outburst genuinely surprised her. She knew he was jealous, but she was astonished and frightened by its depth. What had she done to cause such anger?

"You would've fucked him if I hadn't been here. Bitch."

"Yes, goddamn it. *Yes*. Is that what you want to hear? It was my *intention*. But I didn't *do* it. I didn't commit the *sin*."

"Bitch!" He hit his hand hard against the wall. "Bitch!"

"This isn't going to get us anywhere, baby." Too late, she thought, it's over now. I've lost him now. I've ruined it.

"*Why* did you do it? Why?" He had to know, his jealousy and his curious sense of his own prerogatives as a man who loved this woman required it. Explanation was needed. For he could picture them in bed, the two of them in his bed; she and how many other men he did not know, how many times, and when would it ever stop?

"Why did I do it?" She tried to speak quietly, but she was scared and her voice began to break. "You don't listen. I told you. I picked him up because I was lonely. . . ."

"So was I. I was alone too, for as many days, but I—"

"But you didn't fuck in New Orleans. Well, my angel, I

don't care if you did or not. I frankly don't give a goddamn who you sleep with. I know you love me. You aren't going to leave me because you sleep with some other woman. When you leave me, it'll be to get away from me, not to go to someone else." And I won't be able to stop you, and I think the time has come for you to go, and I cannot think of anything I can do to stop you from leaving me again.

"Jesse, how many others have there been?"

She said nothing.

"Tell me, you whore." His voice was ice hard.

"That's what my father used to say over and over and over again. Jesse, you whore. Maybe it's true. I don't know. I don't care anymore."

"How many men have you slept with?" He grabbed her face and jerked it up. "Look at me!"

"Since when?"

"Since I left you in New York, since my wife and son—"

"That was months ago."

"How many, goddamn it?"

"I don't know."

"Jesus." He slapped his hand against his forehead, laughing sarcastically. "So many you can't even remember them all? Mary and Joseph!"

She shrugged. "I was drugged up most of the time after you left. I don't remember anything. . . ."

"Liar."

"Very little anyway. Mike Rhodes was dying and I wanted to die too. You had walked out on me and . . . I don't know, maybe one or two men, maybe more, maybe none. I felt rotten about myself. I couldn't keep you. I wasn't good enough to keep you. Imagine. I didn't know about your wife and son, if I had. . . . All I knew was that you had promised me so much, and then nothing happened. I don't *like* myself, baby. Somtimes I hate myself. Maybe I do because everybody's always telling me I'm a whore. Maybe that's why. Maybe sometimes I even believe it. Maybe I *want* to believe it. So if

I get drugged up and stoned, it's easy. And if I don't know the guy, if he's a stranger, then I have nothing to answer for in the morning, nobody to throw guilt in my face. I can even pretend it never happened. Sometimes I hate myself so much I want sex with strangers so there's a chance I might get hurt. So I'll be punished for what everybody tells me I am, for what you think I am. When I feel that way, what's crazy is that inside of me I know I'm about eleven years old and that I'm the same girl who was always there before that bastard came at me in the summer house. . . . Hell, I don't know."

"Why? Why?" He paced the room. He did not understand what she was telling him. What did it have to do with him, that is what he wanted to know.

"And every time you leave, Paul, every time, I'm not sure you'll ever come back—"

"You were whoring around all the time I was gone. There was someone here that night I called late from New Orleans."

"—You won't come back because I think you know how really terrible I am, what a whore I really am inside, how I don't deserve love, how dirty my desires are. Hell, hell, how I want to be hated and beaten, you know that and you aren't coming back." She started to cry, putting her hands against her face and crying.

"Tell me! Jesse! Was there someone here with you the night I called?"

"What?" She looked up at him.

"Was there someone here?"

"No."

"I don't believe you."

"Isn't life *shit?*" She stood up and walked across the living room and grabbed the bottle of vodka and poured herself a large drink and then went out on the terrace, carrying the vodka with her. She leaned against the railing, placing the bottle on the floor. The tide was out. The beach stretched far out, seemingly miles toward the horizon, lost in the darkness until one could not tell where the land ended and the

229

ocean began, and above it all, the rumble of the surf, above it all, above the sand and water, above her and him, the dark sky shimmering with a blizzard of stars.

He came up behind her and took the bottle and poured himself more liquor.

"It must be midnight," he said. He sat on a chaise longue behind her and looked at her figure leaning against the railing. She seemed very small and fragile and impermanent. He wondered how he would live without her and go on; that and how he could continue to live with her unless she changed. He did not believe her anymore. He did not know where the truth lay, and his life required it. Doubt spread into paranoia.

"When I was a child," she said, "I used to wonder if the stars I saw were the same everywhere. I decided they weren't. I decided the stars I saw in Minneapolis could only be seen in Minneapolis. They belonged only there, like the lakes. They were winter stars because they were always brightest in the coldest weather, always clearest then. They never ran from it. They were part of it, part of winter. Because they were made of ice. . . ."

She sipped her drink. "Starlight, starbright. . . . How does that song go?"

He didn't answer.

"I can never remember the words to songs. I don't even know the words to 'This Time the Dream's on Me,' and I've heard it a thousand times."

"I still don't know why you cheat on me," he said quietly. Then he wondered why he had bothered to say it. What did it matter? Nothing she said would he believe.

"What do you know about stars?" she asked, turning around and facing him. She leaned her back against the railing and sipped her drink.

"They die. And turn into black holes. They devour themselves."

"Like everything else." She laughed, finding the remark inexplicably funny. "Black holes. Then God fucks them. And His lover gets jealous! Ha-ha. . . ."

230

"Quit laughing at me," he said petulantly. He was feeling sorry for himself and for her. Suddenly it had all gone bad. He wished he had stayed in New Orleans. He wished he had never known.

"What can I do to make it right, my angel? What can I do to make it up to you? I didn't cheat on you while you were gone. Honestly. I only tried."

He distrusted her now too much and loved her too much, and he did not know what to do.

"Finish your drink. We should go to bed."

She took a deep drink. And then a deep breath. She said something, but he did not hear.

"What?" He tensed.

"I don't like sex very much," she said, continuing to lean against the railing, facing away from him, her voice carried on the breeze to him.

"I'm not asking you to have sex tonight."

"When I have it, it's because I'm drunk and feeling terrible about myself, and then I want it to be dirty and cheap, as dirty as I think I am at those moments. Paul, you're too good a man to make it seem dirty—"

"It's lousy, Jesse, to hold what's good about a man against him."

"—I love you because you're good. So sex with you is never good. Isn't that a cruel irony? Maybe in time. . . . Who knows? That's why I'm always drunk. *I don't have any physical feeling for you.*"

"None?"

"Not very much, not when I'm sober. I wish I did. I wish so badly that I did. I want you to love me. I want you to hold me and take care of me. I *need* you, Paul. That's hard for me to say, but it's utterly true. I get drunk and have sex because *you* want it. It's because I love you that I do it with you."

No physical feeling. It cut him deep. And there was nothing, not one goddamn thing he could do about it. In that moment he wished he were every cheap, drunk, dirty stranger she had ever fucked. In that moment he hated himself and

231

her and would have given all to know that she had really wanted him once.

"If you detest sex so much, why the hell do you whore around with other men?"

"I don't. Although you won't believe it."

"Tonight?"

She turned and faced him.

"Tell me!"

"Tonight? I went to Cedars of Lebanon Hospital to see Mike. He's back inside, or rather the doctors never let him out after you sent him there. They finally caught him in their grip, and they'd keep him there now, just as he said they would, until they'd seen him die, full of tubes and comatose and crazy with pain. Then they'd slowly let him drift until he drifted off forever. They'd let him drop cold. . . . I sat by his bed for hours. He was unconscious, Paul. Drugged sleep. They say it's dreamless. Dead but breathing. I held his hand in mine and thought of the places where I had held his hand before, the cities, the beds at night, the beaches, the bars where he was scared and wouldn't say it, and I thought of what I had seen that hand do, hold drinks, flowers, syringes, touch me. . . . It was damp and hot. I could feel his heart beat inside it as I held it, feel it beat away against my palm knowing that in time, so goddamn soon, baby, it would beat no more. When I left the hospital tonight, I tried to call you in New Orleans. There was no answer. I was scared. Alone. I panicked. I got into the car and drove to the parking lot by the pier at Santa Monica. I stood outside the car until whoever that creep was in the Volkswagen bus, until he rolled by and started talking to me. I told him to follow me home. All the time driving home, to keep from thinking of Mike's hand, I tried to imagine what that creep looked like naked, if he was as beautiful as you—"

"Shut up!"

"—and what he'd do to me, and if I'd get hurt. I felt terrible, baby. Because Mike was gone for sure, and there wasn't a goddamn thing I could do about it."

232

She started to cry, angrily.

"I don't believe a word of it. No, maybe I do."

She stared at him, tears running. "What does it matter?"

He hated seeing her cry. It made him want to, although he knew he would not. He stood up and went to her, trying to embrace and comfort her.

"Get the hell away from me!"

He moved back, angry at her rejection.

"You're still in love with him, aren't you?"

She said nothing.

"Say it! Admit it!"

"Yes! Yes! What does it matter?"

She shoved past him and ran toward the beach.

In the morning he left for New Orleans. Before he left, she asked him if he loved her.

"Yes."

"Enough to come back?"

He did not answer.

"What can I do to make you come back?" She grabbed his hand, gripping, kneading it in hers, her eyes red and desperate. "Tell me?"

"Don't worry, love. A few days. I have to think. We'll talk again."

He turned to leave.

"Paul?"

"Yes?"

"Kiss me good-bye?"

He kissed her. She smelled of lilac.

19

He arrived in New Orleans before noon. He took a taxi to his apartment. He sat on the bed for a moment, debating whether to call Jesse. He wanted to have her back, but he also wanted her to be faithful to him. He could not understand how she could love him and cheat on him at the same time. He did not believe her when she said she had been faithful to him. His pride had been damaged, and under it all, gnawing away at him, worst of all, was her saying that she had no physical feeling for him. She was angry when she said it; she didn't mean it; it couldn't be true. But perhaps it was.

Around 3 p.m. McFarland had coffee and doughnuts at the French Market at Decateur and St. Anne, near the Mississippi levee. He sat facing Jackson Square. He thought of Jesse. He wondered if, at that moment, she was missing him. And then he remembered Rhodes, and he knew she would be with him. His suspicion had grown to where he no longer believed Rhodes had cancer. It was another lie, another ploy. Thick as thieves, the two of them, still thick and into it. How he hated him and envied him.

He read the *Times-Picayune*. About an hour after he arrived the boy with the dog, Bartholomew, walked out of Jackson Square, dogless, and stood a moment by the fence seemingly waiting for someone. He was dressed in light cotton trousers and a loose red V-neck sweater, no shirt. He wore sandals.

A few minutes later he crossed through heavy traffic on Decateur and walked toward the outdoor café where McFarland was sitting. He looked at the boy's face, and it reminded him of someone he had known as a boy that age, known or competed against, he was not certain; it called forth an incomplete memory, hinted at some bond between them, a second or third party, or some experience through which they were connected, related perhaps, unawares. On the corner by the café the boy stopped and put his hand on his forehead, making the salute characteristic of Jaime, shading his eyes from the sun. McFarland looked away.

Bartholomew had disappeared when he looked across the street again. Several minutes later McFarland went inside to the toilet. When he returned, the boy was sitting at his table, drinking his coffee and reading his *Times-Picayune*.

Bartholomew made a rather grand gesture with his hand, like a noble granting permission for a courtier to sit.

"I'm starved," he said. In McFarland's absence he had eaten the last doughnut.

"I see." He was amused by the boy's directness.

"I love this place. I knew you'd come here."

"Look, kid. . . ." He was about to ask why he had taken his coffee and doughnut and *Times-Picayune*, who he thought he was, when the boy interrupted him. Just as well. He was glad to see him. When he found him sitting there, he had missed him in a way, and that was a knowledge difficult to accept, discomforting, for it implied the desire for his son, whom he could not replace. Nevertheless, for a moment he looked at the boy and pretended years had passed and Jaime was safe and it was he sitting across the table from his father, alive.

He called the waiter.

"Do you want more doughnuts?"

"No."

They left the French Market. The wind had come up. They stood a moment in the street. The weather seemed colder, the wind biting. He said good-bye to Bartholomew, shaking his hand, the gesture seeming both formal and appropriate.

Bartholomew asked him what he was doing the rest of the afternoon. It was nearly four o'clock.

"I'll be home working."

236

"With your wife?"

"No, alone. My wife's in Los Angeles. . . ." He stopped. He had unthinkingly referred to Jesse as his wife. He had never done that before, but he knew, in saying it, that that was how he saw her.

"Can I come along with you? I got nothing to do." He squinted at him, the sun again, his hand placed above his forehead to keep his hair out of his eyes.

"I really have to work. I'm a writer. I need the solitude." He felt he owed an explanation.

"I know a lot of stories." He smiled. McFarland sensed the boy was extremely lonely. He did not know what to say. He had no room for the boy in his life, no room.

"Some other time." He nodded and walked away.

Moments later he yelled McFarland's name. He turned. The boy came running up. "Tonight"—all out of breath—"I'll meet you, okay?" He grinned hopefully, eagerly, his voice trembling. McFarland felt sorry for him. Had he no one to care for him?

"Some other time."

Bartholomew's smile died. He looked defeated and deeply hurt.

"It's just that I'm busy tonight. . . ."

That evening it began to rain heavily in New Orleans. The temperature dropped. It was damp and cold.

Early evening. McFarland was alone in his apartment. The doorbell rang. He opened it. Priscilla stood in the hall grinning at him. In lieu of a raincoat she was wearing a plastic dry cleaner's bag, the kind that comes with a newly pressed suit, wearing it over her dress, a tight silk sheath the color of the inside of a Bel Air swimming pool, fluorescent Day-Glo turquoise. She wore matching turquoise earrings and turquoise eye shadow. It had begun to run.

"Prissy," he said, honestly happy to see her, "you look terrific." He put his arms around her and kissed her.

"Paul, I. . . ." She could not go on. Instead of speaking she held up her wrist. It was bandaged. So now she had slashed them both.

"It's all right. It doesn't matter." He kissed her again. Priscilla drew protectiveness from him, concern, as easily as drawing a thread from a spool.

"Stupid of me. Another street boy. God help us all. So this time I went to a shrink, and he put me on Valium. I am as calm as. . . . What would be as calm as me? A corpse. Ha-ha. You know what that mouse David said when he saw the new, er, wound? He said, 'If you slash your feet next time and pierce your side, you can found a religion.' Ha-ha. The ass."

"You want a drink? Or dinner?"

"Both, darling. I want it all."

The rain had stoppd by the time they left for dinner, both of them feeling high from several drinks at his apartment. They strolled over to Bourbon Street. The streets were coming to life, the bars bellowing music into the night. They walked slowly up Bourbon toward Lucky Pierre's Bar, where they planned to eat dinner.

About a block from the restaurant he heard his name called.

"Goddamn," he said, recognizing the voice. Bartholomew.

"Wait!" The tremolo voice. "Waaait!"

They stood at the corner of Bourbon and St. Philip streets, by the Lucky Dog stand, a pushcart shaped like a frankfurter.

He introduced Priscilla to Bartholomew.

"My name's Faison B. Smith. Sexiest boy on the muddy Miss!" He bowed. "My friends call me Bartholomew."

Priscilla looked astonished.

"Are you married?" Bartholomew asked. He meant to each other.

"No."

"In a way," Priscilla interjected coyly. She looked at both of them, her expression one of amusement and condescension, a look McFarland had witnessed before with Priscilla when the pangs of jealousy, like stomach gas, attacked.

"Ahhhh," Priscilla murmured, touching Bartholomew's face, "a poet!" She was convinced she had come upon the resurrected Shelley under the saloon lights of Bourbon. It was immediately plain that Priscilla liked the boy, sucker as she was for runaways and hustlers and youths over whom she could maintain some command, over whom she believed, often correctly, some remnants of glamor could be invoked. She found Bartholomew personable and winsome on such little evidence. "Say it again, darling."

"Say what again?"

"Your natal poem."

Bartholomew repeated his dizzy rhyme, his voice going higher and younger with his increased self-consciousness, the tremolo more noticeable.

Priscilla gushed, "Isn't it sweet, but utterly? Couldn't you just eat up the darling thing?"

"You probably will."

"Filthy mind. You're so very common, Paul."

Bartholomew smiled with the required sweetness and too modestly lowered his eyes and took McFarland's right hand, and Priscilla took his left, and the three of them, like the Family of the Year, marched down Bourbon to Lucky Pierre's Bar. On the way Priscilla glanced often and intimately, indeed conspiratorially, at the boy, and he met her look, and the two of them smiled at McFarland because they assumed he shared their mutual delight in their mutual acquaintance. In a sense, he did.

"He looks like Jaime. Like Jaime, well . . ." She stumbled over her words. "Like Jaime would have looked if he had . . . if he hadn't . . . I mean, if. . . ."

"No." He cut her short. She was wandering too close. "Not at all like Jaime."

"Who's Jaime?" Bartholomew asked. No one answered him.

"Yes, like him." Priscilla was adamant. "Like Jaime and someone else, equally beautiful."

On that statement—"and someone else"—he knew where

239

she was headed, despite the Valium fog in her brain—after the latest manic-depressive episode resulted in a mutilated wrist, consequences of another set-up, asked-for Betrayal, the doctor put her heavily on the tranquilizer, and that explained her slow speech and overtolerance, and the benign, placid way she viewed the world that night, her mania blunted—and what her remark told him was that somewhere in the clutter of Priscilla's attic, in that snarl of confused impressions and half-fictionalized, unreliable memory, in that body-face recall, in that night where they're all the same in the dark, somewhere in that mental nest, in that jungle, a space had cleared in the thicket and sunlight broke through too clearly and she was in the ineluctable process of attaching that memory fragment of the Boy Beloved onto Bartholomew, slapping it on as thoughtlessly as one pastes a political sticker to a telephone pole.

Priscilla, like McFarland, was captive to memory, but more completely trapped in it than he, trapped like a dinosaur in a tar pit. She constantly intruded that memory of the first boy she had ever loved onto other boys, infected the young with it like a nurse coughing in a children's ward. Her beguilement was deeply housed in nostalgia, the easiest of lies. She was falling for Bartholomew, and McFarland knew it.

They walked to Lucky Pierre's and took a table in the back room, by the floor-to-ceiling birdcage. Over the bar was a Christmas tree, and a sign that read MERRY CHRISTMAS. McFarland thought of Jesse, and he was lonely. In an hour or two it would be Christmas Eve.

Priscilla complained about sitting so close to the birdcage. She complained about the possibility of getting pigeon mites in her food. "If you won't change tables, at least let me change places with you."

McFarland stood. He had been sitting between the two of them. She took his seat, smiling at Bartholomew as she did. Now she sat next to the boy, and her complaints ceased.

"Perhaps we should eat in my suite. I'm at the Royal Orleans, darling." She patted Bartholomew's cheek. He looked at her, or rather he gazed, star-struck by her glamor.

"Let's!"

"We'll eat here."

They ordered drinks, and McFarland ordered white wine and poured it into a water glass for the boy.

"Darling, are you a virgin?" she asked, squeezing the boy's leg.

Bartholomew blushed and then looked at McFarland for advice.

"Don't look at me. How would I know?"

"Are you, sweet thing?" She smiled.

"A couple of months ago . . ." he began, blushing, his voice high and cracking, the tremolo markedly increased, "a girl, in the church basement, me and my friend. . . ."

"Enough said, darling. We'll get along splendidly." Priscilla was again slurring her words, the liquor mixing with the Valium to send her up.

After dinner he walked them back to her hotel. She asked them both to come up for a drink. She was already drunk, and the Valium was beginning to wear thin, and her panic was beginning to show.

"Darlings, can you spend a few moments with someone . . . someone. . . " She trailed off, touching her head dramatically, self-pityingly, her eyes rolling skyward.

Bartholomew looked confusedly at McFarland. He needed direction.

"We might as well. She'll never go to bed otherwise."

They went up to her suite. Priscilla ordered drinks from room service and then disappeared into the bedroom.

"She's crazy." Bartholomew turned up his nose. He was having second thoughts.

"No, lonely. It's just as bad."

"Where's your wife?" he asked.

"She's in Los Angeles."

"Why isn't she with you? If I had a wife. . . ."

"I know. But she has a job she cannot leave."

241

Priscilla returned to the living room. She was dressed in a white nightgown, with a silk cape, also white, over it. Bartholomew stared.

"Don't you like it?" She looked uncertainly at him. "It cost a fortune."

"That's a vulgar thing to say, Prissy."

"He should know what he's getting."

The doorbell rang. The bellhop entered with the drinks. Priscilla signed the check.

"Merry Christmas," the bellhop said as he left.

"Good Lord. It's Christmas Eve. How drear."

They toasted the holiday.

"Tell me, darling," Priscilla said, sitting on the sofa next to Bartholomew, "where are you spending Christmas?"

He shrugged.

"Shy boy. . . ." She smiled maternally at him. "He means to say, by the slight gesture of his wonderful body, that he will be spending the holidays with me. And you, Paul, I suppose you'll be up there in Shreveport. . . ."

He laughed. "I'll what?" She's gone dizzy, he thought.

"Never mind. It's none of my business, although I cannot imagine a worse stinkhole in which to spend Christmas."

"I *like* Shreveport," Bartholomew said defensively.

"What are you saying, Priscilla?" McFarland asked.

She looked at him, narrowing her eyes. She was jealous now, thinking he would not be with her for the holidays. Her expression became hard and disagreeable. "I never knew what you ever saw in her. Never. I didn't say anything. Oh, no, I let it go on and on. You men are such fools. To fall for someone like what's-her-name. . . ."

"You mean his wife?" Bartholomew asked, looking from one to the other.

"His *wife!* Ha-ha-ha. That's a nice term for it! *I'm* more like a wife to Paul than that bitch will ever be."

McFarland stood up. He had been lonely for Jesse, and he had felt guilty in leaving her in Los Angeles, and now, in the face of Priscilla's words, he was angry. He was in love with Jesse, and there was no help for it.

242

"Priscilla, watch what you say."

"Why the hell *should* I!" She snorted.

"Because I love her—"

"Love? Hell."

"—so keep your goddamn mouth shut about her, or I'll knock you to the floor." He spoke quietly.

"Then you'll have *two* recovery rooms to visit for the holidays. You . . . *God*, are men *stupid*. It isn't love, darling. It's the cheapest kind of masochism."

Priscilla stood up and weaved somewhat unsteadily toward him, smiling wickedly. "Come, kiss Mama, Paul. Kiss Mama. We never made it, did we? Not once in all these years, and I loved you more than Adele and Jesse put together ever did. I love you now. . . ."

McFarland watched her stagger toward him. He felt both pity and contempt. She had never finally known if she had been loved or not, or what she had wanted or why. She had always been too drunk on bathos and self-pity and greeting-card sentimentality ever to discern her own truth. She would never know herself, and therefore, she would never connect.

She put her arms around him. She whispered seductively in his ear, "I'll get rid of the boy. Then fuck me, darling. I'm so lonely. Do it to me like you do to Jesse." She licked his ear.

He thrust her arms from around his neck and pushed her away.

She staggered back several feet, her arms dangling at her side. At first she looked startled, and then contempt and hatred and jealousy came over her. She believed she had loved him too well to little profit, that she had been taken by him and used. That he was laughing at her, as the others had. It was because of him, because of them all, that it never worked, despite how she tried and what she gave, never never er did it work. And now she knew, at her age, that it never would. She held that against him.

"You bastard. Go the hell to Shreveport. I don't give a good goddamn where you go. I hope you rot there!" Her eyes were tearing. They stood for several minutes staring at each other.

243

Priscilla hating him and longing for him. McFarland baffled by her outburst. She's gone crazy, he thought. She's finally run out of gas.

Bartholomew broke the silence. "Why are you going to Shreveport?"

"Because he's *weak*. That's why he's going. Because he's let some nickel tramp blackmail him with sex. Because. . . ."

"What the hell are you talking about?" McFarland shouted. He was thoroughly confused.

"Don't yell at me!" she shouted back. "Shreveport! You know the city north of here? Five hours by car. *Don't deny it.*"

"Deny what?" He was at a loss. And then the premonition of danger overcame him. His stomach tightened.

"Jesse! Jesse!" she yelled as if the name were an obscenity, "Jesse!"

McFarland sat down. He put his head in his hands. He tried to comprehend what the hell she was getting at. He was very nervous now, as if he had awakened in the night hearing a phone ring too many times and lifted the receiver to hear Western Union calling. Priscilla knew something about Jesse that he did not know, and he suspected that what she knew was hurtful.

"Tell me," he said, not looking up. He said it calmly. He was growing depersonalized.

"*Shreveport.* Are you *deaf?*" She leaned down to Bartholomew and in a stage whisper spoke to him, suddenly seeing the boy as her ally in the room. McFarland would leave her, yes, but the boy would stay. One night, at least. Boys were always good for one night. She smiled at Bartholomew, warming toward him, thinking, the boy loves me. This boy. He really loves me. . . . "Paul has gone deaf in the ears," she said, giggling. "Or he never heard of Shreveport. You know," she added conspiratorally, intimately, at once a Southerner with the boy, her voice affected with a thick drawl, "you know how ign'rant some Yankees are—"

McFarland interrupted her. "For the last time, Priscilla,

244

clear the steam from your brain and tell me exactly what you are talking about." He said it coldly. She had heard the tone before when he had attacked Rhodes. It frightened and excited her. And then it occurred to her: *he doesn't know.*

"She didn't tell you?" It was incredible to her that he would not know. She found it astonishing and amusing, and for a moment it gave her a feeling of power over him.

"*What* didn't she tell me?" He glared at her. "Answer me, bitch!" He pounded his hand against the cocktail table in front of him. The ashtray bounced off it onto the carpet.

"Don't shout, darling. I can hear you perfectly well. . . ." She smiled at him, and walked past him toward the door. She stood there a moment, looking down at the fallen ashtray. And then she decided. She gestured toward the door. "Bartholomew's tired. And so am I. I think it's time, Paul, you went home."

He stood up and walked toward her.

"You've damaged the carpet," she continued. "God knows what you'll damage next. Anyway, it's well after midnight—"

He grabbed her unbandaged wrist and squeezed it, pressing his thumb hard against the back of her wrist. "Tell me."

"Tell you what?" She smiled at him condescendingly. She had no intention of telling him, not yet at any rate.

"Tell me. . . ."

"You're hurting me, Paul." She could feel his warm breath against her face. It excited her.

"Tell me, or I'll snap it in two."

"The scar is tearing. Paul, *please*. . . ." It hurt very much; his face so close to hers, his strong hand crushing her wrist; looking into his large eyes, the dark blond eyebrows, the long, straight nose, his full mouth tight and demanding, demanding, the sultry lower lip . . . she wanted to reach her mouth across the inches that separated their faces and nibble on his mouth, have his tongue fill her mouth as his hand crushed her wrist, his breath upon her. . . . "Ahhh. . . ." It hurt too much. She closed her eyes in pain.

He lessened the pressure but maintained his hold.

245

"Jesse is at Bellows Memorial Hospital in Shreveport—"
He let go of her wrist, and as he did, he gasped.

"—I'm amazed you didn't know." She rubbed her wrist. "I'll be bruised tomorrow. How the hell will I explain that?" She looked at him, struck by his expression of alarm and confusion, and then her real affection for him returned. He seemed vulnerable and a little frightened, and she felt sorry for him. Jealous of him as she was, wanting him in a way she knew was beyond her capacity to effect, still she could not bear to see him vulnerable and hurt. She wanted him strong and complete, that is what she loved most about him, she wanted his strength complete even if it meant losing him to Jesse for sure.

"Why?"

"Listen to me, Paul. I gave her money to get there, to pay for it. It was a loan. . . ."

"A loan for what?" He still did not understand, and his lack of comprehension and Priscilla's maddening slowness in telling him angered him.

"For the hospital. I know, she could've had it done in Los Angeles, but she wanted to be near you. Think of it. To be near you. . . ."

"Tell me more," he said impatiently. She looked at him, at his eagerness, his eyes wide and anxious.

"How beautiful you are . . ." she said.

"Goddamn it, tell me what I want to know!"

"I have, for Christ's sake. . . ." She stared at him. He stepped toward her. "Don't hurt me." She moved clumsily back across the room toward Bartholomew, rubbing her wrist as she did, moved toward the boy as though he would protect her from McFarland's confusion.

"Tell me!" Coming toward her.

"What? What do you want to know?" Now she was confused, and she felt rattled and could not pull her thoughts together. She did not know what to tell him because she did not know what he wanted. She began to repeat herself. "She wanted to be near you. I lent her the money. Let me see, uh, the only hospital that does it in New Orleans is Baptist Memorial, but they have no rooms until after the first of the year so my doctor suggested Bellows. . . ."

"That's in Shreveport."

"Yes. It's where all the better Southern ladies go for that sort of thing, I mean. . . ." She took Bartholomew's hand. He tugged at her. She sat down beside him.

"What sort of thing?"

She sighed. It was too much. She desperately wanted to be alone with the boy, to play and fantasize. To forget Rhodes and McFarland and Jesse and David and everyone else who seemed to ruin her happiness. "Oh, Paul. Please do go home."

"It couldn't be abortion," he said to himself, disregarding her, as he went through the possibilities in his mind.

"And why not?" And then she laughed. Foolish man.

"Because Jesse isn't pregnant." He was at a loss.

"Like hell. Good God, Paul, didn't you know she was pregnant?"

"No. . . ." He rubbed his hands over his face. He felt dazed.

"He didn't know. Isn't that extraordinary?" she said to Bartholomew, her voice expressing a kind of wonderment. Bartholomew hadn't known either.

And then suddenly McFarland caught it. *"Rhodes!* I'll *kill* that son of a bitch. This time I'll kill him. . . ." He glared beyond Priscilla at the wall, almost picturing Rhodes there. The muscles of his jaw tightened and bulged; his face was flushed with anger. "I will kill him," he said again, only more quietly this time, with absolute certainty.

Priscilla lit a cigarette.

"It's his child," he said to himself. "He did it to her—"

"He's dead."

"—I'll kill the bastard."

"He *is* deaf," she said to Bartholomew. "Paul, pull yourself together. I said Mike Rhodes is dead."

"What?"

247

"Dead."

"But it's his child."

"Hardly his child, darling. She's only been pregnant for a few months. . . ."

"What the hell does that matter?"

"Don't you know anything? Rhodes hasn't been able to get it up in a year. God knows I tried. . . . Chemotherapy or something equally loathsome took it from him. You were jealous over nothing. No wonder he wanted to die. No, poor darling, I'm afraid the child is yours."

He sat down again. He could not take it in. He felt dizzy and somewhat nauseated. He did not understand what had happened. Why hadn't Jesse told him?

"She came to me this morning," Priscilla said, "after you left for the airport—"

"And?"

"She has no friends, did you know that? None. Only us. God save her from. . . ." She stopped. "I need another drink."

"No, go on," he ordered.

She waited a moment, considering. "Well, Jesse said you two had had an awful fight last night and that she had to get rid of the pregnancy or you wouldn't have her back."

"And?"

"She was scared. You had flown out of Los Angeles hours before, and then she called me, thinking it was over between the two of you. I said, 'Of course not. He's too big a fool to let you go.' Anyway, I said, 'Paul's bark is worse than his bite.' I saw her. She was crying, a terrible, hysterical wreck. Pregnant, and with Rhodes dead. . . ."

"But he was alive when I left."

Priscilla glanced at him and rolled her eyes. She looked over at Bartholomew. Suddenly she was bored with it, bored with McFarland's ignorance and confusion, with his tangled relationship with Jesse, bored with love and the lack of it, bored with life. She wanted McFarland to go away. She wanted it all to go away.

248

"He was alive. . . ."

"This morning? You think he was alive this morning?" She exhaled loudly, expressing her impatience. Oh, why doesn't he go home?

"Yes."

"No. He died last night. Don't you and Jesse talk? God, you're supposed to love each other, and you don't even know. . . . To hell with it. Rhodes died around eight o'clock last night. I'm certain, because Jesse was with him when he kicked. She told me she sat holding Mike's hand until it grew cold, and then she called the nurse. Frankly, I was surprised she called me, but then, darling, she was scared, and she had tried again and again to reach you in New Orleans when Rhodes died. . . ."

"I was on my way to the airport about then."

"So she couldn't reach you. And she panicked. And then later that night you flew home unexpectedly and you two had an argument. It's soooo tiresome, don't you think? Jesse said she had to get rid of the pregnancy. I assume that was what the argument was about. She was afraid of losing you, so I guess she thought she had to do something dramatic to get you back." Priscilla stood up. "Now get out, Paul."

He ignored her and went to the telephone.

He called the hospital in Shreveport. Jesse was asleep, they said. No, we do not put through outside calls after ten o'clock. Has she had the operation? . . . My child, he thought, my child. . . . We do not give out patient information over the telephone, not even to her husband. If you can come in person. . . . But I'm calling long distance . . . We are sorry. Hospital regulations forbid the dispensing of patient information over the telephone. Click.

"Now what the hell are you doing?"

"I'm calling the airport."

There were no planes to Shreveport until nine that morning. Too late.

He then called car rental agencies. None were open.

"Paul, relax, for heaven's sake. Go home. Get some sleep.

Tomorrow's a holiday. They don't do abortions on Christmas Eve. Not Christmas Eve! She won't face it for two days. There's time. . . ." She felt love for him then. She went to him. "Darling, I thought you knew." He was trembling, shaking. She put her arms around him, and he leaned against her. "I know, darling. . . ." She loved him more than she ever had. And she did not know why. Before his weakness had provoked her jealousy. Now his anxiety and unhappiness confirmed her love. She felt needed. "It'll be all right, darling man. You'll be there in time. In time. She loves you, Paul. She has told me that again and again. I envy you two. How goddamn lucky you really are. If only David and I had taken the time. The patience . . . too much blood under our bridge. Too late for us now. . . ."

He pulled away. "I've got to go."

She nodded. His face was drained. His eyes wet. He seemed in panic.

"Wait until morning. There's time."

20

It took him nearly an hour to find a taxi that would drive him to Shreveport that night. On the way out of the city he stopped at the apartment and picked up a package.

He slept most of the trip north to Shreveport, dreaming of her. He was angry with himself and longing for her. He felt a fool, worse, a rogue. A liberal man, a decent man, and yet through pride or arrogance, through misunderstanding, out of the best or most self-protective of intentions the worst had occurred. He believed he had driven her from him, at the time she most needed him, had accused and badgered her until she could not trust him with the truth, and so she sought to destroy it, to have it cut out of her. They never do it on the holidays. Not Christmas Eve. Not to his, hers, ours. Not again. Not another. Face it.

It was after eight in the morning by the time the taxi reached the Bellows Memorial Hospital, a large red-brick Victorian structure set on a hillside in a suburb north of Shreveport.

He gave the driver one hundred dollars in traveler's checks. And then he ran up the white marble steps of the hospital into the waiting room. In the far corner of the room was a painting of Jesus as the Good Shepherd. Near it was a tall plastic Christmas tree covered in colored lights with a huge unlighted papier-mâché star at its top. He went up to the reception desk and inquired about Jesse. He was impatient to see her, wondering fearfully if he had come in time to prevent it.

'One moment. I'll call her floor."

"May I go up?"

251

"No, but you will see her in time."

The receptionist made the call. And then she said, "If you'll sit a few moments. . . . Please." She looked sternly at him.

He went over to a vinyl-covered bench near the tree and sat down. Christmas carols were playing over the public address system, the carols interrupted now and again by calls to doctors. There were several other people in the waiting room, and nurses and doctors walked briskly through. It seemed a rather small private hospital to him, old and comfortable. There was something contradictory and disconcerting about the carols playing and the tree and the white-frocked doctors and nurses; even the warmth of the weather seemed a contradiction to the season, the season itself an affront to his mood, inappropriate and unpleasant.

He sat for nearly an hour, coughing every once in a while, and then the receptionist would smile at him, indicating it would be a few minutes more. Finally, around ten o'clock he was told where he could find Jesse.

He ran down the white marble halls toward the exit. The deeper into the hospital he went, the farther he moved from the waiting room, the stronger became the odor of disinfectant and drugs and other odors equally unpleasant but less defined. It took him several tries to find the right door because the place was old, the white corridors narrow and confusing to him.

Finally, he stepped outside onto the grounds. For a moment his eyes were blinded by the bright sunlight. And then he saw her.

She sat in a chair alone on the great, carefully manicured lawn. She sat with her back to him, sat facing the flat pastures that ran west away from the sun toward the river, which glittered coldly in the distance, the sun silvery-spotted on its wide surface like stars fallen onto brown earth. He stopped, struck by the isolation of her figure, its smallness, its impermanence and contigency; struck by that and memory bounded away and now undone and breaking over him at

252

once, in an instant in the picture of her in her white chair on that vast green expanse. "Jesse," he said. She did not hear him. He walked toward her quietly now, anxious, no longer certain it was she, nervous she might turn suddenly and it would be someone else. He walked up to her. He knew at once. She did not see him, not until he himself was close enough to see a sprig of plastic holly pinned to the collar of her gown.

Then she turned and saw him smiling at her, and her hand went to her lips, her fingers trembling.

He kissed her.

"Merry Christmas."

He took from his jacket pocket a small box tied with a white ribbon. He handed it to her.

"Open it, if you like."

She carefully opened the box.

"Save the ribbon. It's the one you wore that day, remember?"

She took out the gold chain and rainbow pendant.

He placed it around her neck. He kissed her. She smelled of lilac.

He stood behind her for some time, neither of them speaking. He looked in the distance toward the river, its banks lined with leafless winter trees, the fields empty and brown until the eye reached the hospital's grounds where the grass was oddly green, as if the hospital inhabited a special season.

"I love you, Jesse."

"Come where I can see you."

He went and knelt in front of her. She touched his head, and he moved forward and embraced her.

"Oh, baby, no!" She spoke urgently. He had hurt her. Then he knew.

"When?"

"Yesterday. They wanted to get me in before the holiday. It only took a few hours. There were minor complications."

"Will you be all right?"

"In about a week."

"Why didn't you tell me?"

"Because I thought you'd believe it wasn't your baby. No matter what I said. I wanted to prove I loved you. I didn't know how else to do it."

He lay his head on her lap. She caressed him.

"When you left Los Angeles yesterday morning, I thought this misery can't last. This unhappiness, it must end, baby. I couldn't make it end. I didn't know how. I thought I had lost you again, and I sat in the house, trying to remember everything, how you spoke, what your body looked like, how your eyes closed in sleep, the sounds you made in love. And when I came here, all I did was try to remember everything in case you . . . in case I never saw you again and I'd have to make what we'd had last all my life. I knew it wouldn't happen again. You were the only decent man who ever loved me. And I—"

"Love, don't. . . ."

"I prayed you'd come back. I don't even believe in God. I prayed, like a nun."

He raised his head. "Please don't say any more."

"Promise nothing. Nothing anymore."

He touched her face. "Just one unbreakable promise. . . ."

"Is there one?"

"We'll make it work."

She laughed. "That's not a promise, baby. That's a hope."

"It'll do." He kissed her.

Her face clouded over with anxiety. She seemed frightened all at once.

"Are you all right?"

"I'm cold."

He stood and took off his jacket and put it around her shoulders.

"That isn't it?" he said. "It isn't the cold."

"I pawned your bracelet again. I didn't have enough money to pay for all this. . . ."

"It doesn't matter," he said, relieved. He thought she would say something he could not bear, that she did not love him, that she wanted him away. After all this, still he doubted her love because he needed it so much.

"Don't look at me, Paul. Stand behind me so I can't see you. . . . That's right, baby. I want to tell you something because I know if I don't tell you now, it will bother you until I do. And I do not want that between us. I want you to know now, and if you want to leave me, then do it, don't say a word, nothing, simply walk away and I'll pretend you are still there, standing behind me, and when the nurse comes to take me back and I find you gone, I will pretend you've gone to New Orleans and will be back soon, and in a day or so. . . ." She began to cry.

"Jesse, I'll never leave again."

"Don't promise! Don't. Don't touch me. Say nothing. Please, this once, do as I ask." She was quiet for a moment. He stood behind her saying nothing, standing slightly to the side. He could partially see her profile, and he could tell after a few minutes that she was not certain if he was still there.

"Paul," she said. He could barely hear her. "It was your child. It was a boy."

He came up behind her and put his arms around her. "It doesn't matter."

"It matters everything, my angel."

"You matter so much more."

From behind he reached around, lifting her chin, raising her face to his. He leaned down and kissed her.

She looked up at him for some time, as if trying to memorize his face. Then she said, "You are the net and the wire. You always were."

Starry, starry night.